LEAVE MY BONES IN SASKATOON

MICHAEL AFENFIA

PwB
Paperworth Books

Copyright (c) 2023 Michael Afenfia
The right of Michael Afenfia to be identified as the author of this work has been asserted by him in accordance with the copyright laws.

Published in Nigeria by
Paperworth Books Limited
08023130116
www.paperworthbooks.com
info@paperworthbooks.com

A catalogue record of this book is available from the National Library of Nigeria. All rights reserved. No part of this publication may be reproduced, transmitted, or saved in a retrieval system, in any form or by any means, without permission in writing from Paperworth Books Limited.

Maps illustrated by Tolu Shofule.
Cover photos by Bob Holtsman Photography.

The font used in this book is Garamond, a typeface named after Claude Garamond, a sixteenth-century engraver. This font was very popular in the eighteenth and nineteenth centuries and has had many modern adaptations. The choice of this font for this book is a reminder that as we look to the future and hope for change, the past is just as important as the present.

To Iliana Ayana, Anita Ogurlu, Julie Fleming-Juarez and Anahit Fahili. Thank you for all the heart, kindness and warmth you bring to a sometimes cold and wintery city.

To every person who left their home and everything they had to start life afresh in a new land with only the promise of a better tomorrow.

And to Michael Ndiomu, who shared an interesting story idea with me, which became a part of this story.

Thank you.

I Lied

Remember my last photograph
the one you said smile and I did
news flash - that smile was a lie.

The picket fence, the fireplace
the call back home saying everything is fine
that too was a lie.

But the cold
the blistering wind in February
that was true
losing myself in my many identities
that again was true.

It is true
these hands have never
done laundry or shovelled snow
mowed a lawn or lifted heavy things
I have never
driven a cab or dropped off orders.

Because
I burnt every midnight oil
toiled so my voice was heard
loud in the night skies
and echoed in the prairies
until my truth prevailed.

I lied to be here
will my boys lie too?

Michael Afenfia.

MICHAEL AFENFIA

PART ONE

1.

OWOICHO ADAKOLE WAS TERRIBLE WITH DATES. ANYONE who knew anything about him knew two things for certain – he never questioned his bill whenever he made purchases or was out drinking with friends. That was one thing. The second was that memorizing dates and figures was his biggest phobia. He was afraid of numbers and dates and was terrible at adding them together or using them in any way. But he would remember the 7th of July for many reasons, one of which was a secret he would take to his grave.

How could he forget when it was such an important date in his family's life? How could he forget the day he, his wife, and their four children got back their international passports from VFS Global in Abuja? How could he forget the moment he collected the documents that would allow them passage to a new life of wonder and opportunities outside the shores of Nigeria? How could he forget asking the dark-skinned lady with tribal marks on her face to verify the name on the envelope because he didn't want to go home with a set of documents that weren't his? The last thing he wanted was to be called back to return the passports because there had been a mix-up somewhere in the process or the visas were granted in error.

During a previous visit to the intimidating offices of the visa processing agency retained by some embassies and foreign missions in Nigeria to handle visa applications on their behalf, this same woman had been rude to him and his wife. Their visit then was for a Schengen tourist visa. The woman had accused them of shunting and disrupting the queue, which wasn't true, but she insisted. She then got even angrier at his insinuation that her pace was amateurish and that she was holding up non-Abuja residents who had return flights to catch.

Owoicho recalled them having a heated argument for about half an hour. If his memory served him well, it took the intervention of her supervisor to quell the altercation. In the end, they didn't get the visa and so couldn't travel to Switzerland for a short visit that the Nigerian government would have partly paid for because he was selected to accompany the Minister of Agriculture to a one-week global food security summit in Geneva.

Of course, the rest of the team proceeded on the trip without him, and for weeks, he was sad about it. Owoicho's sadness was mostly because he and his wife needed the visa on their passport to establish a credible travel history for future visa applications. And then there was the estacode he had already calculated and spent in his mind and in the physical. He never contemplated their application would be rejected since it was accompanied by a letter of invitation from a United Nations-funded event. Being the only one denied the visa based on a negligible discrepancy between the dates stamped on his passport and what he provided on the application form concerning a previous work-related trip to Accra two years earlier was more than embarrassing. It came across as bad luck, and bad luck made people cranky, speculative, and suspicious of everything and everyone. What if the refusal wasn't entirely administrative but orchestrated by forces and people in the spirit realm, aka village people, who were envious of his good fortune and progress in life? This question lingered on Owoicho's mind for a long time. Why him? Why Ene?

Meanwhile, the Permanent Secretary and three directors from the ministry were on the minister's contingent. Five out of the minister's seven technical assistants, three journalists, his pregnant wife, her younger sister, and his two teenage children were approved to travel. Also on the list was the children's home tutor who accompanied them everywhere they went to ensure the boys didn't stop studying. It was said that the man had been their private teacher since they were in kindergarten because the minister, an alumnus of Harvard University, was determined that all his children attend the same institution as he and his father and continue the "Louis-Nwapa" tradition of graduating from an Ivy League school in America.

Back to VFS and his human obstacle. As they already had a history, Owoicho wasn't expecting her to be nice to him. But this time, he was wrong. She was different. This time she smiled and congratulated him heartily. It was as if they had never met before and that their previous encounter was all in his head. But her face and the hurtful words she hurled at him in front of his wife and everyone else in the room that day were still etched in his memory.

This time though, she was a different person. At first, he couldn't fathom why and what had changed about him since the last time he saw her, but it eventually hit him. His story had changed. Owoicho was certain of it. In that environment, nothing brought instant respect to a person faster than the realization that their visa application was granted and that they were only an airplane ticket away from joining the exclusive club of Nigerians in the diaspora.

Knowing how, for many years, their lives had been a string of hard knocks with the occasional lucky breaks with work and career advancement, Owoicho couldn't wait to get home and show his daughter, Ochanya, the page in her international passport where the single-entry visa valid for nine months only was stamped. He knew she'd be even more ecstatic than he was, so he made a mental note to caution her about telling her friends of the breakthrough until they were ready to let people know. He would also plead with her not to tell her mother or siblings anything about it just yet. He wanted to be the one to break the news to them when they returned. He wanted to capture their reaction with his phone, so he could play it back whenever he wanted a good laugh.

In their conversation the day before, Ene had mentioned that she'd be back in Abuja in the afternoon to make him something special for dinner. He knew it would be yam and fresh fish pepper soup because he had specifically asked her mother to buy him lots of fish since it was cheaper in Makurdi and the sellers usually had more varieties. Ene also said that she had missed him and Ochanya terribly after being away from home for a few days, and that if he could call in sick at work, she'd like all of them to have dinner together as a family. They hadn't done that in a long time because, most evenings, Owoicho was either busy at work at the TV station or out drinking with his friends. As the children grew older too, they preferred to eat dinner in front of the television, a terrible habit their mother's constant nagging couldn't break, so she ate alone. Ene said she missed their dinner table conversations and the lovely memories they made afterward, dancing, playing games, or poking fun at one another while also catching up on what each person in the family was up to during the day. Owoicho missed it too, and he told her so.

Thinking about how they spent their evenings not too long ago made him smile. Back then, weekend nights were like a party. They didn't have much money, but there was laughter, music, and movies. Sometimes there was chicken suya and soft drinks, and when either he or Ene could afford it, they ordered shawarma or pizza from their favourite spot in Wuse 2. Owoicho was happy that his wife was in the mood for a revival of an almost forgotten family tradition. She didn't know about the visas yet, but it felt like she was already in the spirit and setting things up for a celebration even before she and the other children returned to Abuja. He could already picture her jumping and screaming at the top of her lungs. She would break to hug him and the children, and the jumping and screaming would start all over.

Ene loved to dance, so she would do her unique version of the swange dance before finishing things off on her knees with a prayer of thanksgiving to God. There would be tears in her eyes as she thanked Him for answering their prayers and causing the hearts of strangers to favourably consider their permanent residency application. Still, on her knees, she would say something like, "Thank you, Jesus, thank you, Lord. We are going to Canada. We are all going to Canada. Our God did not fail us or put us to shame. Thank you, Jesus. Thank you, Jehovah."

Owoicho saw it all in his mind's eye, and his heart leaped for joy. He was excited. He couldn't wait for the celebration to begin.

2.

AFTER THEIR BRIEF FATHER-DAUGHTER CELEBRATION, Owoicho placed all six passports on the bedroom floor and stared at them. He still couldn't believe it wasn't a dream from which he would wake up angry that his mind had played tricks on him. To convince himself it was real, he allowed his mind to drift back to earlier in the day when he went to pick up the documents at the visa processing office.

After thanking the collections officer and her colleagues profusely, he acknowledged the muffled compliments from the other applicants in the room who all appeared genuinely pleased for him. Though complete strangers, at that moment, they felt like comrades bound by a common desire to acquire a hyphenated identity – in his case, Nigerian-Canadian and, for them, Nigeria and whatever other country they were seeking to settle in.

Owoicho was on a high, and until it dawned on him that some other country wanted him and his family, perhaps even more than his own country did, he chose not to dwell on the uncertainties that awaited them in the magical journey they would soon be embarking on. There was no room for doubt, fear, or even questions about what fate awaited them. It was the 7th of July, and the only things that mattered to him then were the green international passports he was holding and what was stamped on them. And he didn't want to forget that.

To ensure he didn't, Owoicho promptly saved the date on his phone. But phone memory or not, he would never forget that date because of something else that would happen to his family. Something so grave that granting his family Canadian permanent residency was practically insignificant. He didn't know about it at the time, and he wouldn't hear about it until much later in the evening when the story went viral, and even major news networks picked it up as breaking news. By then, the calls and messages to his phone and Ochanya's had become incessant, and their whole world turned upside down. Until that happened, though, Owoicho remained jubilant.

Unable to hold back his excitement, he headed straight to his car after giving a small tip to the security guards at the entrance and exit points of the Garki property of VFS Global.

🍁

It was a glorious end to an arduous journey that began nearly two years earlier, and he was glad the anxious days and nights were finally over for all of them. Typical of him and courtesy of his arithmophobia, he couldn't remember the exact date the seed was planted in his head, but he remembered Ene, his wife of sixteen years, bursting into their bedroom like she was carrying a hot pot of okra soup and had to immediately drop it to the floor because it was burning her fingers.

"Owoicho, you won't believe what I heard when I went out to make my hair today?"

"What did you hear?" he asked with as much interest as he could feign, considering how hectic his day had been at the TV station. There were stories making the rounds earlier that day concerning the President and his vice. Rumour had it that one of them had shoved the other to the ground at Eagle Square during the national congress of their political party, sending their media handlers and aides into a frenzy of lies and coverups. Unnamed eyewitnesses claimed that reporters were beaten up, video cameras were destroyed, and cell phones were seized in a bid to conceal the truth of what transpired between the two men. The instruction, or was it threat, from the owner of the station that he didn't want the story mentioned in their hourly news roundup didn't get to the editor until Owoicho had read the story twice. Forced to take one for the team, he was severely reprimanded by the general manager and given the rest of the day off to reflect on how his actions had embarrassed the station.

Back at home, he thought he had an hour or two for a long bath. He also craved a cold bottle of beer to help him relax and forget his newsroom misadventure. The last thing he wanted to do before calling it a night was lay on the couch in the family room for about an hour or so and watch a couple of informative documentaries about animals and life in the wild on the Smithsonian Channel on YouTube. It was his favourite thing to do whenever he felt stressed or burnt out and needed to unwind. However, Owoicho didn't do any of those things on this particular night. Ene's astonishing news about her friend disrupted all the plans he made.

"Bimpe has gone to Canada, Owoicho. You won't believe that someone I consider a friend and confidant left for Canada two days ago, and I only heard about it from the lady who braids our hair." Ene flung her handbag on the bed as she spoke.

"What do you mean she travelled to Canada? Did she go on holiday or something?" A puzzled Owoicho asked his fuming wife.

"Holiday? Owoicho, Bimpe has relocated to Canada with her husband and child."

"That is good news then. I'm happy for them," Owoicho smiled. "Please, whenever you speak to her, send my congratulations her way."

"Owoicho, you don't seem to get where I am coming from," Ene's frustration was evident from the way she pranced the room. "There's time for us to be happy for her and her family, but that time hasn't come yet. For now, I am trying to process the betrayal."

"Betrayal?" Owoicho asked, perplexed.

"Bimpe kept her relocation plans away from me. That is betrayal. Not in my craziest dreams did I see that coming. You know, on my way back from the salon, I kept wondering if she thought telling me about her plans would jinx it for her."

"She probably thought you might tell someone and that someone will tell another person, and before you know it, the whole Abuja is talking about it."

"Honey, are you calling me amebo? In fact, you are even taking Bimpe's side in this matter when you should be supporting me," Ene undressed as she spoke. Not noticing the disinterested look on his face, she left him in the bedroom to use the bathroom.

"I am angry, very angry," she continued at the top of her voice, leaving the toilet door open so they could continue talking as she took a leak.

"Baby, if I were you, I wouldn't worry too much about Bimpe not telling me she was travelling. You know how secretive people are about such things. They want to be sure they have landed in Canada or America or wherever they are headed before talking about it. What if they tell all their friends and family and, for some reason, they don't travel anymore? Wouldn't that be an embarrassment? People will laugh, and nobody wants that."

"When it comes to Bimpe and me, I am not 'people.' We talk almost every day. We share things, and we visit each other regularly. I was at her place two weeks ago. Owoicho, we even talked about the aso-ebi for a wedding in Lafia next month."

"And during that visit, you didn't observe anything unusual that could have hinted at her plans?"

"Now that I think of it, someone came to take their generator that day."

Ene finished her business in the bathroom, washed and dried her hands before rejoining him in the room.

"She even said they sold their solar panels and inverter as well. Silly me, I didn't even ask her why they were selling the inverter and generator when the electricity situation in the state hadn't improved. I just assumed they were buying new ones. Remember we changed our generator last year, so I didn't read anything to it. It didn't seem out of place at all."

"Well, it is what it is," a still-indifferent Owoicho said. To make her happy, though, he continued with a question. "Did you get her new phone number from the lady in the salon? Is there a way you can reach her to tell her how you feel?"

"What do I need her phone number for? She will see me in Canada."

"Ene, I don't understand. She will see you in Canada? How?"

"We are going to Canada."

"We are?"

"There's a test of English language. They call it IELTS or something like that."

"IELTS? What does that mean?"

"International English Language Testing System, I think. It's a way of testing your proficiency in English and if you know enough of it to function and blend well when you get to Canada. We have to take the test immediately."

"We do?"

"And we must pass with very high scores."

"We must?"

"We will download everything this weekend and get as much information as possible about Canada and how to get there. Honestly, Bimpe will be shocked when she hears that we have joined them there."

"Ene, you hate long flights, remember? And I also hear it is very cold out there." Owoicho protested in a feeble attempt to dissuade his wife from embarking on something he didn't think they were psychologically prepared for or financially equipped to follow through to the end.

"They say children don't pay school fees in Canada," Ene countered immediately as if reading his mind. "They don't take light. Water flows from the tap, and you don't have to own a borehole and pumping machine to have water flowing in your house, nor do you need to buy and fuel a generator daily for electricity. Everywhere is safe, and we can sleep well at night without worrying about kidnappers and armed robbers. The roads are smooth, and there are jobs everywhere. Even sef, there is freedom of speech, and for someone like you who is a journalist, you can say what you want to say and not fear that DSS will come and arrest you."

"But we already know these things about America and Canada."

"Owoicho, there's more. One woman in the salon said that her younger brother lives in Canada and that he told her that the Canadian Prime Minister is begging people to come and take jobs. Look, Canada is sharing jobs like an evangelist shares the gospel, and the country is looking for people like us to come and take the jobs."

"Ene, we have to do our homework and ponder this matter well. We can't rush into this moving-to-Canada business just like that because someone you're not happy with is there now," Owoicho cautioned.

"What is there to think about? Who would insist on remaining here with this low quality of life when we can do much better and have it all somewhere else?"

"Ene, it can't be all that rosy. And remember, even roses have thorns."

"Then why is everyone rushing there? That is the mystery we must go and unravel too."

"Ene, Canada is far from everyone and everything we are familiar with, plus it is extremely cold. I've heard people say that a lot. I've seen reports and read stories at work about what Nigerians and other immigrants are going through. It is not always easy, and the pictures people post on social media don't tell the whole story."

"With all the things I have told you, and there's more, do you think I would be scared of a seventeen-hour flight or the cold weather? Even if it is colder than our deep freezer, people have survived there for generations and people still live there as we speak. See Owoicho, we are going to Canada; we must go to Canada. Our children deserve better than this purposeless life our leaders and greedy politicians are making us live. It's like you wanted to take your bath before I came in?" she asked him, changing the subject.

"You can go ahead if you want; I will go after you."

"Okay."

"Baby," Owoicho went back to the issue at hand. "I like that you have this thing all figured out by yourself. But Ene, I have one small request to make."

"And what is that?"

"When you do your additional research this weekend, can you please find out how we will finance this movement to Canada since you have decided that we must go by fire or by force?"

"Owoicho, if I have to beg, steal or borrow, I will."

"Because you want to prove something to your friend?"

"Because our kids, and even us, deserve to experience this greener pasture everyone in this country wants a taste of. So, my darling husband, this isn't just about Bimpe. So many people I know have left Nigeria for Canada. We have to leave too before we get too old and it becomes harder for us to qualify. And you know this our government, what if they come up with a policy criminalizing migration anytime soon? What would we do then? We would all be stuck in this country forever."

"Well, relocating isn't such a bad idea. And I can't deny thinking about it every now and then, particularly with the children getting older. The problem for me, Ene, is how expensive it is. I don't think we can afford it right now."

"But honey–"

"Please, Ene, let me finish saying what I want to say," Owoicho quietly interjected. "I think we should face the reality of our situation rather than deceiving ourselves. Honestly, based on my salary and yours combined, I don't think we can raise the amount of money required to make your Canadian dream a reality."

Ene remained quiet for a while, and then she said something that gave him hope. Immediately, he began to consider their move to Canada a viable aspiration for her, himself, and their children.

3.

Two years and several millions of naira later in processing fees and agent payment, that aspiration became a reality. Owoicho couldn't wait to show Ene the documents he brought home from VFS Global as proof of their success.

From their last conversation, Owoicho knew not to expect his wife and children until sometime in the afternoon or perhaps even much later, so he didn't think too much about it when she didn't return his calls or reply to his text messages. Besides, he was never one to bother people with too many phone calls when they were in transit. After a while, though, it occurred to him to try and reach his wife through Inalegwu, their oldest child, or through Okopi and Ejuma, the twins, since they were all travelling together. But he changed his mind, remembering how erratic network connectivity sometimes was when traveling from Makurdi to Abuja. He decided to wait patiently for their arrival and not worry that it was getting late. Perhaps he would have maintained his patience if his father-in-law hadn't called.

"Owoicho, are Ene and the children home now? I have tried calling them but their phones are switched off."

Owoicho noticed the slight quiver in the old man's voice. "They are not yet home, Papa. I will see if I can reach them now, then I will call you back."

"Please do, my son. They left Makurdi since morning; they should be in Abuja by now."

"I will call you back, Papa."

"Thank you, my son. I will be waiting to hear from you.'

"No problem, sir."

"We hear that a video is circulating here in Makurdi. Some travellers were attacked by bandits somewhere between Wemba and Abu. There are stories everywhere, Owoicho, but I don't want to listen to these bearers of bad news. Try and call Ene's phone. I will wait until I hear from you."

"Okay, Papa. I will let you know the minute I hear the car at the gate."

Owoicho ended the call with his father-in-law and immediately tried contacting Ene and the children. He tried and tried, but he wasn't successful. Why were all their phone lines unreachable? Suddenly the bed felt uncomfortable, so he got off it and sat on the cold tiled floor. Instead of calling again, he decided to text and send WhatsApp messages to his wife and children, including the driver. He wanted to know when his messages were delivered and read. Owoicho couldn't sit still. His heart wasn't beating right, and he didn't like it at all.

4.

THE IDEA OF VISITING HER PARENTS FOR A FEW DAYS CAME from Owoicho. Ene hadn't been to Makurdi in two years, and her father especially wasn't happy that she had stayed away for that long. Whenever he called to check up on them, he ended the call with a lamentation about not seeing his grandchildren and missing them dearly.

When Owoicho suggested the visit immediately after they completed their medicals and were asked to proceed for biometric capture at VFS Global, Ene knew there was wisdom in going to see her parents. She didn't think her mother and father would like it very much if her last visit with them after staying away for two years was to inform them about relocating to Canada in a few weeks or even days. Naturally, they would be distraught, not knowing how long before they saw themselves again, so this visit was mostly to soften the blow of going away so unexpectedly. In her reckoning, it might be three, four, five, or even longer until they saw one another again, and the mere thought of it was heartbreaking. What would be unpardonable, Ene decided, was if she didn't give them a heads-up about the impending relocation and adequately prepare their minds for the long separation.

She prayed that Canada would be good for them and that she and Owoicho wouldn't have a hard time getting jobs. If her prayers were answered, the whole family could return to Nigeria for a short visit to her parents in Makurdi. Alternatively, they could invite her parents over to Saskatchewan, the province in Canada they applied to and, God willing, the place they would call home in a few months.

Her friend, Bimpe, had confirmed that the stories about the freezing winters were true, so Ene planned that her parents could visit during the warmer months and avoid the miserably cold winter that terrified and frustrated long-time residents and native Saskatchewanians, according to what she was told. However, all that was in the future, and she was even too anxious to let her imagination travel that far.

With relocation and starting life afresh in a new country, she realized it was one anxious moment after another. From the IELTS exam to applying for transcripts and other academic records, getting their credentials verified, finding an agent, sourcing for funds, and waiting to know if they were progressing to the next stage of the application or not, the plan required patience.

Just as it was for her husband, the last two years had been taxing for Ene. Owoicho's job as a newscaster and reporter with Realtime Television Network, a privately owned television station operating from the Federal Capital Territory, meant that he had little time to handle their application himself, so she had to take charge and liaise with Kingsley, the agent Bimpe introduced to them after Owoicho convinced her to swallow her pride and seek guidance from someone who had completed the process successfully and was already in Canada.

All the back and forth, reviewing documents, filling out forms, following up on supporting documents, writing letters, managing bank accounts, and speaking to Kingsley became her responsibility by default. Between her and Owoicho, she had more time on her hands to keep track of things and respond to messages from the agent. Her job allowed her time, and Ene was grateful for it. This way, she stayed on top of things and was able to provide Owoicho with updates when he asked.

The hardest part was making the decision to begin and getting Owoicho on board. For him, it was a question of whether or not they could afford it, and as far as he was concerned, they couldn't. But Ene didn't want to give up without even trying. She recalled her father's words of encouragement to her as a little girl. He used to tell her then that when something was from God and was meant to be, the stars aligned to make it happen, and Ene believed it to be true.

She told Owoicho to allay his concerns about their ability to meet the substantive and ancillary financial requirements, which was the same thing her father told her when she wanted to go for her second degree in the United Kingdom. Her father had told her to just apply. He didn't have the money for her fees and upkeep, but by the time Ene got the admission, he was paid some arrears owed him by the Benue State Government. Thus, miraculously, she was able to complete the one-year postgraduate program in Skin Science and Stem Cell Biology at the University of Bradford.

Ene recalled her husband telling her that they couldn't afford to relocate and that they didn't even have enough assets to sell off if it came to that. That first day she mooted the idea of relocation to her husband, he all but shut down the idea, but she was resolute.

"Can we at least start? Owoicho, miracles still happen to those who believe."

And indeed, a miracle happened. The same week they paid World Education Services to commence their credentials assessment was the same day Ene was appointed by the Benue State Governor as his Personal Assistant in charge of managing his meetings, schedules, and unofficial engagements in Abuja. She was also to double as his Chief Protocol Officer and oversee the day-to-day running of Benue House, the State Governor's official headquarters and residence in Abuja. Just like that, from teaching Biology to senior secondary school students in the Federal Government College, Bwari, Ene became a top government official in charge of access to the most important man in Benue State.

In addition to selling, for large sums of money, access to politicians and contractors wanting to meet with the number one citizen of the state, the position came with a furnished five-bedroom duplex in Maitama, a brand-new Toyota Landcruiser as an official vehicle, a driver, one personal assistant, and a more than generous monthly salary she could only have dreamed of.

Though her father, Elder Erasmus Ejeh-Onoja, a retired Permanent Secretary who served the government and people of Benue State meritoriously until his exit from the state civil service had a hand in the appointment, Ene attributed the timing to God and her own resilience.

By being prudent and keeping her eyes on the ball, Ene had raised close to twenty million naira to fund their Canadian project. It would be more by the time they were ready to leave since she was still gathering more money. At the appropriate time, she would let her husband know how much she had saved, but until then, it was a secret she hoped to surprise him with when they arrived in Canada. She knew he hated surprises, but she enjoyed doing it anyway.

Ene couldn't wait to see Owoicho's face when he realized how much they were worth in Canadian dollars. Knowing him, she was sure he would freak out. It would be such a relief to find out that aside from the money for their plane tickets and other logistics associated with moving abroad, there was money saved up to tide them over for a few months while they looked for suitable employment. The money she had saved so far in the relatively short period she had worked with the governor was enough to rent an apartment in a nice neighbourhood. It would also cover the cost of a good car they could share and still leave them with a reasonable amount to invest in a business and maybe even get a mortgage when they became eligible.

She had spoken to Bimpe again after they were instructed by Immigration Canada to proceed with their medicals. Ene was happy she listened to Owoicho and settled her differences with her friend. Since they aired out their grievances and became friends again, Bimpe was there to provide sound advice and guidance to her every step of the way. Bimpe had everything figured out – picking them up from the airport, where to shop for their immediate needs, a school for the children, and people to speak to about jobs for her and Owoicho. The only thing left was the text message from VFS Global asking them to come for their passports. That was the last and final stage, and Ene was almost certain that by the time she returned to Abuja, that too would be in the bag.

Seeing her parents again, sleeping in her old room in the quaint bungalow in GRA where boys weren't welcomed because of her mother's strictness, as well as reliving her happy childhood memories with them helped take her mind off the anxiety of the last few days of waiting for that all-important message. Sometimes, she wondered how Owoicho was handling the wait, alone in Abuja with Ochanya.

In the five days she and the children spent with her parents, she was tempted to tell them they were relocating to Canada soon, but she restrained herself. She wanted to see the visa in her passport before telling anyone about it.

Ene also pleaded with the children not to tell their grandparents about the plan to move to Canada. With Inalegwu, she had no problem. He was seventeen and old enough to know not to be flippant about things his parents told him not to discuss with others. Thankfully, Ochanya, who was very close to her grandmother, opted out of the trip at the last minute because she was selected to represent her school in an art exhibition being organized by the Federal Ministry of Arts and Culture for secondary schools in Abuja. Her concern was with the twins, Okopi and Ejuma. They were a lively pair of thirteen-year-olds who couldn't keep secrets. They were also fond of their grandparents and might let something slip if they weren't constantly reminded that it wasn't yet time for the big announcement. Ene was worried about them talking because they were at a delicate period in their physical and mental development when being discreet hadn't quite matured into a virtue. She kept a hawkish eye on what they were up to every second they spent with their grandparents.

Until the last day of their stay in Makurdi, Ene was on tenterhooks. It wasn't until the four of them got in the car, said goodbye to her parents, and drove through the inner roads and onto the busier streets and wider highways that led out of the city did she heave a sigh of relief. She promised herself to tell her parents about Canada on her next trip to Makurdi. Ene was certain it wouldn't be long before she returned to do that. Until then, she was only too glad to be going back home to Abuja where her husband and daughter were waiting. Her heart raced with excitement when she thought about Owoicho and Ochanya and the celebration she hoped would happen in a matter of days.

5.

"Odoo, when we get to Keffi, please remind me to buy some yams there. My husband won't forgive me if I don't bring home enough to last us for the rest of the month," Ene said to her driver minutes after they left the city.

"I will do that, madam. The traders there have very big yams that are good for pounding, and they are quite cheap compared to the cost in the other villages along the way," the driver replied gleefully.

"I just knew you would bring pounded yam into this conversation," Ene teased.

Odoo was a distant and much younger cousin she employed to work with her when she joined the Benue State government and had the opportunity to help someone get a job.

"You Idoma men and pounded yam! I wonder what you and Oga Owoicho will do if the government suddenly bans pounded yam in Nigeria and you are forced to eat garri and semovita only."

"We will die. No long talk."

"You will die?" Ene laughed at his reply. "You will die because of food?"

"Honestly, madam, if they try that one, it will be sudden death for many Benue people, and there will be a big protest in this country."

"Odoo, speak for yourself. Me, I will be fine." She laughed again.

"Me, I won't be fine at all if they do that o. In fact, any day I don't eat pounded yam feels incomplete. Even my wife knows it. Like now, as we are going back to Abuja, I know that she has made hot pounded yam and delicious okoho soup to use and take it down. That is her usual way of welcoming me back home whenever I travel. Then me, I will now finish it off with a bottle of cold beer."

"Good for you."

"Madam, thank you for saying that. Me, I don't think any true Benue man can survive without eating pounded yam for a day. I tell you."

"Odoo, I have heard you. Mr. True-Benue-Man, I am not even arguing with you, so please concentrate on getting us home in one piece and take your mind off your wife's pounded yam and okoho soup for the next few hours. Can you do that, please?"

"Yes, ma, I can. No more thinking about pounded yam until we reach Maitama. I am focused on the road ahead."

Ene couldn't stop herself from laughing at the way he went from smiling to keeping a straight face in seconds. She liked Odoo's wit and dedication to his job. He never took advantage of the fact that they were both from Otukpo and related to each other in a very convoluted way only their fathers could explain. Ene also liked that he got along quite well with Owoicho, who could be difficult to please when he wasn't the one behind the wheel. And the kids were very fond of him too, so much so that they nicknamed him "Uncle O."

"I hope you checked the oil and water level in the radiator," Ene said, changing the subject. "I don't want us stopping on the road for any reason. You know how restless Okopi and Ejuma got when we stopped to get fuel on our way from Abuja."

"Don't worry yourself, madam. Everything in the car is in order. I checked the engine, tires, and fuel level before we left papa and mama this morning. By the grace of God, apart from the yams you want us to buy when we get to Keffi, we will not be stopping for any other thing until we get to Abuja."

"Amen."

Satisfied that Odoo had done his job ensuring that the Landcruiser was roadworthy, Ene reached for her phone from her bag. Lost in the flurry of tears and goodbyes and words of advice from her parents to her and the children, she completely forgot to let Owoicho know they were on their way. When they spoke earlier, she was rushing into the bathroom and didn't have time to fill him in on the details of their departure and estimated arrival time in Abuja.

Afraid he might be worried about them, Ene wanted to speak to her husband and let him know they were on their way and already at the outskirts of Makurdi, but her phone was off. Ene grunted in frustration. She remembered plugging in the charger all night, so it was either the phone battery had become faulty or she had not plugged in the charger correctly.

Knowing it was important she reached her husband so he'd be updated on the progress of their journey, she asked Inalegwu for his phone, but the boy had his headphones on and didn't hear her call his name even though he was right in front of her in the front passenger seat of the car. Ene had two guesses: Inalegwu was listening to rap music or watching something on Netflix. Whichever it was, there was no disturbing him when he was engrossed with his phone.

Beside her, the twins were busy with their phones as well. They were absorbed in the fantasy world of augmented reality. It appeared callous to interrupt them and force them to temporarily abandon their guns and castles in whatever game they were playing for the real world. She decided to let them be, expecting that Owoicho would call one of them if he tried reaching her without success. More so, she knew he wasn't one for tracking people when they were in transit. He would rather wait patiently until the traveller got to their destination and then thank God for safe travels.

Replacing her dead phone with the pocket-size Bible she always had in her handbag, Ene opened to Proverbs and began reading from chapter one. She fell asleep while meditating on the wise words of King Solomon and remained asleep until they got to Nasarawa Eggon.

"Madam," Odoo's voice permeated through her subconscious and the dream she was having about haggling with a man dressed in police uniform about the cost of yams and palm oil.

"Odoo, where are we?" Ene asked, trying to shake off the sleep from her eyes. She didn't notice the commotion happening all around them until she became somewhat awake and her sense of comprehension was partially restored.

"Madam, we are at Nasarawa Eggon. We have been here for over twenty minutes now."

"Twenty minutes! And you couldn't wake me up?"

"Sorry, madam, but I didn't want to disturb your sleep."

"Odoo, you should have woken me up."

"I was confused and tired of the whole thing," the driver sounded apologetic and genuinely sorry for his mistake.

"So why aren't we moving?"

"The boys and girls from the community have blocked the road. They are protesting something their chief and local government chairman did to them."

Through the window, Ene noticed the mob and the other vehicles caught up in the impasse between the protesting youths and their local authority figures. Although they looked harmless, the sheer number of them and the fact that her children were in the car instantly aroused her maternal instinct to protect her brood. At that moment, her main concern was getting her children away from the rioters and to safety.

"How long are we going to stay here?" Ene asked with terror in her voice. "I don't think we should be here any longer. Is there another route we can follow?" She frantically scanned her surrounding for an exit or escape route from the rampaging young men and women of Nasarawa Eggon.

"I saw some drivers turning back earlier. Maybe if I reverse and follow the road I think they took, we can catch up with them. Those inner village roads are usually isolated, and it is always better travelling in numbers."

"What road is that?"

"I'm not too sure anymore. I haven't followed that route in a long time, but I think if we go back and make a detour through Arugwadu, Arikia, Wamba, maybe Abu and Gudi, we can still hit Akwanga."

"And from Akwanga?"

"We drive straight to Keffi."

"Are you sure about this road you are talking about?"

"Madam, to be honest, I'm not too sure anymore, like I said. But I can try, and if we get lost, we can always stop and ask for directions."

"Odoo, I trust you. Let us go." Ene said a silent prayer before speaking again. "Thank God the children are still sleeping. I don't want them to wake up and see this crowd. It will terrify them."

"It is good that they are sleeping," Odoo concurred. "So, madam, are you saying I should turn back or you still want me to wait here until the community people allow us move?" Odoo asked to be sure of Ene's final decision.

"Let us turn back. I am not comfortable here at all. These boys look like people who have smoked igbo, and there's no telling what they will do if we stay here for too long."

Odoo did as Ene instructed and deftly meandered his way out of the gridlock and onto an untarred road that was the start of the detour. This time Ene was wide awake. She had no intention of going to sleep again until she was certain they were back in safe and recognizable territory. Until then, she was determined to stay up and vigilant.

Ene wasn't too comfortable that there was just one vehicle behind them, so she asked Odoo to reduce his speed so other cars could catch up with them. The roads were terrible, but the Landcruiser was built for moments like the one they found themselves in. As if reading her mind, Odoo changed the music playing in the car from a lewd dancehall number by Burna Boy to a song by Sinach, and the soothing voice of the popular Nigerian gospel singer lifted Ene's spirit. Their journey progressed smoothly until they got to the junction between Wamba and Abu.

Ene saw the men run out of the bush and head straight for their car. Odoo saw them too. He stopped abruptly and tried reversing to avoid hitting them or running over the spiked plank they placed in front of him, but it was too late. The sticks and stones being hauled at the Landcruiser unsteadied him, and the car fell into a ditch. By now, the children were awake and crying in fear.

At first, Ene counted three men, but they must have been at least twenty by the time they surrounded the car. None of them was masked, and none of them looked older than Inalegwu. But Inalegwu was compassionate and always smiling. That was how she had raised him. The faces around their car were menacing and unkind. Each had a gun or a machete or a stick. Some of the guns looked like those that she had seen Nigerian policemen use to intimidate commuters and innocent citizens at illegal checkpoints in Abuja, while others looked like the sophisticated firepower used by bad guys in American movies.

Odoo was the first one they got. He must have died instantly from the barrage of bullets aimed at him. Inalegwu was also killed in the car. By the time they were done shooting at him, there was no head on his body. The twins were dragged into the bush and butchered like cows to be sold in the market.

Ene saw it all. She kept wondering what she did to them to make them so angry at her and her children. If she could, she would have asked them why they kept her alive to witness the gruesome massacre of her children. She died reciting Psalm 23 and wishing she had told Owoicho about the money.

6.

OWOICHO KEPT DIALLING AND REDIALLING ENE, ODOO, AND the children's phone numbers, but he couldn't reach any of them. By the time he lost count of the number of tries he and Ochanya had between them, he was beside himself with worry. His daughter was worried and grief-stricken, as were Ene's parents. The last time he spoke to his in-laws, they still didn't have cheery news about the situation with the travelling party, which drove him insane. Four members of his family, plus their driver—a married man with a young child and another baby on the way—couldn't be reached and hadn't been heard from in well over ten hours. His stomach was in knots, and he was really afraid for their safety. At a time in the evolution of communication and information sharing when everyone was a phone call or social media post away, the prospect of what that might portend was so nerve-wracking he refused to contemplate it.

While trying his best to ward off the despair and agony, Owoicho waited for news from Ene's parents. He needed to hear something, not just anything but good news. The kind that will cheer him up in the future when the time comes for him to count his blessings and be thankful for the many things God delivered him and his family from. Because there was nothing much he could do until daylight showed its face again in its rotational constellation, Owoicho called Agbenu, the Benue State correspondence for his TV station. She was a dogged and daredevil reporter.

Agbenu and Owoicho got along really well, and in the past, if he had questions about a story she sent from Makurdi, she was always happy to clarify or go back to her sources for more facts. As a journalist, Agbenu always went over and beyond the call of duty. This trait made Owoicho and the writers in the newsroom rely on her reporting. He knew he could count on her to get credible information about where Ene and the children might be. If something bad had befallen them, he trusted her to manage the information in such a way that the dignity and privacy of everyone concerned was protected.

At a little past nine in the evening, Agbenu sent him the video. It was the one his father-in-law had spoken about when he first alerted Owoicho that something might be amiss. Elder Erasmus Ejeh-Onoja and his wife, Elsie, hadn't seen the video. They didn't have it and didn't want anything to do with it either. Owoicho didn't have to ask why. According to the tradition of his people, it was considered taboo for a father and, by association, a mother to see the corpse of their offspring or be directly involved in the transportation for burial or witness the actual interment of a child. It was for the same reason he hesitated pressing the play icon after Agbenu forwarded the video to him. He couldn't bear the thought of the footage confirming something he didn't want to believe about his wife and children. He was a father, too, and the same custom that applied to his in-laws forbade him from seeing the actual or photographed remains of his progeny in the event of death. After struggling with his choices, curiosity and duty got the better of him.

Not minding the images the video in question might contain and the extent of what they confirmed, Owoicho did what was required of him, first as a husband and then as a father. For the sake of his loved ones, he had to be brave and defy the long-held beliefs of his forebears. He couldn't run away from finding out the truth or put it off any longer. He needed to do that to stay sane and also to help Ochanya who was hurting too. The poor girl had come down with a fever and severe headache since he informed her of the situation of things with her mother and siblings on a night they should have been dancing and clinking glasses and dreaming dreams of a new life in North America.

Owoicho closed his eyes, counted to three, and let the video play. As was evident from its grainy resolution, the video was probably shot from a not-too-good quality cell phone of a passenger in a moving vehicle that must have been following the ill-fated black Toyota Landcruiser in focus. The amateur seventeen-second clip showed the SUV struggling to escape from a ditch it had fallen into. Its tires whirled in a desperate attempt to find grip in the sinking blend of dirt and silt, but there was no breaking free.

The license plate number was blurred and undecipherable in the video because the recorder's hands were all over the place. Despite that, Owoicho recognized the two Arsenal Football Club stickers he'd placed on the rear window of the car. He recalled that Inalegwu wasn't happy since he was a Chelsea fan.

The first set of audible voices from the video came from within the vehicle itself. At about the ten-second mark, the audio became a cacophony of gunshots and a chorus of heart-wrenching appeals to Jesus for deliverance. Male and female voices begged the driver of the passenger vehicle to reverse and flee the scene of what was clearly an ambush in a grassy and densely forested location. The final image before the video abruptly ended showed what looked like three male figures dressed from head to toe in some kind of black militarised outfits. Someone not in the frame yelled, "Fire!" The three men took aim at the stationary Landcruiser with their AK-47 rifles while more men dressed like them rushed towards the SUV. There was no doubt in Owoicho's mind that the shots were intended to kill.

As painful as it was to watch, Owoicho replayed the clip three more times before collapsing to the ground. His tears were internal, just like his late father had taught him. He would do his crying in his room and alone so that when his ordeal was over, the world would call him a strong man.

Though gruesome, there were no dead bodies in the short video, and that gave him a glimmer of hope. Owoicho's mind told him that death was the only plausible outcome, but he refused to take abduction off the table. That way, Ene and the children stayed alive in his head, giving him hope. And heaven knew that if he needed anything to help him make it through to the next day when the actual unravelling of his world might begin, it was hope.

Owoicho didn't know how long he remained on the ground after watching the video. Many times, it felt like his heart stopped beating, and his stomach was on fire from eating something really hot and spicy, but it wasn't that. It was pain. Something inside him was refusing to function because of the pain. It was a struggle to breathe and get a hold of himself, but he forced himself to. His legs felt weak, but he dragged himself up from the cold hard floor. Owoicho didn't have a choice but to do it because he anticipated things getting worse in the coming days. That was why he needed to be strong for Ochanya and all the people in their lives that would be impacted badly if the story ended as he feared.

When he felt strong enough to speak without choking up, Owoicho called Agbenu for details.

"Are the shooters bandits or herdsmen?" he asked her.

"Bandits, I suppose, but there really isn't much in the video to work with."

"What is even the difference between the two? Is it the absence of cows in the video?" Owoicho pondered aloud, and Agbenu caught it, compelling her to provide an answer.

"The presence or absence of cattle can be significant in determining who the attackers are," Agbenu said. That didn't sound right to her, so she quickly added, "At the end of the day, though, I guess it is all about semantics and pandering to the dictates of political correctness. Do you want to call them herdsmen? If so, would you be stepping on the toes of the people from the part of the country that are synonymous with that occupation? And if you called them bandits, would you be indicting the person or persons charged with the constitutional responsibility of fighting banditry?"

"Whether bandits or herdsmen, my question is, where were the policemen on highway patrol when these guys went on a rampage? Where were the men of the Nigerian police stationed in the village and its environs when the shooting was going on?" Owoicho couldn't suppress his anger.

"I was told they fled at the sound of the gunshots. You know, most times, the bandits, herdsmen, kidnappers, or whatever they are called, have more ammunition than the police and soldiers, so they do what they consider the most sensible thing to do. I've heard of cases where policemen take off their uniforms and blend in with the villagers because they don't want to be identified and killed."

"That's a nice way of saying that they desert those they are paid to protect," Owoicho shook his head in disappointment. "Speaking of village and villagers, where did the shooting take place?"

"Somewhere around Wamba, I was told," Agbenu answered. "Actually, it is the border between Wamba and Abu."

"And the people who live there, don't tell me they also fled the scene?"

"Like the police, they too are unsure of the amount of ammunition these criminals possess. Seeking refuge in neighbouring communities is always the best course of action until they are told by the police or military that it is safe to return to their homes."

"Do you have any idea what time the attack on my family took place?"

"We've had different accounts so far, but I would say early to mid-afternoon. There was a gridlock throughout the day at Nasarawa Eggon, which made commuters look for alternative routes to their respective destinations."

The framing of his questions and Agbenu's responses made Owoicho feel like they were both live on air discussing another senseless attack by miscreants and criminals on his nightly news program. They had done it many times before, but this time their conversation wasn't a routine for the news on Realtime

Television, and it wasn't about people he didn't know. This attack was on people he knew, lived with, and loved dearly, and it certainly hit differently.

"Where are the eyewitnesses? What are they saying?"

"None of them has gone on record to state what they witnessed, so information is sketchy at the moment. What I can tell you," Agbenu added authoritatively, "is that we have the video I shared with you moments ago, and even that doesn't say much. But I do also know that the authorities are investigating the video for clues that might lead to the source and the identity of the men captured in it."

"If the video was posted on social media, it must show the handle it was first shared from, correct?"

"This particular video first appeared as a forwarded message on WhatsApp, so there's no way of identifying its source. However, I believe that by tomorrow we will know more about the person who shot it and the other actors in the short clip. My request to accompany a detachment of police officers to the scene in the morning was granted by the head office, so I'll be there in Wamba to see things for myself. I'll fill you in on what we find out."

"Thank you, Agbenu. I'll be counting on you."

"No worries, Owoicho. By the grace of God, all our questions will be answered tomorrow. Usually, when things like this happen, some brave villagers familiar with the nooks and crannies of the forests are able to provide useful tips to our security forces, who then take it up from there. Let us hope that it is a case of kidnap and rescue is still possible. Who knows, you might even get a call this night from the criminals demanding that you pay a ransom."

"Agbenu, I don't know what to think anymore. It is all so scary and confusing at the same time."

"Don't lose hope, Owoicho, miracles still happen, and tomorrow we just might have one."

"Thank you again, Agbenu. You've been such a great help."

7.

Owoicho didn't know how, but word quickly got to Ene's boss about the "disappearance" of the manager of his Abuja office and residence. His first thought when he saw the unknown number on his phone very late in the night was that the people holding Ene and the children hostage were ready to negotiate the terms of their release. However, his excitement waned quickly when he realized the call wasn't about ransom but was from someone claiming to be an aide to the governor. Thinking it was a prank call, Owoicho was about to hang up when he heard a different voice in the background ask in fluent Idoma whether he had heard anything new about the missing members of his family. Even though they had never met in person, Owoicho instantly recognized the brash tone in the speaker's voice as Governor Lazarus Ochepo.

It was a voice he frequently heard on television and from Ene's phone. Being in charge of the running of Benue House in Abuja and organizing the governor's schedule and the people he met with whenever he was in the FCT meant Ene and the governor spoke at least three times a week. Due to his loud voice, Ene didn't have to turn on the speaker function on her phone for anyone around her to listen in on his directives or learn details about his travels and movement within Abuja. When the governor and Ene were on a call, no conversation was confidential, certainly not from the perspective of the person on the other end of the phone. The only way to keep things private was if that person had the good sense to lock themselves up in a room, which wasn't always possible with Ene. Many times, she was in bed when the governor's calls came in.

The call caught Owoicho completely off guard. He found himself mumbling for most of it. Thankfully, the awkward conversation lasted only a few minutes because Owoicho simply didn't know enough about the incident in Wamba to provide Ene's boss with a blow-by-blow narrative. However, when the governor told him that his wife was one of the most conscientious staff in his entire team and that his thoughts and prayers were with her and their missing children, Owoicho sensed the pain and sincerity in his voice, and he believed him.

For Owoicho, the surprising thing wasn't that such an important and busy personality would reach out to the spouse of an employee in distress so quickly. The surprise came at the end of the call when Governor Ochepo offered to fly him and Ochanya to Makurdi on a private jet. When Owoicho thanked him and asked how soon the arrangement would be concluded because staying back in Abuja made him feel helpless, the governor assured him there'd be a chartered plane ready to bring him and his daughter to Makurdi as quickly as they could find their way to the airport. He told Owoicho to expect a call from his aide-de-camp with details about the flight and pick-up when they landed in Makurdi.

Upon touching down in Makurdi in the morning, Owoicho assumed that the convoy of six vehicles sent to pick them up from the airport would head straight to Ene's family house. Aware of their coming, his kind in-laws were already waiting to welcome their son-in-law and granddaughter to their home again despite the unhappy circumstances of their visit. Owoicho was also eager to see them and offer what little comfort his and Ochanya's presence would bring. However, instead of driving them directly to the address Owoicho gave to the protocol officer who met them at the foot of the plane, they found themselves speeding with multiple sirens in full blast towards the People's House.

Once inside the government house, they were whisked into the governor's conference room, where an army of reporters with boom microphones, huge cameras with flashing lights, tiny voice recorders, and mobile phones was pushing and shoving one another for a vantage position in the crowded room. Before they could settle in for the spectacle that was about to play out, the ADC to the governor excused Owoicho and hurried him through a side door in the conference room. The door opened to a small passage that led to an exquisitely furnished office that looked like something out of the pages of a home and office magazine.

"Please sit," the ADC said to him politely.

"What is going on?" Owoicho asked, his nervousness obvious in his voice.

"His Excellency asked me to give you this," the ADC, a Deputy Superintendent of Police dressed in a camouflage uniform, handed Owoicho a black bag with the Coat of Arm and the green and white Nigerian flag embossed on it.

"What is in the bag?"

"There's two million naira in the bag. His Excellency wants you to have it. He says it is for the burial."

"Burial? What burial?"

Before the ADC could respond to Owoicho's question, another police officer ran into the room. He appeared frantic and out of breath.

"Oga ADC, His Excellency is on his way to the conference room."

"Okay, we will be there before him," the ADC said to the policeman. He then turned to Owoicho and said, "Just leave the bag on the table; someone will come and take it to the car that brought you and your daughter."

Like someone in a trance, a bewildered Owoicho was led back into the conference room just as Governor Ochepo and the large entourage were being shown their seats.

The event coordinator, a young lady with a screeching voice that didn't require a microphone to amplify, started singing the national anthem, to which the dignitaries in the room stood to reaffirm their love and allegiance to their country. After the anthem, the same lady introduced the top government functionaries in the room. She then proceeded to heap praises on the governor before personally ushering him to the front of the hall for his address to the reporters in the room.

Governor Ochepo adjusted the microphones attached to the podium. His powerful voice boomed through the speakers as he thanked the lady and commended her beauty, singing, and oratory skills. Next, he chanted, "Progress is our right!" the slogan of his political party, Progressive Mandate or PM as it was more popularly called, to which his aides, supporters, and some journalists in the room responded with a thunderous, "Power is our Right!" After the echo died down, the governor started his address.

"Ladies and gentlemen and respected members of the press and the fourth estate of the realm here present, I welcome you all to this press conference to discuss the increasingly troubling trend of farmer versus herder crisis ravaging our dear state and our dear country, Nigeria." The governor waited for the applause to die down before continuing his speech.

"First, I want to send my condolences to the family of my late staff, Mrs. Ene Adakole. Until her death, she ran my Abuja Office, and she did it excellently well. Many of you never met her, but I can tell you that she was such a wonderful, brilliant, and hardworking woman. She and her three children were killed by armed bandits yesterday on their way to Abuja after spending a few days here in Makurdi visiting her frail and aged parents. May their souls rest in peace."

As the crowd chorused a loud "Amen," Owoicho and Ochanya looked at each other with shock and incredulity. No one prepared them for the tragic news Governor Ochepo so casually shared with the reporters covering the press briefing. They couldn't think of a worse way to hear about the death of a loved one, and in their case, four loved ones killed in such a senseless and dastardly manner on the same day. Owoicho wanted to stop the governor and ask him what he knew, how, and when he knew it, but he was afraid the governor's handlers and organizers of the media circus might shut him down, so he forced himself to stay silent.

"Members of the press," Governor Ochepo continued, "their death is an avoidable tragedy, and I cannot even begin to imagine what is going through the minds of the family left behind to mourn them. I understand that Ene's husband, Mr. Adakole, and the one daughter who did not travel with the deceased are here in this hall. Please let them stand up for special recognition wherever they are."

At this point, Owoicho and Ochanya were ushered like royalty to where the governor stood. They were made to flank him on the imposing podium that carried the distinguishing insignia of his office.

"What happened to Ene and her children is a shame, and I blame the federal government for it. Yes, I blame Mr. President and their party's leadership for failing to protect the lives of innocent Nigerians. The level of insecurity in Nigeria today is unprecedented. No one is safe. Our farmers are not safe. Our civil servants are not safe. Even the politicians are not safe. This banditry must stop. The killing and kidnapping of our children in their schools must stop. The killing of our men and women in their farms and in their homes must stop. This domestic terrorism must stop. I am calling on the international community—America, Britain, China, and Canada—please come to our aid. And to our leaders in Abuja, I want to say protect your citizens. It is the job you were voted in to do."

Someone clapped, and the others in the room followed.

"Thank you, thank you. Ladies and gentlemen, members of the press, our people say that every day is for the thief, but one day is for the owner of the house. The day of the owner is coming. The owner's day is only two years away when we go to the polls again to vote for a new president. My people, when that day comes, brothers and sisters, please and please and please, vote wisely. Vote for security. Vote for those who value your lives more than they value the lives of the animals they allow to graze and destroy our farmlands. Vote to put an end to banditry and bigotry. Vote Progressive Mandate."

At the end of the governor's presentation, the applause lasted longer than the speech itself. Reporters raised their hands to ask questions, but the singing lady refused to call them up or give them the microphone so they could speak. The voices of the few grumblers in the hall were drowned by the unending clapping and ululation for Governor Ochepo.

What was described as a press conference to address the growing insecurity in the country ended without the governor taking any questions from the reporters he had invited to take part in the atrocious show of insensitivity to the plight of a father and daughter in anguish. The governor left the room without as much as acknowledging his two special guests. After he was escorted out by his sycophantic followers, Owoicho didn't know whether to be angry at the snobbery or be relieved that he didn't have to pretend to be happy about being used as a prop and puppet in a political game of charades.

Owoicho couldn't believe what he had just witnessed. He couldn't believe Governor Ochepo capitalized on his pain and grief to score a cheap point against his political opponents and detractors who accused him of not doing enough as the Chief Security Officer of his state to protect his people. He thought what the governor did was sad and opportunistic, and he couldn't wait to leave the room. He and Ochanya had just witnessed an ambush, and as far as Owoicho was concerned, it ranked at par with the attack in the bushes of Wamba.

As another protocol officer led them out of the hall, Owoicho thought about the two million naira in the car and felt cheap. He felt bought, used, hoodwinked, and railroaded.

8.

THE DRIVE TO MEET ENE'S PARENTS WAS MADE IN TWO vehicles. Four of the cars in the fleet that accompanied them from the airport to the governor's office didn't make it this time. Every fanfare was dispensed with, leaving just the two drivers for the cars and an extra hand who helped carry the black bag from the ADC. Owoicho concluded that they had become expendable and not quite as important after being used as decorative pieces in the governor's supposed parley with local and international journalists operating in his state capital.

In addition to reducing the size of the convoy, Owoicho also noticed that the sirens were turned off. Perhaps the escort commander or someone else in Governor Ochepo's protocol team thought they did not deserve that kind of honour since the spotlight was no longer on them. Whatever the case, Owoicho was beyond caring. It wasn't a long ride from Benue People's House to where Ene's parents resided, so he wasn't perturbed about the stripped-down vehicular presence or the total absence of armed security personnel in the second car that was actually a police escort vehicle.

Ochanya was inconsolable from the start of the journey to the end. She cried all the way to her grandparents' house, and Owoicho felt terrible that all he could offer for comfort was his hands around her shoulders. He wished there was something more he could do to ease her pain. He was hopeless when it came to expressing emotions with kids. Ene was the one they turned to when things got a certain way. She could handle their mushiness and mood swings. He couldn't. Without her, he wondered how he would raise a forlorn teenager who was more like a younger sister and friend to her late mother. To her siblings, she was a defender and confidant, and it was hard for

Owoicho to imagine a future of just the two of them when, just twenty-four hours before, they were a large family of six.

Owoicho and his daughter walked briskly past the unrecognizable faces perched on the spacious veranda of the Ejeh-Onoja household. From the expression of sadness and how they stared when he and Ochanya alighted from the Toyota Prado that dropped them off, he could tell they were there to sympathize with the family. How they even knew who they were was a mystery to him.

However, he was glad for their presence because he didn't think it was healthy for his elderly in-laws to be alone at such a difficult time. Apparently, the whole of Makurdi was aware of the fate that befell Ene and his three children long before the immediate family members of the deceased did. The news must have spread like wildfire through the city, and as is often the case in such situations, those closest to the victims were the last to find out anything.

Ochanya still had tears streaming down her face as she acknowledged the words of comfort and encouragement from uncles, aunties, and cousins she had never met and didn't know she had. She stopped crying when they entered the living room because of the intimidating presence of the chiefs and elders from their community who were there to commiserate with the family. But the crying started again when Ene's parents, Elsie and Erasmus Ejeh-Onoja, came out of their bedroom to welcome them. This time, it was her grandmother who offered her bosom for comfort and patted down Ochanya's tousled natural hair with her hands as the traumatized fifteen-year-old girl sobbed quietly.

After saluting his in-laws and hearing more sympathizers offer their condolences, Owoicho scanned the living room for a spot he could move to for privacy. The room was jampacked, so he figured he should look for a quiet place where he could get some privacy. His mother-in-law sensed his discomfort and pointed in the direction of Ene's old room.

Stepping into the room he and Ene slept in during past visits to Makurdi, particularly when their family was smaller and the kids were younger, brought back memories of a happier time. But he wasn't ready to dwell on those memories just yet; he only wanted answers to the many questions in his head.

Owoicho had two phone calls to make. He brought out his phone from his pocket and made the first. It was to Agbenu. She was the one he turned to for answers because he trusted her.

"I've been waiting to hear from you."

"So sorry. I wanted to call as soon as we got back from Wamba, but I was informed about the press conference with Governor Ochepo and that you and your daughter would be there. I listened from the office."

Agbenu was quiet for a couple of seconds. When she spoke again, her voice was laden with pain. "You have heard. I am sorry you had to hear it that way."

It was Owoicho's turn to be silent. When he spoke, his voice was laden with something worse than pain. "Did you find out how it happened? Was it quick?"

"They didn't stand a chance. There were too many of them, and they were armed to the teeth with both crude and sophisticated weapons."

"And their remains, did you find out where the police took them?"

Agbenu hesitated again for a bit. She wasn't sure about Owoicho's state of mind and if he was strong enough to hear the rest of what she had to say.

"The driver. They took him to the mortuary in the military hospital. There are no remains for the others."

"What do you mean there are no remains for the others?"

"We saw body parts. Chopped. Scattered in different places. Tiny pieces all over the forest. We brought blood-stained fabrics. Shoes. Things like that for identification, maybe DNA testing."

"Oh my God! Oh my God! Oh my God!"

"I have never seen anything as gruesome as that in my entire life. Everyone was shaking, including the police and soldiers that went with us. Someone even fainted."

Owoicho asked her to stop talking. Clearly, he had heard enough.

"I'm so sorry, Owoicho. I'm sorry there's no better way to relay what we discovered out there."

Before ending the call, he thanked Agbenu for being kind and supportive. In turn, she promised to stay on the investigation and promptly inform him if she found out anything new from those in charge of identifying and apprehending the bandits who murdered his wife and children.

Next, he called Maria, Odoo's wife. Ene had insisted that they both saved her number on their phones for days Odoo couldn't be reached and he was needed urgently in the house or office.

It was a difficult call to make, and Owoicho struggled within himself if his timing was right or not and if he should even be the one to break the news. He couldn't decide which was better, telling her about Odoo when he didn't know if she had a support system with her, or waiting until later and risking her finding out from other sources. In the end, he thought it best that she heard it directly from him. After all, he lost his wife and three children in the same attack that killed her husband.

"Anya."

"Anyachor."

"Oga, dis one you call me like dis, I happy o, no be small. I don dey try my husband number since yesterday. Even dis morning I try am, e still dey switch off. Eee be like say dem still dey that side for Benue because him bin tell me say na yesterday dem go return."

"That is why I am calling."

"Odoo sabi troway phone no be small. Abeg make you and madam no vex for am at all. As I no hear from am so, I know say him don loss him phone again."

"Odoo no loss him phone."

"Him no loss him phone? Oga, abi something bad don happen?"

"Na only you dey house?"

"I no dey house like dis. Na my friend place I dey. She be my neighbour, Mama Comfort. Me and Moses my pikin dey with her so. I come meet her make she help me plait my hair as I go soon born, and I no go get chance to dey go salon like dat again."

Owoicho wanted to speak, but the words were stuck in his throat.

"Oga, you sabi when madam and my husband go return to Abuja? Eee be like say na today or tomorrow dem go come back."

"Maria, Odoo and madam," Owoicho was tongue-tied again, "they are not coming back today or tomorrow."

"Ele!"

Owoicho broke the news of her husband's death to her as gently as he could. He remembered her screaming and asking him so many questions all at once. Questions he didn't have answers to or just couldn't answer over the phone.

He ended the call as politely and tactfully as he could. Minutes after the call with Odoo's wife was over, Owoicho couldn't bring himself to leave Ene's queen-sized bed. The clean red, white, and yellow bedsheet with matching duvet reminded him of a similar design she bought recently for the bed they shared in Abuja. Before closing his eyes to play back the events of the last twenty-four hours, he remembered thinking that he was probably lying down on the same spot Ene had last slept on two nights before.

Still unable to get up from the bed, he squeezed the pillow tight. He didn't need to sniff to get a whiff of the Yves Saint-Laurent perfume he gifted her on her last birthday. It was on the bed and everywhere else in the room. Ene's smell was so strong in the room that for a minute, Owoicho let himself believe that she would walk through the door and say his name in a whisper like she did on the nights he was determined to bring her pleasure.

9.

ALTHOUGH HIS IN-LAWS WOULD HAVE LOVED FOR HIM TO STAY longer, Owoicho had to return to Abuja after about a week with them. Despite the mutual support they found in each other, their lives had to go on.

This time though, as he travelled back to a house that was sure to feel different—lonely and robbed of all joy—like a body missing vital organs, his return wasn't on a private jet. The Benue State government made no special arrangement to drop him off at the airport in Makurdi, and neither was there a welcome party when he arrived at Nnamdi Azikiwe International Airport.

He flew economy class on Dana Air. When he was booking the flight, only the aisle seat was available. The lady by the window seat snored loudly for most of the flight. Even though Owoicho only grunted in response, the passenger in the middle seat couldn't stop gushing about his wife and kids and how he had the most adorable family in the world. One of the flight attendants even spilled water on him. The pilot spoke with a weird accent that wasn't Nigerian, American, or British but a combination of all three. Each time he spoke, Owoicho wanted to scream for him to stop, but he had to contain his irritation because the other passengers on the plane didn't seem to mind the assault on their ears. He found his way home in an airport taxi with faulty air conditioning, non-existent shock absorbers, and no radio, even though the driver assured him before he accepted to join the cab that the Toyota Corona was in tip-top shape. In fact, his return journey was nothing like the red-carpet treatment he and Ochanya got when they left Abuja for Makurdi.

Before returning home, Owoicho helped identify body parts for his own family and coordinated with Odoo's wife and siblings for the driver's burial, which was held on a different day and in another part of Otukpo. Odoo's burial came first. He was laid to rest in his father's compound. It was a sad and quiet gathering of people from all walks of life. People who saw his growth from boy to man.

For Owoicho, it was a struggle just standing there and thinking how vibrant and likable the young man was in life as against how helplessly and silently he lay in his casket that day. He thought of Odoo's little boy, Moses, and the unborn baby who would grow up not knowing their father. He wondered what their lives would be like without Odoo to guide and teach them about life.

The sad ceremony was a precursor to him for what was to come the next day when the coffins being lowered into the ground would be those of Ene, Inalegwu, Okopi, and Ejuma.

Theirs started with a service of songs in the house Ene grew up in. It was such a sad and emotional day for everyone. It was particularly heart-wrenching when Ochanya was called up to read her tribute to her mother and siblings during the funeral. When she finished, there was no dry eye under any of the canopies.

Other people spoke as well—childhood friends, secondary school and university classmates, someone Ene became friends with during her service year in Okija, Anambra State, a former student, and several of her colleagues from places she had worked over the years. They all said the nicest things about her. Be it as a classroom teacher helping kids understand Biology and eventually as a highflyer working with the Benue State government, all the people she worked with agreed that Ene was a good person and that she would be sorely missed. People spoke glowingly about the children too. Like their mother, they would be missed too. The way one woman talked about their untapped potential and unrealized dreams shattered Ochanya completely. She was inconsolable for the rest of the ceremony.

Owoicho's Managing Director and some of the unit heads in RTN insisted on hiring a funeral planner and paying for caskets as their own contribution to the burial. They wanted to make T-shirts too, but he discouraged that because it was supposed to be a non-celebratory gathering of a few friends and family members. Still, they wanted the company's presence felt in a big way. So, even though tradition forbade any form of merriment because of the painful circumstances surrounding the deaths and because the deceased were children and a middle-aged adult, Glorious Chariots Funeral Services sent four hearses and several pallbearers from Lagos.

The team from Lagos came prepared to mesmerize. However, in deference to the wishes of the family and the community, they had to dispense with their large drums and trumpets and ostentatious display of grief. But they were there all the same, and their presence added a certain kind of spookiness to the general mood of the procession and everywhere else in the town. It didn't help that someone in the funeral home suggested the pallbearers come dressed in bright yellow outfits, and no one in the team saw anything wrong with that.

Another person who showed up to the funeral in bright hues was his brother, Onjefu. He came in a fluorescent orange sweatshirt and white jeans, and his sneakers was a shade of red that couldn't have been missed by anyone present at the ceremony. And if somehow those colours got lost in the crowd, the multiple chains around his neck announced their presence. They were golden and chunky, and they looked really expensive. Again, if all that wasn't conspicuous enough in what was clearly a sombre event, Onjefu made sure not to travel alone from Lagos. He was accompanied by his friends. Owoicho counted eight of them, and they were all dressed like him. The only difference was in the colour of their clothes and the number of chains around their necks. Onjefu's were more.

For Owoicho, it wasn't their appearance that shocked him; it was that they came at all. He and Onjefu hadn't talked to each other in more than three years, and the last time they did, his brother warned him to stay out of his life and business and to never get involved in anything concerning him.

In their brief encounter after the service of songs, Owoicho was going to ask his brother how he knew about the funeral, but then he changed his mind. The attack on his family was all over the country's social media space, and even if it wasn't, someone from their family was bound to tell him. Whatever the case, he thought it was kind of Onjefu to show up. What wasn't so kind was that it appeared like he came to show off his big car and rich friends.

Onjefu and his entourage arrived in a convoy of black SUVs and police escort. They also came with their own food and drinks, so Owoicho was told. Someone also told him they came with some scantily clad girls from the polytechnic in Ugbokolo, who, obviously, were misinformed about the kind of event they were invited to. Or maybe they knew and just didn't care. Wedding, naming ceremony, or burial, a party was a party.

But what Owoicho and the immediate family wanted was a solemn walk from the house in Otukpo to the Anglican Church where Ene was baptized as a child. It was a walking distance. The priest would pray over the caskets, and then the bodies would be taken back to the Ejeh-Onoja compound for interment. This was a compromise between Owoicho and his in-laws. According to their tradition, Ene should have been buried in his family compound, but he decided to allow her to rest in her parents' home because she was their only child.

The graves were dug at the back of the family house just that morning because relatives and some community elders couldn't agree, until the very last minute, on the appropriateness of burying people killed by bandits among people who died of natural causes. While some of the elders wanted the bodies taken to a secluded part of the town where people without roots in the village were buried, others felt it didn't really matter where the remains were interred. Eventually, they were allowed to bury the deceased after parting with fifty thousand naira, three bottles of imported gin, and some kola nuts.

With the completion of the burial rites for everyone, Owoicho told himself that his business in Makurdi was done. He knew he wasn't quite ready for the real world yet and that perhaps he was rushing things after the multiple losses he suffered, but he also knew that he had to get his mind busy with work and other things he enjoyed doing. He believed that occupying himself with those things would lessen the pain until it finally went away.

When he told Ene's parents about his decision to leave, they agreed. His initial plan was to stay back in Otukpo for another week, but his in-laws thought it was unnecessary. He had played his part as a husband, father, and son-in-law, and he did well. Owoicho spent one more night with them in Otukpo and left for Makurdi the next day. His return flight to Abuja was scheduled for eleven in the morning, but he was up early to spend some time with Ochanya before leaving her. It might be weeks or months before they saw each other again, so he needed to be sure she was fine with his decision to go back alone.

"It isn't forever. It is just for a little while." That was what he told her and himself, so it didn't seem like he was a bad father who was abandoning his daughter when she needed him the most.

10.

Leaving Ochanya behind was the hardest decision Owoicho had made in his entire life. Quitting his comfortable job in banking to follow his passion for journalism shortly after the birth of his first child, Inalegwu, came close, but it didn't quite compare. Not even the decision to move to Canada gave him the kind of anxiety he felt as he watched through the rear-view mirror of the taxi as his daughter walked back into the house with her grandparents. It ripped his heart in two that she didn't even wave goodbye.

Earlier, when she said to him, "oyaekonaloma," his eyes welled with tears, and he wanted to tell her, "Pack your bags and let's go."

But he remembered his conversation with his in-laws, and it made him feel that he was doing the right thing by allowing her to stay in an environment where she'd have constant companionship. It had to be the best thing. It had to be better than taking her back to a house where it would be just the two of them, and he would be out working most of the time.

More than that, he didn't think he was emotionally ready to raise a female child all by himself. How could he possibly help her when it was that time of the month and she felt cramps in her stomach? What was the solution when boys began to show up at his doorstep and sex came into the equation? How would he handle her first heartbreak or caution her against unwanted pregnancy if she came to him for help or advice? Without Ene, Owoicho knew he was helpless with those kinds of stuff, and he was terrified of making a mistake.

The idea for Ochanya to stay back wasn't originally his. It came from his mother-in-law. On the eve of his departure, she called him into her bedroom for a private chat because sympathizers and well-wishers were still trooping in to pay their respects. Every available space in the parlour and in the canopies outside was taken up by genuine grievers and freeloaders; sometimes, it was hard to tell the difference.

Madam Elsie spoke for close to thirty minutes, and Owoicho listened attentively to everything she said about fathers raising daughters alone. Some of the examples she gave made him really afraid of what was to come. In the end, he was happy that his mother-in-law was willing to help him look after Ochanya until he was ready for the job.

"Ainya enem," Owoicho thanked her after she finished talking.

"You really don't have to thank me. My husband and I have talked about this, and we feel it is the best thing for you and Ochanya right now and maybe in the future. Who knows?"

"Mama, it is as if you read my mind. I have thought about what you just suggested. I just didn't know how to ask or bring it up with you and Papa."

"Owoicho, this house is your house. You should know this by now."

"I know that, Mama. I guess I was just confused because of all the things going on in my head at the same time," Owoicho said honestly. "If my parents were alive, I would have gone to them for help. But with you and Papa, it felt insensitive to do so because you are also going through the same thing as I am. The losses are all ours and the last thing I want to do is impose."

"There is no inconvenience where you and Ochanya are concerned. There is no way we would consider anything you ask us as an imposition."

"I really appreciate that you feel that way, Mama. I don't have anyone else apart from you and Papa. My stepbrother and I don't get along, and I am not particularly close to any of my cousins, either. So, whenever I mention family, I refer to the people in this house. You are the only ones I have."

"We never met your father because you told us that he died when you were in secondary school, but we know his family and they are all very good and responsible people. I know Otukpo is large, but word gets around and we all sort of know one another and the history of our families. Fortunately, in your case, even though your father passed before you and Ene got married, my husband and I met your late mother. She died about six or seven years ago, I think?"

"Seven years ago."

"Yes, seven years ago. She was a good woman too. May her soul rest in peace."

"Amen."

"I remember telling you then, and I will say it again now, in case you do not remember. If there is anything you need from a mother, come to me, and I will do it with gladness."

"Mama, how could I forget such powerful words? How can I repay you and Papa for the way you have embraced me like your own biological child?"

"Owoicho, we had so much respect for your mother, and I am sure if she was here with us still, she would have done the same thing we are doing. She would have offered to bring up Ochanya as her biological child and not let another woman do it. I'm sure Ene would have also wanted this if she could speak and tell us her mind. She would have wanted to spare you the burden of raising your beautiful daughter all by yourself when you have us."

"You are right, Mama. I know that is what Ene would have wanted."

"There you go. We have a nice house in Makurdi, and there are very good schools around where we can enrol her immediately after we return to the city."

"I don't know how to thank you and Papa for this kind gesture. Mama, thank you for allowing Ochanya to live with you for the time being. Honestly, since this thing happened, I've had sleepless nights worrying about her. I keep wondering how she will cope with just me and her in Abuja. There are too many triggers in that place, I tell you," Owoicho admitted to his mother-in-law. "And after what Ochanya has been through this week, I don't want her feeling lonely and sinking into depression on top of everything else."

"Do not trouble your mind, Owoicho. We will not forsake you. Our daughter may have gone, but she brought us a son when you got married. Her daughter is our granddaughter. By the grace of God, we will take good care of her."

"Thank you, Mama. I don't have any doubt about that," Owoicho smiled for the first time in days. "I guess the next hurdle will be how to inform her about this development. I know she's looking forward to our going back to Abuja together. Ochanya will be devastated by this new plan."

"Do not worry about that, my son. You and Ene have raised a very good girl, and you know it. My husband and I will speak to her this evening. She will listen to us and do as we say."

Owoicho couldn't tell if that last statement was an endearment or a threat.

"I can tell you with all confidence, Owoicho," his mother-in-law continued, "without her mother and her siblings, Ochanya would feel terribly lonely. You do not want that for her in this delicate period when she would be adjusting to life without them."

"I just want her to be happy again." Owoicho's words came out sombre.

"Will any of us truly ever get there again?" Madam Elsie mused loud enough for Owoicho to hear her. "Only God and time will tell."

"You are correct on that," he concurred with his mother-in-law. "Mama, I hope this will not be a fresh burden for you to carry at a time when you and Papa should be resting and enjoying your retirement?"

"Owoicho, don't worry about us. We will be fine. A friend of mine, we retired together as directors in the state ministry of education, owns one of the best private schools in the city. She was even around for the burial. I will speak to her about Ochanya next week, and hopefully, she can resume her schooling there immediately. Thank God she still has one more year before her finals, then we can begin to worry about university for her either here in Nigeria or maybe even outside the country. After all, there is nothing we are using our pension money for besides buying foodstuff and drugs."

When his mother-in-law brought up the possibility of overseas schooling for Ochanya, Owoicho saw that as an opportunity to bring up something else troubling his mind, and he took it.

"Mama, there's something else I think you and Papa should know."

"Is that so? If it is something you want me and him to hear at the same time, then he should be here in the bedroom with me. Why don't you go to the parlour and see if you can rescue him from those visitors who do not know that sometimes we just want to be by ourselves?"

Owoicho stood up to go get his father-in-law, leaving Madam Elsie wondering what he wanted to tell her and her husband.

11.

OWOICHO SUCCESSFULLY INTERRUPTED ELDER ERASMUS Ejeh-Onoja's discussion with members of his age grade association. All the four men he was in deep conversation with had on at least one item of clothing made from the traditional red and black woven fabric of the Idoma people. Whenever Owoicho saw his tribesmen dressed that way at gatherings, it always seemed planned and coordinated to him, but it wasn't the case. Most Idoma men and women had the same fabric. Wearing it perpetuated its generational relevance and projected a unique cultural identity in garment form. And he loved it.

"You pulled me out of a very important discussion with my friends. We were analyzing the government's handling of this herdsmen crisis that has wasted so many lives and is threatening to destroy our country," his father-in-law said as he walked into the bedroom. "I hope there isn't another emergency involving another member of the family. The way I am, I do not think I can absorb any more bad news this year. It will be too much for me and Mama Ene."

Owoicho couldn't stop himself from smiling when he heard that. Seeing how happy and in love Ene's elderly parents were warmed his heart. He closed the bedroom door behind him and waited until the old man sat beside his wife before speaking.

"There's no emergency, Papa," Owoicho paused to take a deep breath before continuing. "Papa, Mama, it is about Ene and me. There's something we should have told you long ago, and I take full responsibility for the oversight."

"What is it, Owoicho?" Madam Elsie was visibly agitated.

"We were planning something big before Ene died."

"A divorce?" his mother-in-law blurted out. "You and Ene were going to get a divorce?"

"God forbid!" His father-in-law exclaimed.

"We weren't planning a divorce," Owoicho reassured them quickly. "We were actually planning to relocate to Canada," he revealed. "In fact, we got our visas the very day the attack happened. So, even though it was something we worked on together for about two years, Ene didn't live to see it happen."

"Did I hear you say Canada?" Elder Ejeh-Onoja asked.

"Yes, sir. We were planning to relocate to a state in Canada called Saskatchewan."

"Saska…Saska…what did you call it again?" Madam Elsie struggled to repeat the name she had just heard.

"Saskatchewan?"

"Is that in Canada or Brazil?"

"Mama, it is in Canada," Owoicho replied.

"I have never heard about such a place before. Are there other Nigerians there?" His father-in-law wanted to know.

"There are. We hear the Nigerian population is growing, and there are many other African immigrants there. They also say it is a nice and quiet place, much like Benue is compared to states like Lagos or Kano."

"So, why didn't you people tell us about this move you were making to relocate to Canada? And when were you both planning to leave?" his shocked mother-in-law inquired.

"We have to travel within ninety days of the issuance of the visas; otherwise, they will expire," Owoicho explained. "The way we had it figured out, we would have left Nigeria in August or September when the weather is still warm and so that the children can begin school at the start of the school year."

"This is a big surprise," his father-in-law said, perplexed by the news. "When were you planning to tell us? Ene and the children came to spend a few days here and they left without mentioning Saka or what did you call the name of the place? There wasn't even the slightest hint from them about this thing you said now."

"I can show you the passports if you want to see them, sir."

"I am not saying that I do not believe you. And I most certainly do not need to see your international passports to know you are not lying to us. I just think it is strange that Ene would be planning such a big thing and not tell us even when she was just in Makurdi a few days ago. I mean, she must have known that in a few months, both of you and the children would be leaving for somewhere saner and safer for all of you, and we would have been fine with it."

"Like I said, the process was on, but you are never sure of anything until you get your international passport back with a letter that says your application was successful. That was why we kept it a secret. We didn't want to raise anyone's expectations and have them dashed in the end. Our silence about the Canada thing wasn't intended to disrespect or slight anyone."

"In other words, you wanted to be sure you were going first; that was why you kept the plan to yourselves."

"Exactly. It was meant to be a surprise until everything was set."

"It is okay. There really is no need for long explanations. My husband and I are enlightened enough to know how these things work sometimes," his mother-in-law replied. "So, what will happen now that your wife and the other children are no more?" Mrs. Elsie Ejeh-Onoja couldn't look him in the eye when she got to the last part of her question.

"I don't know. I haven't decided anything yet. To be honest, I can't even think that far. Right now, I just want to take each day as it comes. But I know it is something I must mention to the two of you so you don't go and hear it from somewhere else and think that I was hiding something from you."

"I understand that relocation can be a very expensive venture that requires a lot of money, is that true?" the question was from Ene's father, and it caught Owoicho off guard. However, he managed to nod his head, affirming that it was indeed an expensive undertaking.

"How were you people planning to raise that kind of money?" the old man probed further.

"Well, as you both know, Ene had a good job that came with opportunities for making extra money. On my part, even though we don't get paid much, I have been consistent with my savings, so the burden didn't become too heavy for one person alone. But I must admit, it was mostly Ene funding the entire process. She really wanted it for us."

"Now that this terrible thing has happened to her, do you have access to her bank accounts? Or you operated a joint account?"

"We don't have a joint account, Papa," Owoicho replied his father-in-law. "But from my little understanding, I may have to apply to the courts for Letters of Administration since Ene did not leave a will. The process takes about a month or two to finalize, and then we can have access to whatever she had saved up in the bank. But I will talk to a lawyer to know how it's really done."

"Yes. I know about that from when I lost my elder brother some years ago," the old man said.

"I will start working on it when I get to Abuja. The thing is, with all that has happened, I am unsure what our next move should be. Should Ochanya and I stay back and be close to their memories, or do we move to Canada where we would feel safe and not have to fear that maybe one day, while driving here or even in Abuja, we would be slaughtered by bandits and no one will do anything to our killers."

"God forbid!" Madam Elsie exclaimed.

"To think we are such a blessed country but our leaders keep putting personal interest above our collective good. Just look at how Ene and the children were killed –"

"Did you say killed?" Madam Elsie interrupted her husband. "They weren't killed; they were wasted. If they were killed, we would get justice. But have the police made any arrests? No, they have not and they will not. Those savages will get away with it, waste more innocent lives, and keep terrorizing the citizens, all in the name of looking for where to graze their cows. There was a time I would have reacted differently to this your news about relocating to Canada, but not anymore. I would say go when you have the opportunity and still can. You have my blessing."

"Owoicho, you have heard my wife. Right now, we cannot tell you what to do. Maybe you want to give it some thought and then let us know what you decide. Ours is to support you and continue to pray that God's hands will be in everything you do and every choice you make."

"Amen, sir."

"Naturally, as humans, we would like to have you and Ochanya around us all the time," Elder Erasmus continued, "but then again, as parents and grandparents, we also want you to follow your heart and do what makes you feel safe and happy. So, if you are telling us this because you want our blessing, as your father-in-law, I am telling you that you also have mine. My wife has already given you hers."

"Thank you, Mama. Thank you, Papa."

"Thank you for informing us about your plans, Owoicho. We appreciate your openness and sincerity."

His mother-in-law invited him with open arms for an embrace.

"We trust you, and we know you will do what is best for yourself and Ochanya," his father-in-law reiterated. "For now, as my wife may have already told you, we think Ochanya should remain with us. We shall help her deal with this tragedy as best as we can. By the grace of God, we will take care of her because if we fail the poor girl, we have failed Ene."

Owoicho waited until he was sure Madam Elsie had told Ochanya about the new arrangement before going into her room to tell her that he was still leaving for Abuja in the morning. She begged and cried to follow him, but at that point, it would take more than tears to make him change his mind. It was about doing what was best for her mental and emotional well-being.

12.

For the fifth night in a row, Ochanya cried herself to sleep. She was angry at her father for abandoning her in Makurdi when all she wanted was to be back in the room she shared with Ejuma. She missed sleeping in her soft bed with the really fancy sheets handpicked for her by her mother. She liked the new bedcovers better than the old ones because they weren't all pink and girly. The colours and patterns matched her emotional state, and she was happy her mother listened to her complain of being tired of sleeping on beddings that had Disney princesses on them. She told her mother that she was fifteen and no longer a child.

The last time they went out shopping, her mother let her pick her own clothes, and Ochanya was really glad about that. After months of arguing and making a case for herself, her mother finally acknowledged that she was grown and capable of deciding certain things for herself. The two of them had even started discussing adult stuff, like boys and relationships. They discussed protection for her heart and body when the time came and she was ready for full initiation into womanhood. They even discussed career options for her.

Going back to that house, with its memories of time spent together, bonding as mother and daughter, was good for her and she knew it. Ochanya desperately wanted to hold on to her recollection of the simple things. Like doing laundry, learning to bake, trying out jewellery and makeup, braiding her hair, and discussing her science homework with her mother. Those memories were in that house, and she wanted them just as much as she wanted her mother back.

Ochanya was angry that her father was eager to move on without her. She tried hard not to let her mind stray that far, but knowing that Ejuma and Okopi were his favourite children right after Inalegwu made her wonder whether he would have been happier if she had been the only one on that trip with their mother. She also wished it had been her rather than her siblings. She wished she hadn't been born with artistic talent and hadn't been selected to participate in the art competition that made her stay back in Abuja.

Even though she didn't wish to, it was hard for her not to feel guilty and take responsibility for the incident. On the nights she couldn't sleep, she wondered if things would have turned out differently if she hadn't pulled out of the journey. Perhaps her menstruation might have started that morning, and her heavy flow and discomfort might have made her mother move up their return to Abuja by a day. Knowing how forgetful she could get, maybe she would have forgotten her phone or laptop somewhere in the house, which would have made them return to get it, so it would have been another car in that spot when the bandits struck. But her skills as an artist saved her. Just as it saved her from feeling unworthy and unseen. First as a middle child and then for being different from everyone else in the family.

"Ochanya, where did you come from? You don't look anything like your parents or siblings."

"Ochanya, your sister and brothers are so tall. Where were you when God was sharing height?"

"Ochanya, I love your younger sister's hair. It is so long and curly."

"Ochanya, are those your brothers? They should just leave school and go into modelling."

"Ochanya, you are the darkest in your family; who did you take after?"

"Ochanya, it looks like your younger sister will be more beautiful than you when she grows up. You better do something now o."

"Ochanya, honestly, your parents are like brother and sister. How come they look like Fulani people when they are from Idoma, abi you people have Fulani blood in your lineage?"

Ochanya this, Ochanya that.

It was true her parents could pass for siblings. Her father was tall, light-skinned, and built like a former athlete who had retained his fitness by working out and adhering to a healthy dietary regimen. The glint in his eyes, his neatly groomed hair and his endearing smile made him the darling of viewers in every newsroom he worked. In RTN, he was nicknamed "The Leading Man" because management featured him in most of the programme promos they shot, not minding that he was in his forties and one of the oldest news anchors in the network.

Like her father, her mother too was light-skinned. In fact, they had near-identical skin tones and a presence that made them noticeable and admired whether they appeared separately or together as a couple.

While her father routinely worked out in the gym, her mother only went occasionally. However, after four kids, all in their teens, she still maintained her slender figure from when she was in her mid-twenties. No one could guess from just looking at Ene that she was in her early forties and two years younger than her husband, who still referred to her as his "girlfriend."

Her brothers were just as handsome as their father, and her sister inherited their mother's perfect genes. But she couldn't say proudly that she inherited as many of their features, and it was another thing that made Ochanya stand out in their close-knit family of six.

Ochanya stood out not because she wasn't pretty in her own right but because whenever she looked in the mirror, the little and the slight became magnified. For instance, she was light-skinned too, but her mother and kid sister were a little lighter. Her nose was pointed but slightly less pointy than theirs. She was tall but somewhat shorter than her mother and Ejuma, who was already taller than her at thirteen and almost as tall as their mother. She had luminous eyes, yet she needed just a little more luminousness to match those of her mother and baby sister. Her forehead had to be a bit less prominent to form the right distance between her hairline and the start of her eyes. There was always something she needed just a little bit of, which affected her confidence while growing up.

Her self-consciousness was the reason she avoided taking pictures, and if it wasn't mandatory, she wouldn't have been in any family portrait since turning eleven—the age people's comments really started to get to her. Ochanya was angry at herself. She was angry that she was sometimes jealous of Ejuma and had, on many occasions, wished that she received as much attention as her younger sister did.

Suddenly finding herself an only child with so many people doting on her seemed like that wish came true. But it felt terribly hollow, and she couldn't help thinking that she had wished for something else. Being a budding artist, she had two wishes. One was to have her paintings adorn homes and offices all over the world, and the second was to win a major international art competition while still in her teens. She should have wished for these, but instead, she prayed to outshine her sister, and the prayer was answered, a distraught Ochanya soliloquized.

Ochanya was angry at herself. She was mad that she and Inalegwu didn't speak for days, and on the last day she saw him, she had lied to get into his phone so she could read the text messages between him and her best friend, Irene. Inalegwu and Irene had been dating for weeks but kept it a secret from her.

She was angry for telling on Okopi when the ice cream their mother bought as dessert for them suddenly disappeared from the fridge. If she hadn't told their mother that she saw the empty container under Okopi's bed, maybe he wouldn't have called her ugly, and she wouldn't have told him to go to hell and burn to ashes.

But of all the things and people Ochanya was angry at, her father topped the list. She was mad at him for suggesting the Makurdi visit in the first place. She couldn't communicate her feelings to him or anyone else, but she blamed him for how things turned out for her mother and siblings. Thanks to his decision, her mother wouldn't be there for any of the important milestones of her life. Ochanya also wouldn't be seeing her siblings accomplish all the great things they talked about, and she held her father responsible for that too.

Ochanya was angry at her father for ignoring her mother's reluctance to leave Abuja for Makurdi so close to when they expected to hear back from Canada Immigration. Her mother wanted the visit after they secured the necessary travel approval, but her father would have none of it. Ochanya heard them arguing in their room that night. She overheard everything because the door of their bedroom was slightly ajar.

That night, she stood transfixed outside their door. Ochanya wondered why her mother was crying and why her father accused her of never listening to him and acting like she was the man of the house because she made more money than he did. It was a bitter fight that made her heart sink. It was a fight she wished she had never witnessed because in all the years she had known them as her parents, she had never seen or heard them argue with the viciousness they did that night.

However, to her greatest surprise and bewilderment, when she came down for breakfast the next morning, they were all loved up and acting like everything was dandy between them. Ochanya was surprised to see her parents talking to each other and laughing at something Okopi said, and she heaved a silent sigh of relief. Her parents weren't about to split up and go their separate ways, and their family was still intact. Her spirit was lifted again, and she had convinced herself that the fight was a dream.

13.

Unable to withstand the silence in the house when he got back to Abuja, Owoicho spent his first three nights in a hotel at Garki. He clearly didn't anticipate how incredibly quiet and depressing it would be without the people who made his house a home. He just wasn't prepared for it, so he opted for temporary accommodation elsewhere. He didn't realize until then that without the joy and laughter of family, from one moment to the next, the building in Maitama was just an address to fill out in forms and documents and for receiving parcels and what-nots. The place was nothing more than a meeting place for people wanting to see or track him down for something.

Owoicho learnt quickly, through his grief, that a house in itself didn't have a heart or a soul, or even a spirit. It is all form and no substance until the people in it breathe life into its bones and walls, and then it comes alive and becomes a sanctuary for its dwellers. Until then, it never really dawned on him that the noise the children made, things being constantly out of place, or even the mess in the compound, were essential components in the definition of family and necessary for his own wellness.

So desperate for patterns and the familiar was Owoicho that even the smell of food burning in the kitchen, which used to infuriate him, assumed a nostalgic appeal that he suddenly longed for. Ejuma was usually the culprit.

"Close the kitchen door!" was a familiar refrain around the house whenever she volunteered to help out in the kitchen. There was nothing Owoicho wouldn't do to say those words again if it would bring his favourite daughter back to him.

Tired of paying the bills, he was finally forced to check out of the hotel and head to Maitama. On his first day back, he ordered food from Jevinik Restaurant in Wuse 2. By the time he got home, the food had gone cold because he lingered at the fuel station talking to a friend who wasn't a friend in the true sense of the word. He had run into this person when he stopped at the NNPC Filling Station to fuel his car. Because they didn't really know each other well, there wasn't much to talk about other than the offer and acceptance of condolences. But Owoicho made sure to prolong the conversation by going off on a tirade about the state of insecurity in the country and how the President lied when he said on national TV that the government was winning the battle against insurgency and terrorism. The discussion was a desperate ploy to delay his return to his empty house.

Eventually, they ran out of things to say and Owoicho drove home. It was the slowest he had ever done the distance from the filling station to his house since moving to Maitama. Being someone who didn't enjoy eating from takeaway packs and disposable spoons, Owoicho went into the kitchen to fetch proper tableware and heat up the pounded yam, egusi, and the extra spicy snails he ordered for himself.

For as long as he could remember being a husband and father, there had always been a "daddy's plate and cutlery" reserved for every time he ate. His meals were never served in anything else, and food somehow tasted different if he used another fork or spoon from the kitchen. Again, he searched for patterns and the familiar. Although his foray into the kitchen was his first time after a long time, Owoicho found his way around without much trouble.

At night, he kept hearing noises. First, he thought it was Ene flushing the toilet or running a bath for him, and he smiled. But as quickly as he smiled, his heart sank. And then it sounded like the children were in the hallway and outside his window. He thought he heard their voices, but it wasn't them. It was a combination of the house settling in for the night and the wind rustling and asserting its dominance of the elements at play in the dark. Every other sound he thought he heard was in his head.

In order to drown out the voices tormenting him, Owoicho turned on the TV in his room and the one in the living room as well. He increased their volume so he could simultaneously listen to the panellists' conversation on CNN and the voice of the gospel singer Nathaniel Bassey on the other. On CNN, Don Lemon, two white ladies, and a Black gentleman were discussing the hypocrisy of the Republican Party in refusing to back a policy they had previously supported just because they lost the presidency to the Democratic Party in the just concluded presidential elections in America.

Hearing their voices above Nathaniel Bassey's saxophone without actually listening to the merits of what they were saying made Owoicho feel like he had other people in the house with him. It was the vibe he needed to chase away the spirits messing with his head, so the house didn't feel haunted by invisible people anymore. At five o'clock in the morning, still unable to sleep, he texted Maria, Odoo's wife, to find out when she would be back in Abuja. To his surprise, she texted back immediately to say she would be back in Kuje by the weekend.

That Sunday, Owoicho went to Kuje to visit Maria and her son. She expressed surprise when he asked for her account number and transferred the sum of two million naira to her bank account. He told her that since she didn't have the support of a husband anymore, the money was to help with any business ideas she could have after the baby was born. Maria thanked him profusely and prayed for God to bless him and send a befitting helpmate to replace the one he lost. She asked God to give him long life and fill his home with many children and grandchildren. To all of these prayers, Owoicho said a silent Amen. Maria equally prayed that his pocket never experienced dryness and for God to replenish the source from where the money came. Of course, she had no idea the money came from Governor Ochepo. It was the money in the black bag the governor's ADC had given to Owoicho in Makurdi.

Owoicho had the money in his account for days. At some point, he was tempted to give a part of it to Ene's parents, seeing that they had spent quite some money on the burial. He was going to keep the rest for himself; however, when he remembered the shabby way he and Ochanya were treated by the governor and his aides, even after using them as a gambit in his publicity stunt, Owoicho decided that he wanted none of it. Besides, with the tragic reduction in the size of his family, he didn't need any of that money. If anybody needed it, it was the poor widow suddenly turned breadwinner and her children who would grow up without their father's love and protection.

14.

"Seriously, Alegwu, you shouldn't have bothered travelling all the way from Lagos just to say sorry to me. In any case, we don dey talk for phone since the thing happen. I swear, if to say you tell me say you dey come see me, I for discourage you. It's not necessary. And you've done enough already."

"Haba, I no sabi my friend again? Dat na why I didn't give you any hint of my coming, because it is something I must do. You would have done the same thing for me if the tables were turned."

"Okay, if you say so. But as you don show now, wetin you think say go happen? You go fit bring Ene and the children back to life? In fact, na donation you do for those Air Peace people. You just dash them money for nothing. Your three hundred phone calls day and night in the last couple of days don do."

"Fifteen, why you dey talk like this?" Alegwu addressed his friend by the nickname that started way back in their university days when Owoicho would rip his notebooks and handouts fifteen minutes before every exam as a show of confidence in his ability to recall what he had read. His coursemates had nicknamed him "Fifteen."

Again, because he graduated with a second-class upper and never had a carryover as an undergraduate, the name and strategy perfectly worked for him. Over the years, some people would hear the number and imagine it referred to how long he lasted during sex, but they were wrong. In later years, Owoicho would continue with the ritual of arriving at the venue of events fifteen minutes before the start time, and he was always fifteen minutes early to work.

"Tor, wetin you want make I talk?"

"You mean say I for no travel come see you face-to-face and say my condolences? What are we friends for? In short, you don't know how terrible I feel not being here earlier to support you right from when you thought they were missing until now. Imagine me, Alegwu Francis, a whole me, missing Ene's burial. Two of your kids are my godchildren o, remember?"

"The twins."

"Yes, the twins. I still remember when they were born. Mercy and I came all the way from Lagos for their naming and dedication. We were still trusting God for a child after five years of marriage and four miscarriages. We didn't want to come at all because we felt somehow about being godparents to Okopi and Ejuma when we didn't have children of our own. We felt being there with you guys would remind us of our childlessness and leave us sad rather than happy for you and Ene."

"How can I forget?"

"In the end, we came because of Ene's persuasiveness. She convinced us that we would be doing the right thing by accepting to stand with both of you as godparents to the twins. She told us that not having children of our own didn't disqualify us from accepting the responsibility and honour. In fact, I vividly remember her saying that she believed our taking up the role of godparents would bring us good luck. She told us that we would have our own children and they would stay. And she was right. Divine-Favour was born that same year and Prince-Shammah came two years later. God used that child dedication to visit us because as your pastor prayed for all the childless couples in the church that day, Mercy and I tapped into the prayer. If Ene hadn't insisted that we came, we wouldn't have been blessed. Owoicho, your wife was a good woman. Ene na angel, I no go lie."

"That means that her assignment was over on earth, and God has called her back to continue her angelic duties in heaven," Owoicho said solemnly.

"Ene is gone," Alegwu lamented. "God, I still don't believe Ene is gone. Beautiful, understanding, patient, prayerful, ever-smiling Ene that would bend over backwards for people, even strangers."

"That is why they say good people don't last. I know that now."

Owoicho was in the living room with his best friend, Alegwu. Their friendship started way back when they were coursemates and later roommates at the university. Alegwu was there when he and Ene started dating. He was there as the best man when they got married, and until he moved to Lagos to take up a job with the Nigerian Ports Authority on the recommendation of his step-father, a retired comptroller of customs, they worked as tellers in the defunct Hallmark Bank. Whenever Owoicho was in-between jobs or changing careers and things were difficult for him financially, Alegwu was the one he called on. Alegwu was that friend that became a brother, and deep down inside, Owoicho was happy that he came around to see him. If nothing else, Alegwu's presence meant he would have company for a few days.

"I hope say you know why I dey here sha?"

"Tor, why are you here, abeg?"

"I am here so you can talk to someone about everything going on in your head right now. With everything you have been through in the last few weeks, I think you need someone you trust to pour it all out on and be completely human with. You know, as men, our greatest fear is to be perceived as weak, and, in our minds, nothing screams "weak" louder than showing our vulnerability."

"My friend don turn Dr. Phil abi Oprah Winfrey."

"No be like that. I just feel say you need a real friend right now. That was why I wanted to come since all these days, but my oga for office dey on leave and na me dey deputize for am."

"Alegwu, I am fine if that is where you're going with this."

"I haven't said you're not."

"You don't have to say it," Owoicho played with the can of Heineken in his hands as he spoke. "You've been acting like I'm an invalid or a nutcase since you got here."

Alegwu placed his drink on the table like he wanted his friend to see how serious he was about the conversation they were about having.

"I'm only wondering if you've grieved, Owoicho. Apart from losing my dad when I was in secondary school and maybe Mercy's miscarriages, I haven't had anyone close to me die, so I can't pretend to know the exact way you feel about losing Ene and the children. But as a close family friend for many years, I feel something too," Alegwu said.

"Does anyone really?"

"Come on, Fifteen. I know your feelings are a million times more than any pain, anger, and sadness the rest of us feel, but it is hard for us to process too. Look, Owoicho, me, I don cry for this their death tire. I don ask God plenty questions even though I know say I no supposed to do that kind of thing. Have you?"

"Have I what?"

"Have you taken time to ask God why it had to be them and why it has to be you going through this painful experience?"

"Alegwu, I said I am fine," Owoicho answered stubbornly.

"Fifteen, I know you. Na so you go dey form hard guy, hard guy like say the thing no touch you, but meanwhile you dey feel am oh. Even as we dey together since, you just dey take style dodge some of the questions wey I dey ask, as if nothing happen. Owoicho, get emotional if you must. Cry, shout, and if you want to talk to somebody, we dey here. Just don't bottle up your pain. Na that one dey quick cause wahala for people."

"Alegwu, I dey all right."

"Have you started thinking about the lifestyle changes you might be compelled to make? Have you even requested time off from work for these things?"

"I have done that."

"Owoicho, you went back to work as if nothing happened."

"Now you want to teach me how to mourn, abi?" Owoicho was starting to get upset. "Please, allow me deal with this thing in my own way. Cry, cry, shout. That is what people keep saying to me. If I start crying now, what will Ochanya do? What will Ene's old parents, who lost their only child, do? Alegwu, I am a man. It hurts, what I have been through, but I will take it like a man."

"I'm sorry, Owoicho. I came here to offer comfort and not to agitate you," Alegwu immediately apologized when he noticed the change in his friend's countenance.

"I am hurting. I am sad. I am grieving. I am lonely. I am angry. I am miserable. I am all those things you said, but I am also in denial because I am afraid of admitting my mistake to myself. I don't want to face the fact that I am responsible for their death. It was me. Alegwu, I caused it, and now you have heard me admit it. I sent Ene and those innocent children to their death."

"What do you mean?" Alegwu couldn't mask his surprise.

"Ene never wanted to go to Makurdi that weekend. I made her go. I forced her to go on that trip and ensured she carried the children along. In fact, we fought over that particular decision for days, but in the end, she did what I wanted because that's who Ene was. She listened to me."

"Why were you determined to get them to travel to Makurdi?" a perplexed Alegwu asked.

"Because we could be migrating to Canada, and her parents didn't know. I wanted them to warm up to the idea of our leaving and not just have us spring a surprise on them a few weeks or even days before we left Nigeria for good. If we did that, I know they would automatically assume I put Ene to it. It would never occur to them that the whole migration thing was her idea in the first place and that she was always drumming it in my ears not to allow anyone in on the secret until the process was finalized and we obtained our Canadian PR papers."

"You guys are migrating to Canada?" Alegwu almost screamed.

Owoicho felt it was a night of bombshells and surprises for his friend, who let it show by literally letting his jaw drop.

"Alegwu, what you just did now is why I don't speak about it to anyone. You should have seen the look on your face when I mentioned Canada and immigration in one sentence."

"I won't say I wasn't shocked hearing this now. I'm also thinking how it feels like Canada is on another planet and that I'd need a spaceship if I wanted to visit," Alegwu said.

Owoicho could tell he was still unable to hide his disappointment at being kept in the dark over something he felt he should have been told sooner.

"With that being said, I respect your decision to keep certain things about your family private, so I won't go into that conversation with you today. However, Fifteen, just so you know, I'm happy you found an escape route out of this country. It is the best thing any father can do for his child right now when it feels like the government isn't doing anything to make this country work again. Our leaders have no idea how to solve the many problems besetting us as a nation, and that's scary as hell," Alegwu said after getting over his initial shock and disappointment.

"Thank you, Alegwu. I appreciate that you understand why we kept it hush-hush."

"Concerning what you said about being the one who convinced Ene to travel with the kids to see her parents, all I can say is that God knows best. What will be will be. Shebi that is how they say it in English," Alegwu smiled. "Please don't be too hard on yourself. And can you stop blaming yourself that things took the sad turn they did? Stop taking responsibility for what may have been divinely programmed to happen, whether you suggested it or not. If it was preordained as their destiny, then they would have still been in that spot one way or the other."

"But I should have listened to her."

"You meant well suggesting she visited with her parents. That's the most important thing you should tell yourself when these bad thoughts come."

"Thank you, Alegwu. Thank you."

15.

ALEGWU ARRIVED IN ABUJA ON A FRIDAY EVENING AND LEFT for Lagos on Sunday morning. He stayed for just two nights, and Owoicho was sad to see him leave. But he understood that his friend had to go back to work and to his wife and kids in Lagos. That was life. It keeps moving. Everyone moves on. In the end, you are left to deal with your problems yourself. No matter how much concern people show, be it real or fake, when the time comes for them to leave, they leave. Since becoming a widower, this was one reality he understood better.

When he returned home after dropping off his friend at the airport, he headed straight to his room and did as Alegwu advised. He went under the duvet and let it all out. Owoicho cried like he had never cried before in his life. He wept because of the pain and the hollow it left in his heart and for the silence and emptiness in his home. He wept for being unable to share his guilt with anyone else and for bottling it up for so long. He wept because he really wanted to tell Alegwu everything but some things were better left unsaid. He wept because in the early hours of the seventh of July, a day he would never forget, for the fifth time in his eighteen years of marriage, he cheated on his wife. He wept because that night, while Ochanya slept peacefully in her room, he snuck his neighbour's twenty-two-year-old niece into the guestroom downstairs, and they made love till five in the morning.

When it was over, Owoicho hated himself. He should have known better. He should never have sent that text message but something stronger than his will to resist took control of him. He was way older and wiser. He was on TV almost every night and when he turned on the charm like he did in the car that day, the poor girl didn't stand a chance.

This was the secret he swore to take with him to the grave.

His indiscretion and desecration of his home, in the manner he did that night, even if it was his first and only time, with a girl he barely even knew, a girl he only gave a ride to Jabi because it was raining that morning, was the reason God struck him with a punishment so severe it left him broken and scarred for life.

Owoicho knew that his action that night, behind Ene's back, and with his daughter under the same roof, was the reason for the catastrophe that befell his family. It was the reason God took Ene and the children away from him. He was the reason his wife died; nothing anyone said to him would convince him otherwise.

Owoicho wept uncontrollably for bringing a curse on his family.

16.

THE NEXT ONE MONTH WENT BY REALLY FAST. OWOICHO WAS thankful for work and the fact that it kept him busy. Considering the tragic circumstances surrounding the passing of his wife and three of his children, no one had expected him back in the newsroom and in front of the camera so soon, but Owoicho needed the adrenaline rush that came with deadlines and breaking stories in a twenty-four-hour news circle. He needed to stay active. Do something, anything to stop himself from thinking about Ene and the children all the time. He needed to be among people so he didn't feel lost and alone. He needed to keep his mind focused on being exceptional at work and delivering every time he was scheduled to read the news, interview a public figure, or work on a special report.

The first few weeks were incredibly tough for him. His biggest challenge was having to report new cases of kidnapping, banditry, and attacks by herdsmen almost every other day, similar to his own experience. But Owoicho was a seasoned professional, and, if nothing else, his own ordeal meant he could empathize and approach such stories from a perspective most other news anchors couldn't.

Apart from the demands of his job, perhaps the other equally pressing thing on his plate was moving house. It was something he knew would happen at some point, but he didn't expect it would happen with the alacrity it did.

The house in Maitama was owned by the Benue State government. It was originally intended as an annex for accommodating top-ranking political appointees and their friends whenever the main Benue House in Abuja was occupied. But because the men always came with their girlfriends, and the women too sometimes had male companions, they feared that stories of their philandering could get back to their spouses in

Makurdi, so they abandoned the property. However, the main reason the building was shunned by visiting appointees was the knowledge that they were entitled to lodge in any five-star hotel in Abuja at the expense of Benue State's taxpayers. Certainly, it was easier to inflate travel and out-of-station allowances when one stayed in a hotel than in a government-run guest house.

Expectedly, the more the number of official visits to the FCT an appointee or elected functionary made, the more government money there was to fleece and misappropriate to the detriment of the generality of the people of the state.

For many years before Owoicho's family moved in, the house remained deserted by previous administrations. The guest and pool houses were used as storage for old government files, which was quite unfortunate considering the value of property in Abuja. There were the occasional stragglers from God knows where, though, who paid money to someone in charge of the building at some point so they could use the place for short-term sexual encounters. This went on for quite a while, and it would be the only thing the building was known for because someone in a government office in Makurdi was profiting from the hotel arrangement. The mansion that would later become home to him and his family was a monument of waste and an exemplification of a mindset that prioritized profligacy over education, security, social infrastructure, and healthcare.

The call to Owoicho's phone came on a Monday afternoon, just before he went into the studio to read the four o'clock news recap. The caller with the strange number that had a lot of threes in it arrogantly introduced himself as the Deputy Chief of Staff to the Governor of Benue State. There was no salutation or pleasantries. The voice went straight to the purpose of the call.

"His Excellency, Governor Lazarus Ochepo has appointed a new head of protocol and manager for Benue House. The appointment of the replacement for the late Mrs. Ene Adakole is with immediate effect. To this end, you are kindly requested to vacate the house at Number 4 Jamaica Crescent, Maitama, which is your current residence, to enable the new appointee, Mr.

Dominic Ochepo Junior, take possession of the house. Please do this within the next two weeks of this phone call to avoid embarrassment to you and your family."

Owoicho could have sworn that it was a robocall or the caller read out the message verbatim from a printed letter someone forgot to mail out to him. But what did it matter? The important thing was that they wanted him out of the house immediately, and he must comply.

In the two weeks they gave him to find a new place and hand over the keys to the Dominic fellow who shared the same last name with the governor, he contacted a property agent he found online. True to her word, the lady found him a decent two-bedroom apartment in Gwarimpa.

Before moving out of the old house, he called Ochanya to brief her on the development and to ask if there were some of her mother's and sister's stuff she would like to keep. Her response was an unenthusiastic "no."

Since returning to Abuja, he endeavoured to speak to her every day, although he noticed that he did all the calling and most of the talking. She never initiated contact, and when he did, she had very little to say. She seemed distracted and disinterested in the things happening in his life. Owoicho thought it was unlike his daughter, but he was too frightened to bring up his observations with her grandparents. He thought they were doing enough keeping her, and bringing this up might come across as ungrateful.

Still, it hit him hard that the gulf between him and Ochanya was widening by the day, and he needed to do something about it. But that was something for a later day. His immediate headache was how to fit all the furniture, clothes, and sundry assets from the big house into this smaller one.

Even more worrisome was his inability to figure out what to do with the things that belonged to Inalegwu, Okopi, and Ejuma. Burn them? Give them away? Keep them for their emotional value? He was confused and uncertain about what to do with their clothes, toys, and books. Eventually, he gave everything away to the cleaners and security guards in the office. He had no use for them, but they did and seeing their faces light up as they made their pick brought a large smile to his face. He hoped their children's faces would light up too when they saw the things.

The day he took down the picture frames was by far the hardest. He was alone, so he didn't feel bad about talking to himself and shedding a tear. Looking at their wedding photos made his heart sink. Reliving the memories of that special day sent sharp darts through his heart, and Owoicho took a short break to gather his wits again.

Ene looked lovely in her wedding dress and in all the dresses she wore in the other pictures as well. She looked lovely in the dress she wore the first day they met. That picture didn't have to be on the wall; it was framed in his soul.

The dress she wore that day was short. It was a sleeveless denim ensemble with patched pockets and large buttons from top to bottom. It was their first lecture as students at the Federal University, Makurdi. Even though he was in Mass Communications and she was studying Microbiology, all freshers converged in a large hall for English 101. They sat beside each other. He offered to buy her a drink after class, and she accepted. They became friends, dated throughout the university, broke up when they went for national service in different states, reconnected after her post-graduate program in the UK, and married shortly after. They had loved each other long and hard, and there was no getting over her and the life they created together.

The final thing that kept Owoicho occupied was the running around and waiting for the Letters of Administration concerning his late wife's estate from the courts. He had applied for it immediately after he got back to Abuja so he could have access to the money Ene had saved up for their relocation. The banks needed the Letters of Administration to make any arrangements with him without getting themselves into trouble. He was told the process took about two months, but it could be concluded within a month under special arrangements. Owoicho opted for the special arrangement so he didn't have to wait too long.

With all the things going on around him, he had to put off taking a position on Canada until he heard back from the banks. There were so many other things to consider, but money had become the prime factor in whether he and Ochanya travelled out or stayed back in Nigeria. Owoicho had to be sure there was enough of it to see them through the first year of their new life in Saskatoon in relative comfort. His plan, if he decided to move, was to register for some course in journalism and communications that would enable him to get back into radio or television. The money would enable him to do that with ease.

Owoicho secured the letter on a Tuesday afternoon but decided to wait until the next day before going to the banks with the authorization. There was no rush. An excited Owoicho arrived at the first bank early the next morning. He didn't know how much Ene had with the banks because they never really discussed it, so he could only speculate. She did all their Canada immigration application herself, and he only showed up when he had to do something personal, like medicals and getting his biometrics taken. But based on what she told him before she left for Makurdi on that final journey, he would say, at the very minimum, that her balances would total around ten to fifteen million naira.

The manager of the GTBank branch in Wuse ushered him into his office and handed over the statement to him in a sealed envelope. Owoicho thanked him and promptly left his office for Fidelity Bank in Garki, the second and only other place that confirmed holding her account. Again, because of his popularity as a newscaster on national television, the bank's branch manager was all smiles when welcoming him into her office. She also gave him the statement he requested in a sealed envelope.

In search of the perfect atmosphere to open both envelopes, Owoicho drove straight home in his red Honda CR-V. Grabbing a chilled can of Heineken from the refrigerator, he relaxed on the sofa and began the deliberately slow process of ending the suspense like he was Ebuka on the final eviction episode of the Big Brother Naija reality show.

Not all moments are rushed. Some are meant to be experienced in slow motion, and this was one of them. Owoicho took his time. He was gentle with the seal to avoid ripping the paper inside the branded envelopes. When it was time to unfold the statements, he did so even more delicately.

Owoicho's eyes popped wide open, and they stayed that way as if dilating them would help him better understand the documents he was holding. Wanting better illumination in case the problem was with where he sat, he moved closer to one of the bigger windows that allowed the most light into the living room. The figures didn't change. His eyes weren't playing tricks on him.

Instead of the ten or fifteen million naira he expected to see when he added the balances from the two banks, the total he got was two hundred and seventy-two-thousand naira, twenty-one kobo! The first thought that came to his head was that he and Ochanya would never get to Canada with that amount of money. Two hundred- and seventy-two-thousand-naira, twenty-one kobo might land them in Sagamu, but certainly not Saskatoon.

In spite of the temperature in the room and the cold beer he had sipped just moments before, Owoicho broke into a sweat, and his heart began to palpitate. His head was filled with questions, many of which were meant for one person – his late wife. Of all the questions he needed answers to, the most pressing was the one he repeated over and over again to himself as he folded the bank papers and put them back in their envelopes.

"Ene, where on earth did you keep the damn money?"

17.

"OCHANYA, WHERE ARE YOU COMING FROM? WE HAVE looked everywhere in the compound for you?"

"Grandma, I went for a walk."

"Ochanya, you went for a walk at this time of the night? Ehn, Ochanya, when will you stop acting like this? Ehn, when?"

Madam Elsie was starting to get frustrated by her granddaughter's attitude, and she couldn't hide it anymore. Since the death of the girl's mother and siblings and asking Owoicho to let her stay with them, Ochanya had been nothing but trouble. It was always one thing or another with her, and the old woman was tired of talking to her about it. Her husband was also tired of her constant nagging, so she no longer went to him with her observations and complaints. The last time Ochanya acted up and she spoke to him about it, he told her categorically that he didn't have the heart to scold or discipline a child that was still dealing with a traumatic situation way above her years.

It started with the crying that went on for weeks. After her father left for Abuja, all Ochanya did was cry. From the start of the day until the end, people in the house hardly saw her because she would lock herself up in her room, and if she bothered coming out for meals at all, her eyes would be bloodshot and swollen. Then she refused to go with them for the mandatory written test and oral interview requirement for the new school they found for her because, according to Ochanya, they didn't let her say goodbye to her friends and teachers in her old school. It took almost one week and the intervention of her father to get her to change her mind about the test and interview and accept that Makurdi was her new home, at least for the time being.

After the crying and refusing to enrol in school phases, next came the sleeping-and-not-wanting-to-help-out-with-chores-around-the-house phase. When Madam Elsie brought this up with Owoicho, he told her he was shocked to hear that his daughter was suddenly acting lazy because, at home, she was the hardworking and responsible one they counted on to maintain order and cleanliness. Again, he intervened, but it didn't yield much success this time.

The next thing was with Ochanya's phone and the television in her room. This time it was Owoicho himself who called to complain to his in-laws because he noticed from her WhatsApp status that she was online most nights. And that, as far as he was concerned, could only mean one thing. She wasn't sleeping, and maybe there was a boy she was talking to.

When he brought this to their attention, Madam Elsie and her husband decided they would take turns opening her door intermittently to ensure Ochanya was asleep and not on her phone. It was during these checks they found out about her TV addiction. Ochanya told them she couldn't sleep without the TV on and that she had nightmares about her mother and siblings whenever it was quiet in the room. There was very little they could do about this because she linked the problem to the death of her mother and other siblings. So, they would sometimes monitor the sound coming from her room and go in to turn off the television when it looked like she had slept off. At other times, though, they just let her be.

The most worrisome development was the disappearing act. Madam Elsie wasn't comfortable with Ochanya's description of the countless times she left the house within the last month as "mere walks to clear her head." She suspected strongly that there was more to the walks than her granddaughter was letting on because Ochanya wouldn't let anyone know when she left the house or be specific about the duration or destination of her nightly solo outings. However, Madam Elsie was hesitant to stop her granddaughter from staying out after sundown because she didn't have proof that they weren't as harmless as they were meant to believe.

"Grandma, the way you emphasize this night thing, anyone listening to you would think the time was 11 PM or something like that. It's just 7:30 in the evening, and it's really not that dark outside."

"It is dark outside, Ochanya. The whole street is pitch black!"

"But I was just around the corner," Ochanya defended herself. "And if you must know, I've only been away for an hour and a half. I time my walk, grandma, I time my walk!"

"Young girl, you keep missing the point whenever I talk to you about these things. This country is not the way it used to be."

"I know, grandma, but it was really hot inside the house. I couldn't stay in my room because of the heat, and everything I was studying was just entering my head and evaporating again. Grandma, you know how restless I get when there is no electricity in the house, and you won't allow Mr. Samuel to turn on the generator until seven o'clock. What was I supposed to do, take off my dress and sit on the bare floor?"

"This girl, the way you talk sometimes, I just wonder," Madam Elsie shook her head in frustration. "If I am concerned about you being out in the dark, it is because this country is not how it used to be when I was your age. I keep telling you this, but you will not listen. Even this GRA is not like it used to be when we first moved here many years ago. Today, there are a lot of funny characters all over the place. Please, Ochanya, be careful. That is all I am saying. If it is dark and you must take these your nocturnal walks, please let someone know before you leave the house. It will not cost me anything to ask someone to accompany you."

"Grandma, I don't need an escort for a short walk around my own neighbourhood. After all, I am still on my street," Ochanya protested. "I didn't even cross into the next street."

"Then try not to always forget your phone, even if you are just standing in front of the gate," Madam Elsie retorted. "Nobody is saying you should not exercise your mind and body if that is what you go out to do. What we are saying is that you should inform the people in the house before you step out of the gate. It is the responsible thing for a girl your age to do. In fact, it is the responsible thing for anyone anywhere in the world. Even your grandfather cannot just get up, enter his car, and drive out without letting me or someone else in the house know where he is going. What if something happens while you are out? Where will we begin to look for you?"

"But I thought Mr. Samuel saw me leave. Shouldn't he always be at the gate when people come in or go out? Isn't that what he's being paid for?"

"Ochanya, at this point, you should simply say, 'I have heard you, grandma, I will not do it again,' and end this long talk."

"Grandma, I've heard you, and I am sorry. Next time, I will make an announcement so the whole house knows I am going out to take fresh air."

"Now that you've said those words, have you died?" Madam Elsie said, ignoring the sarcasm in her granddaughter's voice.

"So, you were looking for me. Did you want me to do something for you?" Ochanya asked, changing the subject.

"No. It was Sisi who was looking for you. She wanted to do the dishes, and she needed some help."

"Okay, and that was why you were looking for me? Am I now expected to hold her hands while she does the dishes?" Ochanya asked rather rudely.

"Ochanya. Ochanya, calm down."

"Grandma, I am calm. I just don't see the connection between me and the plates Sisi needed to wash. Did she need me to sing her a song while she did the washing?"

"Sisi said you didn't eat in the dining room this afternoon?"

"No, I didn't. I took my food to my room because I wanted to eat and study at the same time."

"After eating, you did not take the plates to the kitchen so Sisi could wash them. That was why she was looking for you."

"Okay, did she find the plates she was looking for in my room?"

"Yes. She found the ones for today, the ones from last night, and the ones you used in the morning. They were all under your reading table."

"Grandma, this is so wrong. So, so wrong. Why would Sisi be allowed into my room when I wasn't even there? What if she took something or found something I don't want her to see?"

"Like what, the boy you have been hiding from us?"

"I am not hiding Oche. He is my friend. He lives on the next street, and I met him in church. Your church. You know his parents. He and I would be in the same class when school resumes in September. And he has only been here twice. And if you must know, he was telling me about the school and the kind of people who go there. We sat down together here at the dining table all through his visits. Everyone could see us!"

"Still, you did not get our permission before allowing him into the house," Madam Elsie insisted.

"Grandma, can I go to my room now? Please?"

Ochanya didn't wait for her request to be granted. She stormed out of her grandmother's presence and into her room. She didn't slam the door behind her, but the scream she let out when she entered her room had the same effect.

18.

OCHANYA LOCKED HERSELF UP IN HER ROOM. SHE DIDN'T COME out until after the generator was turned off, and her grandparents and the rest of the household had retired for the night. She hated that she did that and that it was becoming a pattern, but she couldn't help herself. When her father decided she was better off staying back in Makurdi without seeking her opinion, he left her with two unpleasant options. One was to recoil into her shell and stay there, the obedient daughter meekly accepting his wishes. The other was to become difficult, put on an act, and lash out at her grandparents as if they were responsible for the tragic demise of her mother and siblings. Ochanya chose the latter. The strategy she opted for was to stay aloof and frustrate everyone around her, especially her grandparents, with her faux obstinacy and outspokenness. When they did everything to get through to her without success, her grandparents would be left with no other choice but to send her back to her father.

She longed for the familiarity of Abuja and the environment she grew up in. Her longing intensified when her father told her about the new house in Gwarinpa. There was nothing she wanted more than to join him there and be a part of his new beginning. But she found herself unable to communicate her needs to him in a way that he would understand where she was coming from and what was going through her teenage mind.

Her grandparents too didn't quite comprehend the extent of her angst and frustration. Ochanya wished they did. She also wished she didn't have to pretend to be something she wasn't whenever they reached out to her with the special kind of love and kindness grandparents reserved for their grandchildren. It wasn't always easy keeping up with the whole difficult adolescent charade that was her strategy for getting out, but she thought it the best way to grab her father's attention. She believed wholeheartedly that it was the only way to get him to see how unhappy she was in this new home when her desired life was elsewhere.

On several occasions, Ochanya was tempted to knock on her grandmother's door and ask to spend time with her. She wanted to listen as the old woman told stories of what her life was like growing up. Ochanya longed to hear her grandmother's stories, and she missed her hugs too. She missed having Madam Elsie as her confidante and companion, the way every granddaughter wanted their grandmother to be. She missed the closeness they shared before the incident at Wamba happened and shattered their lives.

Ochanya wished they could sit outside in the evenings, and maybe even cook dinner together sometimes. She wished she could brighten her grandmother's dark days and say something funny and comforting to her and her grandfather because they were hurting too. But she just couldn't bring herself to do it. Ochanya may have hardened her heart to the truth, but deep down, she knew they wanted her to stay with them because it kept them connected to her mother. Having her in their home and seeing her daily was like having their own daughter still. She knew this because she overheard some things they said when they thought she wasn't listening. Painfully though, because she was consumed by her mission of escaping Makurdi and going back to her father, she chose to place purpose over emotions.

Occasionally though, Ochanya wondered if they could see through her tantrums and discern what was really going on with her. She wondered if her wise grandparents could tell that her attitude was an act, the distancing and resistance to elderly counsel and parental supervision a cry to her father. She knew that her grandparents spoke with him often and that they reported to him every time she did something wrong. That was why she was upset by his refusal to acknowledge her bad behaviour. It was as if he had moved on with his life and couldn't be bothered about her childish drama.

Their daily conversations since he left were mostly peripheral. It was lots of monosyllables and no substance except when he wanted to know why she stopped painting.

"Are you taking a break?"

"I'm not taking a break, dad. I just don't see myself painting ever again."

"I think it's too soon to speak about a talent God gave you with that much finality. The last couple of weeks have been tough for all of us, no doubt, but I'm sure you'll feel differently a few months down the line."

"Dad, I won't."

"Ochanya, drawing and painting is your life. You were born to be an artist. It is something we have known since you were seven."

"But you and mum have always said that you wanted me to study Medicine and that painting can be a hobby."

At that point, she should have told him about her guilt, but she didn't. She didn't think he would understand, no matter how hard she tried to make him see that her being alive was because of the stupid arts competition her school signed her up for. He would say it was God's will and that they couldn't question God. But Ochanya couldn't understand why God would spare her from that attack only to afflict her with the burden of survivor's guilt. Sometimes the feeling got really acute and overwhelming, and all she could think about was cutting herself and ending it all.

"Still, your mother and I spent a lot of money setting up a studio for you in the boys' quarters of the old house," her father said. "So now that you are in Makurdi waiting for school to resume, why don't you just let me send the things in the studio across to you? I know your grandparents are willing to convert one of the rooms in their house into a studio for you."

"How did you know that?"

"Because we talked about it."

"I'm not sure I want that, dad. I don't think I can work on any art piece ever again. I already told you."

"But you can; it's what you've been doing since you were a little girl. You can't just give up painting because you are unhappy right now. It has always kept you busy, plus you are really good at it."

Once more, her father prevailed, and she had her makeshift studio set up in Makurdi. Except no one saw her go in there or create any art. She preferred sneaking into the studio when everyone in the house was asleep just to stare at her old works. She didn't touch anything; she just stared.

The paintings, arranged neatly on the floor of the studio, evoked memories of a happier time when she was experimental with colours. The more vibrant they were, the better and more beautiful a piece of art was to her. But since her life unravelled, the only colour stuck in her head was red. The blood-red splattered in the car and on the decapitated corpses in the forests of Wamba.

With just the backlight from her phone guiding her, Ochanya tiptoed down the hallway and into the room beside the one Sisi and the other house-help slept. It was the room her grandparents turned into a makeshift art studio for her.

Ochanya picked a brush from the stand and walked towards the easel with the twelve-by-twelve blank canvas. It had been that way for weeks. She closed her eyes and conjured up an image for the canvas. It was of a boy and a girl entangled in an awkward embrace on a dark street. The girl had several red butterflies fluttering in her stomach because it was her first time being so close to a boy, and she didn't know whether to enjoy it or be scared. In her imagination, the girl's eyes were closed. Ochanya couldn't tell if it meant anything, so she was afraid to transfer it from her head onto the canvas. How does an artist portray uncertainty in a painting? Ochanya wondered. She let the brush fall to the floor. She wasn't supposed to be painting or even thinking about it.

As she tiptoed back to her room, Ochanya wondered what she would do if Oche asked to kiss her.

19.

Call Onjefu. Call Onjefu. Call Onjefu…

Owoicho didn't know why he kept hearing those words repeatedly in his head. He heard them in his dream and even when he was awake. Since finding out that Ene didn't have the money meant for their travel in the bank, it was all he could think about. He thought about it when he was alone and when he was in the midst of people. Those two bank statements flashed before his eyes, whether at work, preparing to go on air, or in the house praying for sleep to rescue him from the emptiness that had become his life. And every time they did, something in his heart tightened like a noose threatening to restrict air supply to the rest of his body.

Finding out Ene might have kept the money somewhere he didn't know about was such a big blow, and he couldn't even begin to process it. It hurt. It hurt every single time he thought about it. A devasted Owoicho couldn't tell which was worse—that she didn't trust him enough to let him in on the details of her finances or that some fraudulent bank staff might have tampered with the funds.

Whatever the situation, the significant thing was that he was in great pain, and that much was certain. What was opaque, however, was whether the pain came from watching their Canadian dream get buried together with Ene or if it was something worse. He needed a lot of money to make that dream a reality, and if he was unable to raise a substantial amount before the expiration of their visas, then he might as well kiss that dream goodbye.

Where was the money? Why didn't Ene tell him where she kept it?

Those questions and many more tormented him night and day.

Call Onjefu. Call Onjefu. Call Onjefu…

Though it was way past midnight, Owoicho decided to obey the voice. He asked Siri to call his brother, Onjefu Adakole. He knew it was late, but he figured calling at that time of the night would signal to Onjefu that he wanted to speak to him about something serious. Something that had to be attended to immediately and couldn't be put off for when the rest of the world was awake.

"Hey, bro," Owoicho could hear voices and music in the background.

I shouldn't have been worried about disturbing his sleep.

Expectedly, his brother was partying or out clubbing with friends.

"Owoicho!" Abeg, hold on small. Let me find somewhere quiet so we can hear ourselves better."

"No wahala, I'll hold," Owoicho said, reaching for his Air Pods to help improve the audio quality from his own end. He almost didn't recognize his brother's voice because it had been long since they last spoke to each other on the phone. And apart from their brief exchange at the burial, they also hadn't seen themselves in years.

"Hello. Hello. Can you hear me now?" Onjefu's voice sounded different.

Thicker. Settled. Confident. Prosperous. Happy, maybe? He is rich now.

"Yes. It is better now. So, how are you?"

"Owoicho, you are just calling me now to ask how I am? Why are you even calling me at this time of the night?"

Because I need your help.

"Because…because I suspect you live a busy life, and this might be a good time," Owoicho blurted out. "Bro, I am sorry I didn't call you after Otukpo. It has been rough. But I made a thank you post on Facebook and tagged as many people as I could. I also sent out a personalized text to everyone on my contact list. I sent one to you; you never responded."

"You didn't tell me about the burial, remember? I heard about it from strangers. Look, let's not even talk about it. It's all in the past now. Besides, it's about death. I wasn't close to your wife, but I respected her. And those kids? They were my nephew and nieces. I can't be forming enmity with you when I know what you went through. I thought you'd call me when you got back to Abuja to thank me for showing up and for the money I gave to your in-laws."

Thank you? You came to show off.

"Thank you, Onjefu. Your presence meant a lot."

"You're welcome. Anyway, that one don pass. Back to my question. Why is Mr. Perfect calling me at this time of the night?"

Mistake. This is a mistake...

At this point, Owoicho was torn between telling his brother the real reason for the call and making up a story about just wanting to check up on him or something. He already felt small reaching out to him. He could imagine how much smaller he would feel if he asked his step-brother for financial assistance.

You've got to ask! It's your emancipation money we're talking about here.

"Big bro, you are still not saying anything."

Owoicho was happy his brother couldn't see how nervous he was. He didn't know how to ask for favours from people, not even from his brother. He had no idea where to begin or what to say to Onjefu. It had always been that way since they were kids. They were two brothers with nothing in common.

Their relationship had been strained since they were young boys growing up in Makurdi. As they grew older, things got even worse between them. His mother used to tell him that it wasn't his fault they didn't like each other. He was good; Onjefu was bad. That was it.

Onjefu had always been the stubborn one. The child who was a disgrace to the family. He was the son who always went out to look for trouble and brought embarrassment home. He was that boy who would never do well or amount to anything good in life. Then and even when they grew older, Owoicho couldn't bring himself to accept his deviant ways, even if they were related by blood—their father's blood.

Onjefu came to live with them when he was eleven. Owoicho was seventeen and just finishing secondary school when he knew he had a brother. His father, a driver with Benue Links, worked for the Western Region department in the parastatal, which meant he did a lot of travelling across the Yoruba-speaking states in Nigeria. For most of his time, driving from Benue to states in the west, he plied the incredibly busy and lucrative Lagos-Makurdi route. That was how he met Onjefu's mother, Morenikeji. She had a canteen in the motor park at Mile 2, where drivers from the corporation congregated for the night. Most of them would sleep in their vehicles or anywhere in the park they found space to lie down for a few hours. They did that to save the extra money the government gave them for accommodation in whatever city they anchored for the night.

Morenikeji made the best ewedu and gbegiri soup, but that wasn't what she was famous for. Nearly all the drivers were smitten by her heavy bosom and big backside, which drew them to her business. But of all the admirers that flock to her like bees to honey, it was Anebi Adakole, the handsome, bearded one from Otukpo, she gave her body and affection. She was a widow with no children, so Anebi offered her comfort and companionship. In return, she gave him good food and something to look forward to at night. When she got pregnant and had a son, Anebi married her, but he didn't tell his first wife in Makurdi about this situation.

After she had Owoicho, his mother, Grace, had wanted to give her husband more children, but sadly it never happened. But she knew her husband wanted at least one more son and maybe even a daughter because he sometimes said hurtful things to her when he was drunk. One day, while emptying the pocket of some clothes he wanted her to wash for him, she saw a piece of paper that caught her attention. It was a list of things his son needed for school, and she was happy that he was making back-to-school plans for their boy without her asking. The only problem, though, was that when she examined the list more closely, she discovered that the name on the paper wasn't Owoicho but Onjefu.

Who on earth was Onjefu?

They fought about it, but in the end, his mother accepted her fate. She knew almost all the other drivers had women and children in the cities they frequented, and she had always suspected that her husband was no exception. She was prepared for the inevitable just as long as her position as the first wife wasn't threatened and his father didn't shirk his responsibilities to them.

The same year his mother found out about her husband's dalliance, Morenikeji died. The hospital said she died of natural causes even though she was sick for a long time and doctors couldn't fathom what was wrong with her.

Initially, Onjefu stayed with his maternal aunt and her family in Mushin. But as an only child of a woman who had given up on having children, Morenikeji had indulged him. The ten-year-old was so stubborn and spoilt that he didn't last a year with his aunt.

After they rejected him and he had nowhere else to go, Anebi was asked to come and take his child. Onjefu was trouble from the get-go. Neighbours complained about things disappearing under mysterious circumstances. Money, shoes, chicken, soup, soap—nothing was safe. And it all started when he moved into the neighbourhood.

Tragedy struck the Adakoles household a year after Onjefu joined them. Anebi died of renal failure. His dying wish to Owoicho's mother as he took his last breath was that she took care of Onjefu like he was her own son. And his mother did exactly that. She hounded him so he didn't drop out of secondary school. She borrowed money several times to bail him out when he got into trouble and was arrested by the police.

When he was rusticated from the University of Jos for engaging in secret cult activities, she looked for money and encouraged him to start again at another university. In his final year at the Lagos State University, he was caught cheating in the exam hall and would have been rusticated if his mother hadn't sold her farmland in the village to raise the money demanded as a bribe by the lecturer and his cohorts in the exams and records office.

During his national youth service program in Lagos, Onjefu was involved in a ghastly road accident on a night out drinking with friends, and it was Owoicho's mother who bought a wheelchair for him. Everyone thought being paralyzed from the accident would slow Onjefu down and maybe even change him completely, but they were wrong. Yes, other people with similar experiences repented and even became a born-again Christian, but not Onjefu. If anything, he became even more engrafted in his quick money-making schemes. From his wheelchair, Onjefu concocted ingenious ways of committing crimes and defrauding people. What he couldn't accomplish because of his lack of mobility, he did with technology and brain power.

In spite of all these, until her death, Owoicho's mother would send Onjefu money whenever he complained to her about being broke. She continued to send him money and foodstuff from Makurdi even after he secured a job as a lab technician with the Lagos State Government three years after the accident. The job was to fill a disability quota in the state's ministry of health.

Owoicho wasn't in touch with many people from his past, but every now and then, he would run into someone from their old compound, church, or school, and they would tell him that his mother died when she did because of the trouble Onjefu gave her. That was why he couldn't stand his younger brother. Like those people, he believed that Onjefu contributed to his mother's death from cardiac arrest. And that was something he was still angry about.

But then again, he was happy that she wasn't alive to see her beloved stepson resign from his government job in preference for the dark and nefarious world of cybercrime. People kept coming to him with stories that his step-brother had become a yahoo-yahoo boy. Onjefu didn't deny it when Owoicho confronted him with the allegation. Still, they occasionally spoke about life and other things because he knew his mother would expect that from him.

However, the final straw that made him sever ties with Onjefu happened when he catfished a Senior Advocate of Nigeria. He had created a fake Facebook account where he was this pretty girl studying law at Birmingham University. He became friends with the SAN, and the two began an online affair involving sexting and lewd pictures. When he felt he had enough compromising pictures and text messages to work with, Onjefu struck. Refusing to succumb to blackmail, the SAN went to the police and Onjefu was arrested. He called Owoicho from the police station, begging and crying for his brother's help.

Owoicho left work and everything he was doing at the time to be by his brother's side in Lagos. Fortunately for him, the SAN was someone he had interviewed many times in RTN about legal issues and the state of Nigeria. Owoicho went down on his knees and pleaded with the seasoned lawyer to forgive his brother's attempt at extortion. With his intervention, the case was abandoned, and Onjefu got only a slap on the wrist. That day, Owoicho told himself he didn't have a brother anymore.

Onjefu remained Onjefu. He continued his catfishing, cryptocurrency scams, and other illegal quick-money schemes on the internet. Every now and then, Owoicho would see him on social media flaunting his ill-gotten wealth. He had houses on the Island in Lagos, cars he bought brand-new, and all the celebrities were his friends. He constantly did giveaways on Instagram where it looked like money would never be his problem again.

But my problem right now is money. Lots of it. Ask and take what he gives you. You can even tell him it is a loan, so it doesn't feel like you are completely helpless.

Owoicho thought it ironic that he spent so many years condemning his brother for duping innocent people and living off the proceeds of his innumerable fraudulent machinations only to find himself calling on that same person for financial assistance.

It isn't financial assistance. It is payment for making mama suffer.

The one question he found himself asking was whether he would be able to sleep at night if he took money from Onjefu. What moral high ground would he stand on if, out of desperation to travel abroad, he accepted to become a beneficiary of the lifestyle he had criticized for so long. And in wanting to give Ochanya a better opportunity than he and her mother had growing up, was there a line he wouldn't cross? Was there a breaking point for his conscience? Owoicho's heart pounded as he contemplated these questions.

Ask him for help. Ask him for help. Ask him for help…

"Bro, was there something you wanted to ask or tell me?"

"No. Nothing at all," Owoicho said to his brother. "I know I should have called to thank you for coming to the burial weeks ago, but I got back to Abuja, and other things came up. I apologize for my oversight."

He needed money, but he wouldn't sell his soul to the devil.

Owoicho said goodbye and hung up the phone before his brother could say anything more.

20.

"I DON'T UNDERSTAND, OWOICHO? WHAT DOES THIS EVEN MEAN for you and Ochanya's relocation plan?"

"Alegwu, honestly, I'm just as confused as you are about this matter. There I was expecting some cool millions from Ene's accounts, only to discover when I heard back from her bankers that she didn't have any money. I'm still in shock," Owoicho confessed to the only person he felt comfortable opening up to about the disturbing discovery.

"Ene didn't have any money in the bank? I thought I heard you say something earlier about a couple of hundreds being in her accounts."

Owoicho felt like his friend was making light of the situation, and he didn't hide his irritation. "You've obviously not been paying attention. Two hundred and seventy-two-thousand-naira, twenty-one kobo. Alegwu, that one na wetin? To relocate to Canada, we need a lot more than that. We need millions; that's what we freaking need. And all my mind be say we don get am already and na to dey plan how we go take waka remain."

"No vex say e be like say I dey take the matter joke. Na serious question I been dey ask you," Alegwu clarified. "This thing when you dey talk so, e shock me too I no go lie," Alegwu said to an obviously troubled Owoicho.

He had several questions he wanted to ask his friend about Ene. He was curious about the state of their relationship before she died, as well as the position with Owoicho's personal finances. However, he thought it best not to stir a hornet's nest. Since he was unsure how best to react to his friend's narrative and what to say to him for comfort, he stayed quiet and waited for Owoicho to provide him with more information.

"Shock doesn't even begin to describe how I feel right now. I am devastated. Where do I start? All of my calculations since we decided on this path were based on Ene coming through for us. In fact, I had my fears, and whenever I expressed them to her, she would assure me that everything was under control and that money wasn't a problem."

"Could she have lied about having money just to keep your hopes high?"

"No. I know she had money. We had to include the bank statements in our application, and the money must remain untouched until we got our permanent residence visa or until we landed in Canada even."

"So, where's the money?"

"Search me. Actually, our last conversation about money and expenses when we got to Canada happened a few days before she travelled to Makurdi. Based on what she told me that day, I knew she had everything worked out. Since she got the appointment with the government, her concern was not about the money but the success of our application. She handled the application, so I don't even know the bank where the proof of fund money is, or maybe she moved it from one of these accounts that I have now into another one I am unaware of."

"How do we tackle this problem now?"

"The way I see it, it must be one of two things. It's either fraud by the banks, or she has the money in another account I don't know about."

"What if it made it to the bank but the money is in someone else's name?"

Owoicho paused to think for a bit.

"You have a point there, seriously. But I doubt it. The much I know about this Canada thing, the money has to be in the account of the principal applicant, which, in our case, was Ene. What do you think I should do now? How do I get to the bottom of this mystery?"

Alegwu gave it some thought, and then he voiced out his opinion.

"The banks have told you how much Ene has with them. You can't challenge that because, apparently, she never told you how much she had saved up or where she was saving it. If you were certain about the facts or even had proof, I would have said to sue both banks, but taking legal action against them would only be a journey in futility at this rate. First, you don't have proof, then you'd spend more money and time locked up in unending litigation."

"I agree with you completely."

"With everything going on in this country today, I would say focus your attention on raising the money from elsewhere. I think you and your daughter should leave this country now that you have the opportunity."

"I'm tired, Alegwu. Maybe I should just forget about this abroad matter. At this rate, it is as if God Himself doesn't want us to leave Nigeria."

"Even Abraham and Moses in the Bible left their people to start life again somewhere else. Please, don't lose this opportunity to escape. Abi, you don't follow the news? What am I even saying, sef? You people are the ones who read the news to us na. You know that things are not getting better in almost every sector you can think of. Yesterday it was Chibok. Today it is Kankara and Jangebe. Who knows what tomorrow will bring? As one set of students are being killed or released under very suspicious circumstances, another set are being abducted. Fifteen, no one is safe, not even our children."

"You are right," Owoicho concurred. "If I had known things would turn out this way, honestly, I wouldn't have rented such an expensive apartment. What do I do now? How can we make it to Canada before our visas expire?"

"I can lend you some money and help you sell your car and anything else you'd like to dispose of if that would help."

"Thank you, Alegwu. That would go a long way. I don't even know how to thank you."

"What are friends for? Let's talk again tomorrow. We must get you and Ochanya out of this country by fire by force."

21.

"You really don't like it here, do you?"

"No, I don't," Ochanya responded to her new friend, Oche. "I don't like it here one bit. In fact, I really, really dislike this place. I dislike everything about this neighbourhood and this city. I dislike the people; I dislike the way they stare. I can't stand the food. I dislike the way they dress –"

"Hey, hey, small girl, hold it there. I say hold it there," Oche shushed her in faux outrage. "I hate it here, I dislike the people, I dislike the rain, I dislike the sun, I dislike the moon, I dislike this, I dislike that," he mimicked Ochanya's rant. "You can't just be running down my quiet, beautiful city in my very before, girl. Chill!"

"Dude, I'm chilled like something straight out of the fridge," Ochanya said, pulling a face that had both of them in stitches.

"And while we're still on the subject of likes and dislikes, let me get something straight. Ochanya, are you trying to tell me that you dislike me too?"

"I didn't say I dislike you, Oche. I just don't like it here. Period. My life is in Abuja. I was born there." The intense, frightened, and traumatized fifteen-year-old replaced the blithe and chirpy teenage girl that was her persona when they started the evening.

"I've lived all my life there. I've not stayed elsewhere for more than one week, and being here indefinitely terrifies me. Oche, you know I don't like talking about what happened to my mother, my kid sister, and my brothers, right?"

"I do."

"But the truth is, not a day passes that I don't blame this state and its government for the horrible way they--the horrible way they –" Ochanya couldn't bring herself to say the word that followed.

"Am I wrong for thinking that they would still be alive if they didn't come on a short visit to Makurdi?" A distraught Ochanya asked Oche as they approached their usual rendezvous spot in the abandoned building that once housed a popular private nursery and primary school in the government-reserved area of Makurdi.

Oche once told Ochanya that the property was owned by the first wife of a former senator from the state who was killed in a plane crash a few years before. Once bustling with progressive ideas and learning activities, the building was now a shadow of its old glory. Since her untimely demise, the school had been converted into a free-for-all quasi-community centre where young people from all walks of life and all parts of the city, but mostly from the affluent end of the community, hung out and connected with each other for fun and games.

Every now and then, the senator would get mad and kick out miscreants and squatters from the premises in hopes of reviving the school again, but his plan never came to fruition. Word on the street had it that his younger wife opposed reopening the school. It was rumoured that she would rather see the massive campus in ruins and the school shut down forever than encourage her husband to propagate the legacy of her late rival and sworn enemy, a woman who mocked her childlessness. They said the first wife hated her while she was alive, so when she died, the second wife decided to return the favour by manipulating the senator's attention away from the school and other assets owned by the deceased woman.

Apart from its field used for football practice and the occasional church crusade, the rest of the facilities, including the classrooms in Radiant Educational and Child Development Centre or RecDC as it was more popularly called, were balkanized into territories by its users.

Teenage boys who were Oche's age and maybe slightly older gathered in the classrooms on the third floor of the four-storey classroom block. This was their territory. It was where they brought their girlfriends and the girls they fancied for some quiet time and romantic chitchats. Most times, they only just talked, but if the girls allowed, then they did other things their parents might not be too happy to discover they were into.

The bathroom on that floor was designated the "fire zone." According to Oche, it was called that because it was where boys and girls considered "bad" or "hardened" smoked or initiated others into smoking regular cigarettes and marijuana. And if anyone needed some other kind of drug or even guns, whether locally made or imported, it was where they went.

Now, as a result of the layout of the building, it was inevitable that the two young friends passed by some of these people on their way up or down the stairs, but Oche never joined them or took her anywhere near the "zone." He told her he didn't smoke and wasn't a member of any cult group in school or the neighbourhood.

He told her that his father, a former Vice-Chancellor of the Federal University of Agriculture, Makurdi, and his mother, a lecturer at the same university, were born-again Christians. What he said was that they would disown him if they as much as saw him on the streets with someone holding a cigarette, let alone if he was the one smoking. That was how strict his parents were, and the only reason he was permitted to visit RecDC occasionally was that they had no idea it had this other dark side.

If some adults in the community were oblivious to the other side of the place, most young people were well aware of its existence. However, that didn't stop them from hanging out there because they didn't have to pay or buy a drink to get in, and it was far removed from the prying eyes of the adults in the city. As far as the youths were concerned, RecDC was still considered safe and secure for socializing in that there were always other people around to prevent molestation or violence.

Whenever fights broke out, and fights could happen anytime and anywhere, there was always that one sane person who ensured things didn't get out of hand and that no one got hurt. For that reason, the police never got called to intervene or arrest anyone.

"Abuja, Abuja, Abuja. That's all you ever talk about. If I didn't know better, I would have thought Abuja was in Europe or North America."

By choosing to say something silly in order to steer the conversation away from her pain and grief, Oche hoped he succeeded in uplifting Ochanya's spirits. He wanted her to see him as a friend. Someone she could trust. Someone who cared a lot about her.

"I'm sorry if I can't stop talking about Abuja; that's where all my friends are, duh!"

"Are you saying I'm not your friend?" Oche acted surprised. "Silly me! There I was, thinking my text messages and midnight calls, all the funny videos and memes I send you and our regular evening walks have endeared me to you. Too bad I was wrong. I don see am say all the data when I dey burn on top your head na waste."

"Well, if it makes you feel better, I didn't mean it like that. You are different," Ochanya smiled coyly. "You're not silly. You just have a very big nose and really white teeth. And you're too tall for your age. I wonder what your parents feed you!"

Oche smiled too. He reached for her left hand, and Ochanya didn't pull away. She let him lead the way to the spot in the classroom they had colonized. It was the spot they wound up each night she joined him for their regular stroll. She knew she shouldn't be doing it or even be with him since her grandmother loathed RecDC and anyone associated with the place, but Ochanya chose defiance over obedience. If the old woman didn't want her anywhere near RecDC because she had heard bad things about the abandoned property, then she would make sure to go there every day. In her heart, she was convinced that the only way to get her grandparents to send her back to Abuja was by giving them a hard time. She prayed that the plan worked.

Ochanya watched as Oche wiped the desk clean with his white handkerchief. He said he didn't want their clothes to get stained or dirty. She liked that he was thoughtful like that. When he finished, Oche waited for her to sit and then sat beside her.

She liked that he was gentlemanly and did the most chivalrous things even though he had a tough look and hardly smiled.

"So, where were we?" Oche asked when they both settled down to have a conversation and trade funny stories. "Yes, I remember now. You were saying how I was different. Now is that a good or bad thing?"

"It's a compliment, Monsieur Oche; take it."

"With all pleasure. I get it that you miss your dad and your home in Abuja, but that isn't enough reason for you to be so resentful of us. Level with me, Ochanya. Why do you hate this place so much, and don't tell me it is because of what happened to your mother and siblings?" Oche smiled again. "It's a boy, right? You have a boyfriend in Abuja?"

"Go, jor, I don't have a boyfriend. I've told you this before," Ochanya shoved him playfully. "Really, you said you've been to Abuja several times, so you must understand why I feel stifled in this place."

"Ochanya, say the truth and let the devil be ashamed. When you say it feels stifling, is it Makurdi that stifles you, abi your grandparents?"

Ochanya laughed. "If I should say the truth, I would say my grandparents."

"In that case, you mustn't tell them about the party next week."

"What party are you talking about?"

"My seventeenth birthday party. My parents will be in London for my cousin's wedding so we kids will have the house to ourselves. I'm planning a pool party in our backyard on Saturday evening, and afterwards, my friends are organizing something for me at Le Bistro Lounge."

"Le Bistro Lounge? That sounds like the name of a nightclub."

"It is a nightclub, and I'd like you to join us. Ochanya, nothing will make me happier on my birthday than having you beside me as my date."

"But how are we going to get into a nightclub? We are underage."

"I know we are, but that isn't going to be a problem. The manager of the club and I are first cousins," Oche explained. "I've already told him about the party, and he's fine with it as long as we are not more than fifteen, we don't drink alcohol, and we leave by midnight. Also, our parents must not find out."

"You want me to join you at a nightclub for a party that doesn't end until midnight? Come on, Oche, there's no way that's going to happen. Number one, I've never been to a night party, ever. Number two, your parents will not be in the country then, but the people I live with will be very much around. What will I tell them? Where will I say I am going to?"

"We could say there's a programme in church."

"A programme taking place in her church that she doesn't know about? Oche, this isn't going to work," Ochanya was emphatic in her refusal.

"Please, please, Ochanya, say you'll be my date to the party. I understand that staying out until midnight might get you into trouble with your grandparents, but I can't imagine having a party and you not being there. Please say yes. Just say yes, and I'll figure out how we'll sneak you out of your house without getting you into trouble with your folks."

Ochanya looked away from him so she could properly process what he was asking of her. She needed to weigh the pros and cons before giving him an answer.

The obvious con was that her grandparents would be cross and disappointed in her if they discovered what she did, and they might. Then her dad will hear of it as well, and he too will be furious at her. But she didn't know what action he might take against her when he found out she snuck out with a boy and stayed out until pretty late. If he got really angry at her and decided he had had enough and that she should join him in Abuja, would she still consider it a con? Ochanya wondered to herself. As for the pros, she could only think of one. She gets to experience a wild night with a boy her age. A boy she was already fond of and who could make her like Makurdi if the care and attention he lavished on her didn't stop.

It was either of two things for Ochanya. Turn down Oche's invitation and risk losing his friendship and growing affection, or accept the invitation and face her father's and grandparents' wrath.

Since their friendship began that day in church when he stopped to ask for the time, and she, in turn, asked him for directions to where drinks were sold, he had been her sole source of support. And for as long as she was in Makurdi, she needed that support and friendship.

"Okay, Oche, I'll come to the party with you."

"Awesome! Don't worry about your folks. I'll definitely think of something. There must be a way of getting you out of the house without them knowing. That your security guy, Mr. Samuel, that is his name, right?"

"Yes, Mr. Samuel."

"We might have to involve him somehow. Maybe if we gave him some money, he could keep your gate open or be on the lookout until you get back home."

"One more thing, Oche. I think twelve is too late for me. I'll like to be home by nine or ten pm if you don't mind."

"Noted. I'll get you home anytime you feel like leaving the party."

They stayed in the classroom for a little longer, talking about everything from music to movies and what they were starting to feel about each other. Ochanya was tempted to tell him about Canada, but since it wasn't going to happen again, she decided it wasn't something she should discuss with anyone.

Starting to worry that her grandparents might have started worrying about her, Ochanya told Oche that it was getting late, and he walked her home.

When they arrived at her gate, Oche gently squeezed her hands and told her not to worry about Saturday because he had everything under control. He waited until Ochanya closed the gate behind her, and then he went back to the place he told her he never did.

"Hey, Bakris!" Oche called out to his friend he had asked to wait for him there. He had to raise his voice to be heard amidst the cacophony of sounds coming from within and outside the bathroom stalls.

Not counting the number of people in individual stalls, he counted nine boys standing or leaning against the sink, and Bakris was one of them. Entranced by the smoke emanating from the wraps some of the boys had in their hands and the strong smell of marijuana oozing from them, he called out impatiently to his friend again.

"Bakris!"

"Hey, dude!"

"Please pass me your joint."

Bakris left his spot in front of the last stall to join Oche by the main entrance door to the bathroom.

"I haven't paid for it yet," he informed Oche.

"Don't worry about that. We'll split the cost."

Bakris handed him the wrap, and Oche took a long drag before handing it back.

"You brought the new girl here again," Bakris pointed out the obvious. "What is going on between the two of you? Is she now your girlfriend? Dude, what is it with you and every new girl that comes to our school or this area?"

Oche laughed. "This one is different; she's decent, and she's going through stuff. But we vibe, so I don't know. She has agreed to join us when we go out on Friday, so let's see how it goes?"

"Dude, so what is it going to be? Will you just catch cruise and dump her like all the other new girls you have made out with?"

"I don't even have to think about it. Guy, you know Vero is my main girl, and I'm not ready to break up with her yet. So, with this one, it is the usual formula – make-out and japa. What I don't know is if it will happen this Saturday or if I have to carry on with my Prince Charming act for a little longer."

22.

It was Wednesday, and Ochanya still couldn't decide what to wear for Oche's birthday party on Saturday. She had started the day with six sets of clothes in mind but had it narrowed down to two by lunchtime. She thought the four she eliminated were cute outfits, though, but they were either short dresses or a skirt and blouse combination that were somewhat revealing.

Ochanya would have preferred something short and girly on this first major outing with Oche, but her mother's words the last time they went out shopping together kept ringing in her ears as if she was standing right there in front of her: "Don't ever wear a short or revealing dress to a date until you are certain the boy can be trusted."

The two outfits on her final shortlist were trousers and fitted tops because her mother would have wanted that. One option paired a black long-sleeve turtle neck pullover with a moderately distressed blue and flared bottom Levi Straus jeans and orange sneakers that popped and jazzed up the ensemble. It didn't scream dress to kill, but it gave off a tomboyish vibe she liked. The second of her top two choices was a melange of white, blue, and yellow patterned ankara slim-fit slack and an oversized white t-shirt she was going to accessorize with a black cinch belt and black pumps. If Ejuma had been around, Ochanya was certain what her sister's choice would have been. Her kid sister would have opted for the latter get-up. The girl loved vibrant colours and grown-up clothes, but Ejuma was no more, and she had no one else to help her choose.

For a minute, Ochanya was overcome with sadness, and once that feeling crept in, it was always an effort to shake it off. This time, however, she acted swiftly. She straightaway brushed all thoughts of melancholy and loneliness aside, and instead of thinking grim thoughts, she willed herself to think happy thoughts. She thought about Saturday.

Saturday was special for Oche. Ochanya was flattered that he wanted her to be a part of such an important day for him. He didn't tell her about any other girl he liked or may have dated, but she thought it was significant, and it meant a lot to her that he wanted her in all the activities he had lined up to celebrate with his friends.

When he told her that her presence meant a lot to him, Ochanya's heart almost exploded with joy, but she couldn't let him see it. Not just yet. But come Saturday, if he asked, and she had a funny feeling he would, she was ready to let him know how elated she was to be his girl.

The thing, though, was that the party was three days away, and Oche still hadn't come up with a concrete plan for how she would escape the hawkish eyes of her grandparents. Knowing them, there was no way on earth she was getting their permission. Sneaking out was the only way she and Oche could be together that night. Being all in on the idea of having fun, dancing, and doing all the crazy things teenagers do when they are in an unchaperoned gathering, Ochanya was worried that something might go terribly wrong with the escape plan. If that happened, not only would she miss the party, she'd be grounded for life!

As if on cue, she heard her grandmother call her name, and she went to meet her in the family room. After about ten minutes with the elderly woman, Ochanya ran back to her room, all giddy with excitement. She grabbed her phone from the bed and called Oche.

"Guess what?"

"You know I'm terrible with guessing. Please tell me already. What is it?"

"My grandmother just told me that she and my grandfather would be travelling to Otukpo on Friday. They're going for a wedding." Ochanya couldn't contain her elation.

"Oh my God! This is the best news ever."

"It is. Now we don't have to worry about them. We only have to worry about Mr. Samuel, and I know I can bribe him to keep quiet."

"This is good, this is good," Oche also sounded really excited.

"I have to go. My grandma wants me to help her with her luggage, but I thought to break the good news to you first before going to help her."

Ochanya hung up the phone, thinking the heavens were rooting for her and her new best friend. In her head, that best friend would soon be her boyfriend.

🍁

On the other end of the phone, Oche was thinking about something entirely different. He was thinking the night could go better than he expected, and he could get lucky.

He took out his wallet from his back pocket and checked to see that it contained what he was looking for. Satisfied he had protection, he smiled and slid the wallet back into his pocket. Ochanya just made his day, and he was sure he would have an even better birthday celebration because of her. She would be giving him the best birthday present of the night, though she didn't know it yet.

Oche put on his headphones and returned to the game he was playing before Ochanya's call came in, all the while wondering how many new girls he had to shag before his friends started calling him KONG – King of New Girls. He thought he had earned the title, and if anyone doubted him, he would prove it again on Saturday. Saturday would be the day it stopped being a chase but another conquest for him.

23.

"Hi, Bimpe. Good morning, or is it evening there sef?"

"Hey, Owoicho. It's actually morning, and I'm just getting out of bed."

"Oh, dear! Should I call back later?" Owoicho asked apologetically.

"No, there's no need to do that. I'm up already," Bimpe, his late wife's friend, answered in a sleepy voice.

"Seriously, I could call back. I mean, if you're just waking up, you may want to make breakfast or get your kid ready for school."

"I slept in, so my husband should have taken care of that," Bimpe informed Owoicho, still sounding tired.

"I'm really sorry for calling at such a bad time."

"Owoicho, it's fine. I'm fine. I should be apologizing for not taking your call the last time you tried reaching me. I had just gotten back from work that day, and I was super exhausted. But I should have called you back." She ended without telling him why she didn't return his call, but Owoicho didn't take offence.

"My bad. I don't know why I keep getting the timing wrong?" Owoicho laughed. He thought doing so would make this gaffe less awkward for both of them. "You said it's a seven-hour time difference, right?"

"Yes, seven hours and you guys are ahead of us."

"Abeg, so when is the absolute best time to call you? And I promise not to get it wrong the next time."

"Let's say when it's like five or six in the evening for you, then it'd be something like ten or eleven in the morning here in Saskatoon. That would be the absolute best time to call."

"Monday to Friday?"

"Monday to Sunday. I sometimes have to be at work on the weekends as well."

LEAVE MY BONES IN SASKATOON

"Great. Honestly, I feel bad disturbing your rest."

"No worries."

Owoicho picked up Bimpe's new accent, and he thought it was strange that she would use it on him. He wanted to comment about it, but they weren't that close, and she might not see the humour in what he might say or how he said it, so he let his observation slide. The last time they spoke over the phone, which was two or three days after Ene and the kids were killed, she had her strong Nigerian accent. And now, all of a sudden, she sounded Canadian, or was it American? He couldn't tell which it was.

He also couldn't tell if it came naturally to her or if she was struggling to maintain it, but it was sort of jarring, and he wished she just went back to sounding like her old self. He did notice, though, that the longer they stayed on the phone, the less foreign she sounded until her attempt at impressing or intimidating him became whittled down to a strange blend of accents—Nigerian-Canadian.

"Thank you for everything. I just can't thank you enough for the phone call and the money you sent," Owoicho said.

"Oh, please! That's not even necessary. I even feel bad that I didn't do enough. Ene's death is devastating, I tell you. And if I don't call you as often as I should, it is because it still hurts, and I don't even want to acknowledge to myself or anyone else that she and those beautiful children are no more."

"God gives, God takes. Who are we to question Him?"

"Believe it or not, I still wake up most nights thinking it's all a dream. Owoicho, we even spoke that day. Well, we didn't exactly speak, but she left a voice note on my phone. She was really excited about you guys coming here. She was so looking forward to it."

"I know. It was her dream for two whole years, and it was the only thing she talked about."

"And then she gets killed on the day-- Please, let's not even go there. It's too painful. Please, how's my daughter, Ochanya?"

"She's still in Makurdi with Ene's parents. But I've been running around trying to raise the money we need so we can join you guys in Saskatoon soon. Things haven't been easy, but friends are helping out, and I'm selling some of our stuff so there will be enough money for rent, a car, and other things we will need when we get there."

Bimpe was silent for a while, and when she spoke, Oche noticed her stutter.

"Sounds--sounds good. I--I--I wish Damiete and I could help, but we have some projects in Nigeria draining all our money."

"Bimpe, I understand. I won't even collect money from you guys. It's enough that you introduced us to your agent."

"We thank God. So, have you decided on a date?"

"Yes, that is partly why I called. Can you help us get a place we can stay when we arrive? I don't want to waste money staying in a hotel until we can rent an apartment. We don't even have that kind of money to spare."

"If you tell me your budget, I can go online and start looking at places. We can either do a townhouse or a basement unit."

"Ok. I don't know what those are, but I trust you to make the right call."

Owoicho told Bimpe the amount he was hoping to spend on rent monthly, and she promised to make some inquiries and get back to him.

"When you land, you and Damiete can talk about work and all that, and I'll help Ochanya with school. You guys will be fine. We've got you."

24.

OCHANYA WAS THE FIRST ONE UP ON THURSDAY MORNING. She had fallen asleep to A song she really liked. It was A Whole New World by Zayn Malik and Zharia Ward from one of her favourite movies, Aladdin. The movie starred Will Smith as the Genie and a young actor she crushed on for the longest time, Mena Massoud, as Aladdin. That particular song from the film soundtrack still played in her head when she woke up. And although she couldn't remember what she dreamt about or if she even dreamt at all, her spirit was filled with a cheerfulness it hadn't felt in a long time.

At first, she couldn't identify the source of her happiness or place her finger on why she was excited, so she attributed it to the miracle of waking up hale and hearty. But gradually, she started to figure it out. It was Oche. He was the reason her heart beat with a vigour she thought she'd never experience again. He was the reason for her song and the spring in her steps. He was the Aladdin to her Jasmine. And even though he didn't have a magic carpet or a mystery lamp with a genie that granted his wishes, she knew she'd follow him out on Saturday and any other day he wanted to spend time with her.

On other days, she was the last one out for morning devotion, but this Thursday was different. Not only did she get to the family room first, but by the time her grandparents and the other people in the compound joined her, Ochanya was already seated. As if that wasn't enough surprise, an even bigger shocker came when she offered to lead the praise and worship session even though Sisi was all geared up to do it. In the past, she didn't even sing out loud or clap her hands until she got the special look from her grandmother.

After the singing and praying and the short message her grandfather preached about God's love and genuine repentance from the Bible verse of the day, Ochanya didn't return to her room. She followed Sisi to the kitchen and helped her prepare breakfast. She also cleaned up afterwards and asked if she could help during lunch.

Everyone noticed she was acting out of character, but the only person that said anything was her grandmother.

"Ochanya, did you hit your head against anything yesterday?" Her grandmother asked after her husband left the breakfast table for the veranda, which was his favourite spot for reading the papers and meeting up with early callers who showed up at his house for money or advice.

"Grandma," Ochanya laughed. "I think I know why you're saying that. No, I didn't hit my head on anything yesterday. And before you ask again, nothing hit my head either. I am fine. Is there anything wrong with being happy and useful around the house? After all, that's what you've always wanted me to do, right?"

"I've always wanted you to do that, yes. But that doesn't mean I shouldn't be surprised when it happens. I mean, you led praise and worship this morning, you prayed, you cooked. You cleaned! Ochanya, please tell me what is going on. Is it because your father is coming today? You've really missed him, haven't you?" Her grandmother asked.

"My dad is coming where?" This piece of news caught Ochanya by surprise, and her grandmother noticed.

"Here, of course! Didn't you know?" Her grandmother replied. "I thought he called you last night after he told us about his visit to Makurdi today."

"No, he didn't. Did he say why he was coming?" Ochanya asked, still perplexed her father didn't speak to her about his visit.

"If he didn't call you, then I can't tell you anything o. You have to wait until he gets here and hear it directly from his mouth," her grandmother answered, getting up from the dining table to join her husband on the veranda.

"Hear what, grandma? What does he want to tell me?"

"Seriously, Ochanya, when you said you didn't fall or hit your head on something, I automatically concluded that your father told you he would be here today. I also assumed he already told you the reason for his rather impromptu visit."

"My dad and I didn't speak yesterday or even this morning. If you didn't mention it just now, I wouldn't have known he was coming today." The way Ochanya said it, it was more like a protest against her father for being kept in the dark than anything else.

"If you didn't know your father was on his way here, why were you so excited and acting like some special anointing fell on you?" Her grandmother asked, trying to tease out a response from her. This time though, she was the one with a look of surprise on her face.

"Grandma! Can I go to my room now?"

Ochanya didn't wait to hear her grandmother's response before storming out of the living room. She didn't know why, but she had a bad feeling about her father's sudden trip back to Makurdi. If he had something to say to her or even her grandparents, he could have just told them over the phone. Why did he have to come all the way from Abuja just to pass on some information to her, which he could have done with a text, voice or video call? And if it was something he felt must be done in person, why did it have to be two days before Oche's special day?

"Why do you have to come now, dad? Please don't spoil my plans." Ochanya muttered under her breath.

Ochanya was still sulking over her grandmother's bombshell announcement about her father and Oche not responding to her messages for him to call her when Sisi knocked on her door around noon to tell her that her father had just arrived and was with her grandparents in the living room. She quickly jumped out of bed, brushed her hair back, and went out to meet him.

"Good afternoon, dad," Ochanya greeted her father.

They were both happy to see each other, and when he opened his arms, she walked right into it.

"My daughter, I've missed you."

"I've missed you too, dad. You didn't tell me you were coming, and we spoke on Tuesday."

"I'm so sorry, Ochanya, I was going to call you after I spoke to Mama and Papa yesterday, but I thought it was late and you might be sleeping," Owoicho explained to his daughter. "So, how have you been? I hope you're not making your grandparents worry about you anymore?"

"No, Ochanya has been doing really good these past few weeks. I think setting up a place for her to paint and do her artwork was what did the trick," her grandfather said.

"That's very correct," Madam Elsie concurred. "She has been very useful to all of us in the house, and we would definitely be sad to see her go."

"Go where?" There was no masking the confusion on Ochanya's face. She turned to her father and asked. "Dad, where are you taking me?"

"Like I said to your grandparents yesterday, and I was just saying to them again before you came in, I have come to take you back home."

"Home? I don't understand, dad. What do you mean you've come to take me home?" Ochanya didn't realize it, but she was starting to sweat and get really antsy despite the air conditioning in the living room. She also couldn't sit still, so she circled her father and grandparents. "Didn't you say this was home for me now, dad?"

"I know I said that, but your real home is in Abuja, and I've come to take you back there. I thought you'd be happy about this development?"

"Are you saying I should go into my room right now and pack my things?" Ochanya was almost in tears. "It's not fair, dad; it really isn't."

"Who said we are leaving right now? Ochanya, we'll be leaving on Saturday morning," Owoicho declared, smiling, thinking his daughter may have misunderstood his good intentions for her.

"This isn't fair, dad. This isn't fair at all."

"Why do you complain about everything, Ochanya? It isn't as if you have any friends here you will miss and want to say goodbye to, or is there?" A perplexed Owoicho asked his daughter. "Please, you don't have to start packing immediately, but just know that we are leaving on Saturday, so when you are done acting out, start putting your things together."

Ochanya stormed out without replying her father. She knew that begging him for an extra day wouldn't change anything since apparently his mind was made up, so she jumped on her bed, brought out her phone and tried calling Oche again.

25.

OWOICHO BELIEVED HE WAS A BEARER OF GOOD TIDINGS, so Ochanya's reaction came to him as a huge surprise. He had expected her to be thrilled at his news because it was what she had always wanted, but obviously, he was wrong. Since he couldn't figure out what was responsible for her rather shocking and disappointing response to what he thought was happy news for her and the elderly Ejeh-Onojas, he turned to them for help. Unfortunately, they too were just as astonished as he was by Ochanya's attitude.

"She was happy. Even this morning, she was laughing and singing and dancing all over the place," his mother-in-law said, shaking her head in disbelief at how quickly her granddaughter reverted to her taciturn ways.

"What can be the problem now? Why is she acting like this all of a sudden?" Owoicho threw his hands up in the air in frustration. "God, please help me understand this child."

"I think she made a friend. There is this boy in the neighbourhood she sees most evenings. I think they are sort of close," Madam Elsie explained, so he didn't feel too bad about his daughter's unexpected behaviour.

"There's a boy?" Owoicho was taken aback by this information, and he was going to ask his mother-in-law why he was hearing this for the first time, but he bridled his tongue out of respect for her and her husband and also in appreciation for all the help they offered with Ochanya.

"I do not know if there is anything going on between them," Madam Elsie added quickly. "But I think he might have something to do with how she acted just now. You know these children of nowadays, their ways are so hard to understand. If she has made a friend here or is starting to make friends, she might feel like you asking her to pack her things and return to Abuja so abruptly and without warning is insensitive."

"I think she is just going through a phase all girls her age pass through. She will calm down once you speak to her again and it sinks in that whatever you do is in her best interest and not to punish her or deprive her of something important," Elder Erasmus offered a counter-justification to his wife's position.

"Papa, I really hope you are right."

"I think I am right on this one," his father-in-law responded confidently. "Besides, for all you know, she might not even be ready to face the ghost of her mother and siblings back in Abuja. Maybe that is why she wants to stay with us a little longer. Talk to her, Owoicho. Just don't put her under any pressure or make her feel like her opinion does not count or that you do not even care about her feelings. My son, I am sure she will understand if you speak to her. I know how difficult she has been since she started staying with us, but deep down inside, I see a very considerate and well-brought-up girl. I think you and Ene raised a good child. Talk to her," Elder Erasmus concluded.

"I don't know why she is acting up like this, honestly. It is not as if I am taking her to the old house. I don't even live there anymore! There're no ghosts in this new address."

"Then give her some time and then go in and have a conversation with her. Let her understand that this has come up because everything is set for you and her to travel to Canada. I am sure that is something that will cheer her up. I do not know much about these young people, but from what I see on Facebook and on the news, I want to believe that every young Nigerian today will give anything to be in her shoes right now."

"Thank you, Papa. I have heard everything you and Mama have to say about this matter, and I know you are both right. I will allow her to process everything and then speak to her again later. Hopefully, she'd understand why I'm doing this."

Back in her room, Ochanya was finally able to speak with Oche. He listened as she ranted and raved about her father and his decision to forcibly take her back to Abuja, even though that wasn't what she wanted. When she was done talking, she waited for him to offer up words of consolation and perhaps come up with a plan that would ensure that she was still in Makurdi for his party on Saturday, but Oche had nothing to say about her predicament. When she pressed him to say something, he was tight-lipped. He told her he was tired and needed to rest after spending the entire day cleaning his father's poultry and delivering eggs to buyers all over the city. His blasé reaction to her tirade made Ochanya feel like she had let him down and he was mad at her.

Unsure of what else to say to him about the situation, Ochanya got off the phone with Oche and went in search of her father in the guest room. This time, she decided to go down on her knees and plead with him to let her stay two more nights. And if that wasn't enough to persuade him, she was prepared to throw in some tears. It was a trick she learnt from her sister, Ejuma, and it worked like magic every time.

However, this time it failed because her father was adamant.

"Ochanya, this isn't about me being wicked or insensitive. I wouldn't be here if it wasn't necessary. I didn't want to get your hopes high until I was certain it was going to happen; that was why I didn't say anything these past weeks. Ochanya, things have started to happen really fast, and we have to leave for Canada next weekend. I've bought the ticket, and everything is set."

"Dad--"

"I know I should have told you. I shouldn't have kept you in the loop, and I am sorry," her father explained.

"Do we have to go to Canada, dad? Do we have to leave them here? Would we ever come back to visit their graves, bring them flowers, dad? Doesn't it feel like we are abandoning them and just moving on as if they don't matter?" A distraught Ochanya asked her father.

"I don't think so. I don't think so at all. Remember this whole Canada thing was your mother's idea in the first place. It was what she wanted for all of us, so I don't see her being angry that we are living her dream. If anything, I think it will make her and your brothers and sister very happy wherever they are."

"They are in heaven."

"Heaven. For sure, they are in heaven."

Her father explained why they couldn't leave for Abuja on Sunday or the day after. He told her that he had paid for their flight and he wasn't able to reschedule it because he was expected back at work on Saturday evening and that they had less than ten days to pack the few things they'd be travelling to Canada with and say their final goodbyes to family and friends. He insisted that they must leave Makurdi together and that it had to be done sooner rather than later.

Ochanya wanted to be the first to wish Oche a happy birthday, so she stayed up. But Oche didn't take her calls. He didn't text her back even though she could see that he had read her goodbye message to him. Even then, she knew he would be in her heart for a long time because he was the closest she had come to having a boyfriend.

Unknown to Ochanya, her father's resolve saved her from the heartache and misery Oche had planned for her. While she was angry and broken-hearted about Oche, he was with his girlfriend, Vero, discussing their plans for Saturday. To Oche, Ochanya was an already erased memory of an adventure that almost happened.

BOOK TWO

26.

OWOICHO AND HIS DAUGHTER ARRIVED IN SASKATOON ON A Sunday afternoon in mid-august. Their expected arrival time was 3:45pm, but the pilots were able to bring the plane to a halt eleven minutes ahead of schedule. Unlike other passengers in the Air Canada aircraft, father and daughter weren't revved up by the early touchdown. While their co-travellers scrambled for bags and other personal items in the overhead cabin, they remained rooted to their seats. Each lost in thoughts.

Other than the relief of landing safely and the eagerness to exit the plane after hours of being stuck in one position, there really wasn't much excitement on their faces and in their hearts. For Ochanya, not even the allure of the picturesque outdoors visible from where she sat could erase the sadness of not having her mother and siblings present for the special moment.

In place of excitement, Owoicho felt fear. He was afraid of the unknown. He was afraid of what the future held for him and his daughter in a land people back home spoke so affectionately about.

For Ochanya, she had never really been in close proximity to anyone that wasn't black, so she feared not being liked or accepted. It didn't help her nerves that only about a third of the people on the plane were black, brown, or from a visible minority. Was it a sign of things to come? She wondered.

In a matter of minutes, Owoicho and Ochanya would exit the plane and pick up their checked-in luggage from a designated carousel in the John G. Diefenbaker International Airport. They were minutes away from starting a new life, and it frightened Owoicho. Similar fear gripped him when they deplaned at Toronto Pearson International Airport for their connecting flight to Saskatoon. The longer they were in line to be served in Toronto, the more Owoicho feared that an error would be discovered in their landing documents and they would be denied entry into Canada.

Thankfully, the immigration officer who attended to them was brisk and extremely polite. When he was done stamping their passports and handed them the separate letters containing their Social Insurance Numbers, he looked Owoicho in the eye, smiled at him and Ochanya, and then uttered the three magical words a lot of people in his circle would give anything to be told.

"Welcome to Canada."

Those words should have comforted Owoicho, but they had the opposite effect. Yes, he was in Canada. He and Ochanya had accomplished something many people back home would give an arm and a foot for, but did it mean they would find happiness in Saskatoon? Owoicho questioned himself.

His countenance didn't give anything away, but Owoicho was terrified of what awaited them outside the airport doors. He knew from when they taxied down the runway of the Murtala Muhammad International Airport in Abuja that there was no turning back. What terrified him the most was not knowing if it was his last time in Nigeria and if he'd ever see his homeland again. And even if he were to return, would his country be the same way he left it? Would the people he was leaving behind be safe? Was there a promise of a better future for them, and would the government change its ways and put an end to corruption, bad governance, and all the other terrible things that had held back the most populous country in Africa for so long?

A part of him was glad to be leaving. After everything that happened to his family, being in Canada was definitely an escape for him and Ochanya. If Owoicho needed convincing about his decision to relocate abroad, the news of insecurity in Nigeria and the failing economy, which he commented on constantly during the TV programs he anchored, was sufficient proof that he was on the right path. Still, Owoicho felt guilty about leaving his motherland.

In many ways, it felt like he was abandoning Nigeria and taking the easy way out, and it tugged at his conscience. He knew he should have worked more with like-minded people, but how much impact would a handful of people with little resources have made? Owoicho wished he had engaged more with the influencers and politicians he came in contact with socially and through work. He regretted not doing enough. And now, with the little money he had saved and the rest he borrowed from his friend, Alegwu, he too had jumped ship.

He'd often hear people speak of greener pastures. Owoicho wasn't always sure that "greener" was equivalent to more happiness or meant greater fulfillment in any shape or form to the would-be-immigrant and those who left already.

While helping Ochanya bring down her carry-on bag from the overhead compartment, Owoicho made a note to look out for any green patch he saw on their way from the airport. He wanted to be sure that the grasses in Saskatoon were truly greener than those in Abuja. It was a crazy thought, and just thinking it brought a smile to his face. However, if he was being honest, it would certainly make him feel better if he noticed enough green and lushness on his first day in his new city. For whatever it was worth, it will be the welcome he imagined Ene would have wanted if she had made it to Saskatchewan.

"Canada shall be green for us," he muttered a prayer.

The noise in the plane cut through Owoicho's reverie. Most of it came from people making phone calls to family members and loved ones. The lady standing behind Ochanya could have been in a music concert going by how loud her voice was. And though she spoke perfect English, he guessed from her accent and features that she was Latin American. Owoicho knew he guessed right when she referred to the person on the other end of the phone as mi vida, a Spanish phrase he was familiar with from a movie he had watched at the university. For a couple of seconds, the woman went on about how she hated being in the middle seat and how miserable the flight was. She ended the call when the line started moving, but just before she did, she told her "vida" that she'd meet him outside in a few minutes.

Hearing those words reminded Owoicho that they also had someone waiting to take them to their new home in Saskatoon. As if reading his thoughts, Ochanya touched her father's elbow. A travel-weary Owoicho turned to look at her.

"Are we forgetting anything on the plane?" he asked.

"No, dad. I think we have everything," Ochanya replied. "I just wanted to know if there's a way you can let Aunty Bimpe know that we have landed and if she will even recognize us when we head out to the airport."

"Why wouldn't she recognize us? It's only been three or four years since she left Nigeria, and I don't think we have changed that much since then, have we?"

"Speak for yourself, dad. Me, I grew taller."

"Well, if she doesn't recognize us, I will certainly recognize her. She has her pictures on her WhatsApp status all the time, so there's no way I wouldn't know it's her when the time comes for that. For now, let's try and leave this plane."

"Okay, dad."

"And if by chance we miss ourselves, we'd just take a cab to the house. I have the address on my phone."

27.

WHEN OROMA ELEMELE LEFT THE HOUSE TO GO SHOPPING, her intention was to stop at Winners on Eight Street East for dresses before heading to Shoe Warehouse in Centre Mall. She figured buying five or six pairs of good office shoes there wouldn't dent her savings too much as she prepared for her first day at her new job. On her way back home, she made a quick stop at Dairy Queen on 22nd Street West. The stop wasn't in her plan, but her taste buds craved her favourite dessert, the Oreo Cookie Blizzard cake. Though an indulgence guaranteed to earn her a few unwanted pounds, Oroma couldn't resist the temptation. She was in a celebratory mood.

Days after she got the call, it still felt surreal that she didn't have to apply and be interviewed in several places before landing her first proper job in Saskatoon. It was her first application and job since completing her master's program in Public Health at the University of Saskatchewan, and she felt really lucky. She felt lucky because the position was posted five days after she received her certificate from the university. One month later, she was invited to come in for a chat with some top managers of the organization, after which she was called back for a written test. Two weeks later, she was notified that the job was hers, and if she wanted to, she could resume at their offices in Lawson Heights the following Monday.

Oroma felt truly lucky about the job, but she knew her deaconess mother wouldn't use that word. She would say blessed, and this time, Oroma wouldn't argue with her that both words meant the same thing. In fact, she felt so blessed that she went to church that morning. It would be her first time going to a place of worship in a little over a year, but she felt compelled by the dictates of her Christian faith and upbringing to do the right thing. And the right thing was for her to hand over the job, together with all the people she would be working with, to God. The right thing was for her to pray for favour in the sight of her supervisors and managers and for her position to be made permanent after the three-month probationary period.

Even more than that, she went to church that morning to show gratitude to God and return the honour and glory to Him because she didn't feel deserving of such a miraculous breakthrough after the heartache and pain she endured and the difficulties she went through when Chike moved to Vancouver.

Oroma was happy she could go to church again after months of running away from God and from people in the city familiar with her story. However, she knew she couldn't hide forever. At some point, she knew she must find the strength to put the past behind her and live again. Chike had moved on. Why shouldn't she?

Nevertheless, that Sunday morning, Oroma didn't return to the glamorous Pentecostal Nigerian church Chike took her to when she first joined him in Canada two years ago. No, she couldn't go there anymore. She knew that place and the people that fellowshipped there all too well. Besides, that auditorium held too many unhappy memories for her, and it contained far too many nosy people who would smile and say one thing to her face, only to say the exact opposite thing the moment she had her back to them.

So, instead of God's Alabaster Ministry, she went to a small Baptist church downtown. She chose Holy Trinity Baptist Church because it was close to her house, and its members were mostly old white people. Old white people would mind their business. Old white people didn't know Chike Chike-Uchendu. And even if they did, because Saskatoon is such a small city, she doubted they would know the whole story or care very much about the details of their seven-year relationship.

The people she saw in the church didn't strike her as the judgmental type; if nothing else, they had no reason or basis to judge her. Except she told them, and she didn't plan on doing so. The congregants of Holy Trinity Baptist Church didn't have to know that she resigned from her well-paying job with all the perks and opportunities that came with it to move to Canada.

They didn't have to know that she sold her car and everything else she owned to move to Saskatoon because a man professed love to her and would often say to her, "Oroms, what are you still doing in Nigeria? This place is too cold for a man to be alone. Please come and join me so we can start a family and help each other grow."

28.

ONCE OUT OF THE PLANE, OWOICHO AND OCHANYA FOLLOWED the directions indicated BY the green and white arrows lining the four walls of the concourse. The signs led them straight to the spacious baggage claim area that looked nothing like the confined spaces he was used to seeing, even in the biggest airports in Nigeria. Owoicho counted five carousels. By the time he located the one assigned to their plane, other passengers had taken up the best spots around it. It was obvious from how quickly they got there that most of them were familiar with the geography of the facility.

While Ochanya went in search of a porter, her father positioned himself between an elderly Indian couple and a Chinese woman who didn't look like she was a day older than thirty, even though he knew she was. He knew this because he sat opposite her and her teenage granddaughter in the departure lounge in Toronto while waiting for their connecting flight to Saskatoon.

Owoicho chose that spot between the Indians and the Chinese because it gave him enough room to grab and maneuver his suitcases off the carousel without holding up anyone or interrupting the baggage flow. It also gave him a good view of all the items coming out of the chute linked to the whirling metal and protective neoprene contraption.

By the time Ochanya returned with a porter, her father was already pulling the first of their six bags to the ground. The fellow, dressed in his crisp all-blue janitorial uniform and a black-crested hat, was all smiles as he helped Owoicho with the remaining suitcases. Because the man had an unmistakable Ghanaian accent, Owoicho thanked him in Pidgin English every time he came back to stand beside him after dropping a bag in his cart.

The very last item out of the conveyor belt belonged to the Adakoles. It was a brown customized Ghana-must-go bag containing the best of their enlarged family photos. Because he didn't know where to keep them, and he didn't wish to throw them away either, Owoicho wrapped as many framed photographs as the bag could contain, and he was glad he did. Even more than the documents and clothes they travelled with, what he treasured the most were the happy memories in each photo that made it to Saskatoon.

The love he and Ene shared was captured in their wedding photograph. The fruit of that love was evident in each individual portrait of the four children God blessed their union with. And although they didn't have money for lavish birthday parties at the time, he and Ene made it a tradition to have a portrait of each child made when they turned one. It became their one indulgence every time there was something to celebrate in the family. No doubt some of the frames hadn't aged well, and the portraits had become old and faded, but the memories they evoked remained everlasting.

"Is that everything?" the porter inquired.

Owoicho saw him size up the last bag as if wondering whether or not he should ask for help to get it off the ground and onto his cart.

"Yes, John. That's all we've got." Owoicho called him by his name, to which the Ghanaian acted visibly surprised.

"You know my name?" the thirtyish-looking, bearded, and well-spoken airport auxiliary employee asked with a resolute smile plastered on his face.

"The tag on your shirt, it says you are Jonathan Dumelo," Owoicho pointed out. "Are you related to John Dumelo, the Ghanaian actor?"

"I get asked that a lot, but no, we're not related, and in fact, I've never met him. I am also not an actor, although I used to be on television a lot before I moved from Kumasi to Saskatoon about three years ago."

"Really?" It was Owoicho's turn to be surprised. "What did you do on TV?"

"I used to sing for one of the most powerful tele-evangelists back in Ghana. He was a popular pastor, and he would call me up to sing before he started preaching. That is how I became popular too, and most people in Ghana know me as the Salvation Place singer, after the name of his church. I mean, I'm walking on the streets, and people are shouting the name of the church, shouting my name, and begging me to sing for them. I was doing very well, I tell you. I was also a chartered accountant in my municipal government, and the job paid very well. Honestly, it paid really well, and I was comfortable."

The smile didn't leave his face though Owoicho saw traces of sadness in his eyes as he told his story.

"If so, what are you doing here working as a porter?"

"Brother, you will soon learn," John replied ominously. He kept the smile, but this time it didn't match the gloominess on the rest of his face.

At this point, Owoicho concluded that John's smile was dubious. It was part of his uniform and not at all from his heart. Obviously, it was an act he had to put up for his bosses if he wanted to stay employed. In his head, Owoicho could see the exact page and paragraph in the office handbook where it was written. "You will lose your job the day we get a complaint that you are not smiling."

Though Owoicho wasn't Ghanaian, he knew that in West Africa, no well-educated person would be smiling and happily doing a job that could be considered lower than their educational qualification and perceived status in society. People aspire to go higher, get better jobs and move on to bigger things. The reverse was never the case. The journalist in him couldn't help wondering what John's backstory was, what the singer slash accountant turned porter wasn't telling him, and what the young man truly felt about the job he did at the airport. Owoicho wondered why he didn't just change jobs if he wasn't happy with the current one.

"What do you mean by that statement – 'you will soon learn?'" Owoicho asked, wanting to tease out some more information from his fellow African.

"I take it you and your daughter are permanent residents arriving in Saskatoon for the first time. Brother, all I can say is, welcome to Canada."

Before Owoicho could ask if he was being sarcastic or if he genuinely wished him and Ochanya well, the porter deftly changed the subject.

"Now, if there's no other bag coming out, I'll just ask you to assist me so we can lift this one together, and we'll be all done here."

"Okay." Owoicho did as he was asked.

"Would you like to confirm the number of bags again, please?"

"Confirmed. Six bags in total. Nothing is missing."

Owoicho couldn't tell if it was the porter's tone or if it was something else, but he found himself reflecting on how the entirety of his and Ochanya's life up until that moment had been reduced to five padlocked suitcases of documents, clothes, and shoes and one Ghana-must-go bag containing old photographs.

"Perfect," came the response from Jonathan. "If there's nothing else here, maybe we can be on our way to the taxi stand, or do you have anyone picking you up?"

"A friend…a friend from my country who has lived here for a while. She should be outside waiting for us, I believe." Owoicho sounded tentative in his response, and John picked up on his hesitancy.

"You didn't call to let them know you've arrived?"

"I don't have a Canadian number yet, but I spoke to her just before my daughter and I left Nigeria. I texted our estimated time of arrival to her days ago, so she should be out there at arrival waiting for us."

"Perfect," Jonathan said, adjusting the bags so nothing rolled over when it was time to push the cart. "I saw your child go into the washroom.

"The washroom?"
"Yes, the washroom. That is what they call the bathrooms here. We will proceed as soon as they come out."
"They?"
"In this country, we don't assume. You have to ask people their preferred pronouns; otherwise, refer to people as 'they' and 'them' until you are told otherwise."
"Oh, okay," Owoicho said, making a mental note of what he had just learned. "So, which is your pronoun?"
"I am a man. 'He' and 'Him' is fine with me."
Minutes later, Owoicho sighted Ochanya walking briskly towards them from where he assumed was the direction of the bathroom. She wasn't alone.
"Hi, my name is Isabella. Isabella Ramos." The lady accompanying Ochanya stretched her right hand to him for a handshake. Owoicho recognized her instantly. It was Vida! Vida from earlier when they were disembarking from the plane. Vida who couldn't wait to see her "Vida."
Owoicho wondered what this woman was doing with his daughter and if Ochanya was already in trouble with the Canadian authorities before they even exited the airport.
"Owoicho Adakole is the name," he offered his right hand too. The lady gripped, squeezed gently, and then released it immediately. Though all three steps were completed in nanoseconds, the confidence she exuded with that small act wasn't lost on a travel-weary Owoicho.
"Nice to meet you, Ada…Adakola?" She struggled with his name.
"Close enough, but I really do prefer Owoicho. That is my first name," Owoicho said, still curious about her and Ochanya and what might have transpired in the female toilet to make this stranger want to have a word with him. "Is there any problem?" he asked, shifting his gaze from the woman to his daughter and then back to the woman again. "Did my daughter do anything wrong?"

"There's no problem," the lady smiled. "Your beautiful daughter and I got talking in the washroom, and she mentioned to me that it is your first day in Canada today."

"Yes, it is."

"A few years ago, I was just like you, but now I work as a Settlement Advisor for an organization called Newcomers Outreach Network of Saskatoon. NONS for short. We provide support and render assistance to refugees and economic immigrants arriving in Saskatoon for the first time. In a nutshell, we help newcomers, such as yourself, make friends and become a part of the community in no time. We've been doing this for many years now."

"Oh wow, this is interesting. Do I have to pay for this service, and does it also cover my daughter?" Owoicho asked.

Before the lady could respond, Jonathan cleared his throat loudly. Owoicho was already engrossed in what he was hearing from his new acquaintance that he missed the cue.

Jonathan cleared his throat again, and when Owoicho still didn't decode the gesture, he spoke up. "We need to get going, sir. We don't have too many of these carts here, and they are also meant for other travellers. Besides, my shift ends in a few minutes, and I need to write my report before heading home."

"My bad, it looks like I am the one holding everyone up," Isabella said. "Let me walk with you guys to the arrival so I can quickly fill you in on how we operate and how you might contact us tomorrow if you wish. Do you have an arrangement for getting to your destination in the city?"

"Yes, we do. A family friend is picking us up."

"Perfect. My husband is also waiting for me at the arrival, and I can bet my last dollar he's wondering why I'm not coming out. One more minute, and my phone will ring."

Isabella looked around as she spoke. "It looks like everyone from our plane is out already, and we're the last ones here. We better get going."

29.

An excited Oroma tried on the dresses she had just bought from winners. One after the other, she let the perfectly tailored cut of each outfit rest on her petite frame. Some were meant to accentuate her curves, others not so much. Her goal with each look was to come across as casual, approachable, yet professional. For the ones that made her look serious, she picked colours and patterns that complimented her glistering brown skin. One thing she knew was that every look was beautiful. She was beautiful, though she hadn't heard that from anyone in a long time.

Staring at the mirror in the last of the dresses, she wished it possessed human attributes so she could ask for confirmation that she was still the resourceful and confident person she was before moving to Canada. She wanted reassurance that she was still the same loveable and smart woman who turned heads and managed a portfolio of pharmaceutical products worth over three hundred million naira. Oroma closed her eyes and wished the mirror could tell her that despite everything she had been through since arriving in Saskatoon two years ago, good things could still happen to her, and she could feel excitement again.

She couldn't decide which of the dresses would make the best first impression when she showed up for work in the morning because they all fit perfectly. In the end, she thought any of them would do. Oroma was beside herself with joy and excitement, knowing she didn't have to wear the same dreary blue and orange t-shirt she wore every day to the coffee shop on College Drive that had been her job for the last seven months. In a few hours, she'd be trading the uniform for beautiful dresses. Instead of cleaning tables, she'd have a desk and a computer all to herself, and hopefully, after her introduction and orientation, she'd be assigned a task that would make her feel like she was contributing to something important.

With her eyes still closed, she let her mind travel back to the last time she felt this excited about anything, and her mind didn't have to travel far because it already knew. The last time her heart thumped with this much expectation was because of Chike Chike-Uchendu. It was meeting and falling in love with him.

They met on a Sunday afternoon at Studio 24 in Victoria Island. She was there for a photo shoot because she needed a couple of headshots for her Twitter and LinkedIn accounts while he came in to pick up the passport photographs he had taken the previous day.

She had received a call from someone trying to convince her that her bank account had been compromised and that she risked losing all her money if she didn't provide a pin that would be sent to her phone number while the call continued.

"Really?" Oromo had asked, feigning ignorance. "Which of my accounts, sir? I mean, what bank is that?"

The caller went on rambling about how it was important for her to call out a pin which had truly been sent to her phone. If she was at home and had some time on her hand to spare, she would have engaged the caller until he realized he was being played and ended the call. But she had more important things on her mind and was not ready to play along this time.

"Oga, abeg shift! You still dey learn work. No be only pin, na needle. Wait, I'll even send my BVN to you too. No go find better work do, idiot!" Oroma said and ended the call.

"You must have received a couple of those kinds of call," Chike had said and laughed.

"Don't mind the yeye scammer. I wonder who falls for the dumb calls."

"You'd be surprised. Anyway, you handled that pretty good. My name is Chike."

She responded with her name too, and they got talking. Some minutes later, Chike told her the photos he came to pick up were for his permanent residency application to Canada.

And that caught her attention. "So, you are one of those people, eh?" she asked.

"Which people?" Chike had wondered where she was going with the question.

"The lazy Nigerian youth who don't want to stay to build this nation?"

"I want to go and hone my nation-building skills so I can join other builders to build us a better country when I come back."

"Then you're not running away for good?"

"Run to where? This country sweet die, I won't lie," Chike smiled at her. "Think of it as a sabbatical. In short, my plan is to live abroad for a few years, work hard, make plenty of money, and then come back home to spend it on myself, my family, and friends."

"If that is the case, how soon can we become friends?"

"Sorry, we have exceeded our friendship quota for the year. But, for the right amount and incentive, I can reserve a spot for you next year."

From the way he said it, Oroma understood he was teasing, and it made her laugh. The attraction was instantaneous and mutual. Best of all, it felt genuine.

Chike was thirty-five years old at the time, and she was thirty-one. He was tall and dark and had the chiselled look of someone whose livelihood depended on maintaining a certain muscular frame and looking good all the time. Oroma confirmed this when he told her that he owned a gym on the Island and, together with some of his friends, also ran a media company that specialized in advertising, artist management, and show promotion. However, his ambition was to upraise his passion for a more global and diverse clientele, which was his reason for contemplating a move to the United States, Canada or the United Kingdom where he had friends.

"Oroma, you know you look so much like your sister. I follow her on Instagram," Chike said after the bout of laughter subsided.

She had a look-alike sister, a popular socialite and an acclaimed number-one online aphrodisiac seller in Nigeria. Apparently, her name had come up a while back on blogs and gossip magazines, which she didn't follow or read, by the way. The story was about her being unmarried and in her thirties. Since her elder sister, Ratamma, had a young husband she paraded on Instagram all the time, a husband she claimed was kept in check because she was the mistress of seduction in Nigeria, internet trolls did their investigation and dug up information about Oroma's last two breakups as proof that her sister's kayanmata business was suspect. If one sister's love medicine and sex toys couldn't bring the other sister a man that would stay with her forever, then the whole aphrodisiac thing she was brandishing all over the place was a sham.

The trolling got so bad that whenever the efficacy of Ratamma's beads, sweets, scented oil and lotions were questioned, Oroma automatically became the topic of conversation. Chike told her he knew that much about her already, and if she wanted, his company could help her and her sister with strategies to combat the bad press and even turn it into fresh endorsement opportunities for Ratamma.

Oroma introduced Chike to Ratamma and her husband, and before long, he got the job as their brand manager. Through them, his company also got inroads into other Nigerian celebrities and influencers. On her part, because she would do anything to dissociate herself from her celebrity sister and the erotic products she sold, Oroma let Chike into her world, where she was a high-flying sales and marketing executive in one of Nigeria's largest pharmaceutical companies. She put in a good word for him there as well, and Human Resources accepted her recommendation that the company, Rahab and Cross Pharmaceuticals, sign up with CCU Fitness and Aerobics for a three-year gym and fitness training deal for all its employees as part of their welfare package.

   Oroma typically wouldn't open up to a man that quickly, but with Chike, it was different. He was easy to talk to, which wasn't even what she liked the most about him. She liked that he was affectionate and he listened. She liked that he had a sense of humour that pretty much anyone could relate to. Most of all, he was driven, which she found most attractive in men. She hadn't been in many relationships, but of the few people she had dated, the two most common causes of friction were inferiority complex and greed. It was either the men were intimidated by her success, or they saw her as a meal ticket. Chike wasn't intimidated by her, and he didn't want her money.

When his permanent residency application to Canada was declined after months of waiting and feeling confident that it would be successful, Oroma was the one who suggested he changed strategy. Since some of her colleagues had successfully entered Europe and parts of North America as international students, she suggested that her boyfriend try the same route. The day he was accepted into the MBA programme at the University of Saskatchewan, she treated him to a lavish dinner at Eko Sky Restaurant and Lounge, where she let him know how happy she was that his dream of going global with the things he was passionate about had finally begun and she was there to support him every step of the way.

Chike and Oroma dated for three years before he left for Canada. Of the three years they were together in Nigeria, he lived in her house for two. And apart from those in their inner circle, most people who knew them from a distance assumed they were already a married couple.

Oroma didn't realize how much she missed Chike until he left for Saskatoon. Her body yearned for his, and it sucked not having him physically present for companionship, conversations about her job, and all of the family drama going on with Ratamma and her other not-so-notorious siblings. Even worse, the challenge of being in a long-distance relationship was compounded by the seven-hour time difference between Lagos and Saskatoon. It meant that when she was done for the day and ready to call or chat with the love of her life, Chike was engrossed in school work or busy at the part time job he did detailing cars to help with his bills.

After he graduated from the University of Saskatoon, Chike told her he got a better job working in the university library. He also ventured into talent management after he became friends with an upcoming Nigerian rapper he met at a music festival in Saskatoon. He also managed a duo of Nigerian-Canadian teenagers popular on Tiktok for recreating iconic scenes in movies and TV shows, and another extremely talented Nigerian girl known in his province for her poetry.

When he started making money from his side gig, Chike occasionally sent her dollars even if she wasn't in need and never complained to him about being broke. He also relied on her to check on his gym and give him feedback on how things were going with the business. He made her feel like she was a part of his life and that he needed her even though they were worlds apart. Whenever they were on a voice call or face-timing, Chike would tell her how much he missed her. He complained about food and not eating right because he couldn't cook. He constantly went on about the weather in Saskatchewan and how he struggled with cold and depression though he had a couple of friends, including Bailey, the bubbly Pakistani medical student he shared an apartment with.

Every time Chike spoke about being lonely, Oroma felt guilty about not being there with him. She wanted nothing more than to love and take care of him. And though they spent hours talking on the phone when they both had the time, it was never the same as being together physically.

Chike talked about starting a family and having kids a couple of times. He spoke about her joining him in Saskatoon once he sorted out his permanent residency and was certain of his status in Canada. But that was it. He would hint at marriage, raise her expectation, make her wait and stay loyal, but he never proposed or took active steps to bring their families together, and this troubled her.

Between them, they knew they were fine and that their relationship was in a good place, but other people weren't seeing it that way. Chike's long absence from Nigeria and her life had become a concern to close friends and family members. It sent tongues wagging and sparked talks about an imminent breakup and her inability to keep a man.

The talks and rumours upset Oroma more than she let herself admit. It drove her crazy. Confused and unsure of how to handle the situation, she turned to the expert in all things love, seduction, and manipulated relationships—Ratamma.

30.

"Any sign of your friend?" Isabella asked, minutes after they exited the baggage claim area of the airport.

"No, I haven't seen her yet," Owoicho said, peering through the faces of the many people waiting on the other side to welcome family members, business associates, and friends, whether they be residents or first-time visitors to Saskatoon.

"I wish I had a way of reaching her, but contrary to what I was told in Nigeria, my phone has refused to roam, and it isn't picking up signal from any of the local networks here."

"That happens," Isabella said to Owoicho, seeing as he was already looking downcast and agitated, like a child whose parents didn't remember to pick them up after school and they were the only kid left in the playground.

"Honestly, this is so frustrating. I wasn't prepared for this at all."

"Tell you what?" she spoke to him again. "Why don't you let me have this woman's number? I'll call her to find out if she's somewhere waiting for you and your daughter, or maybe she's still on her way and you have to wait a little bit longer for her to get here. Whatever it is, until we speak to her, we wouldn't know what to do next."

Owoicho thought she made a lot of sense, so he asked Ochanya to give Bimpe's number to the kind lady God sent to rescue them from what should have been an unpleasant and hopeless situation.

While Isabella stepped away from all of the noise and backslapping going on in the arrival to make the call, Owoicho fixed his gaze on the crowd for the one familiar face that ought to have been there to give them the boisterous Nigerian welcome to Saskatoon he had hoped for. He also used the opportunity to plead with Jonathan to be patient with his cart.

The last thing he wanted was to allow this particular porter to leave when he was certain they'd need his assistance to move their belongings to Bimpe's car when she eventually showed up. Luckily, Jonathan understood his predicament and was willing to wait a few more minutes with them.

"Good news and bad news," Isabella said, walking back to the spot the trio chose as their rallying point when she went off to call Bimpe.

"Good news first, please," Ochanya pleaded, pausing the game she was playing on her phone, so she could hear what Isabella had to say.

"Please, start with the bad news," Owoicho overruled his daughter's request. "Did you speak to her? What did she say? Does she know we have landed?" he continued.

"Yes. We spoke, and now she's aware of your safe arrival to Saskatoon," Isabella informed the Adakoles. "The bad news, I'm afraid, is that she picked up an extra shift that opened up unexpectedly this morning at her job, so she's still there. She asked me to tell you that she can't leave until the close of work at eight o'clock tonight. So, unfortunately, your friend won't be coming to pick you up, and she didn't have anything arranged either."

"Did she forget we were coming in today or something?" Ochanya threw her hands up in the air, demonstrably appalled and disappointed at the unfortunate turn of events with her mother's friend. "Please, can we hear the good news already?"

"The good news is that my husband came with his big truck. It can fit all of us and our bags quite conveniently. Your dad's friend gave me the address of the house you'd be staying, and it's on our way. I already talked to Miguel, and he's happy to drop the two of you there before we head home."

Miguel's vehicle was a shining silver Ram 2500 heavy-duty pickup truck that still smelled like something straight out of the assembly line. Isabella waited until the porter turned to re-enter the building after dropping the bags by the side of the truck before doing the introductions. Miguel Ramos smiled at Ochanya and shook hands with Owoicho.

Between the two men, loading all the bags into the back of the truck took only a few minutes. Isabella sat in the front passenger side beside her tall and muscular husband while Owoicho and Ochanya got into the back seat.

"So, welcome to Canada, guys."

"Thank you, sir," came the chorus from father and daughter.

"And is this your first time here?" Miguel inquired.

"Yes, it is," Owoicho replied. "You and your wife have been very kind. I don't know if there's anything we can do to show how grateful we are for all the help we have received from you today."

"Repay us?" Miguel laughed. "You don't know Isabella. She does this all the time. I honestly can't recall an occasion when we didn't help some newcomer family arriving in the city for the first time or some random people stranded at the airport. In fact, I'd have been shocked if she had come out of that building alone."

"Miguel!"

"Honey, you know I'm not even messing with you," her husband gave her a playful look from the corner of his eyes. "And whenever I tease her or ask her why she does it, she just says it's her passion and her job."

"Speaking of jobs," Isabella turned to speak to Owoicho, "I already told you I work as a Settlement Advisor, right?"

Owoicho responded in the affirmative. "I was going to ask if your services are free, though."

Isabella laughed. "We don't charge our clients anything. Our services are free because we are fully funded by the government at all levels – federal, provincial and municipal. And before you even ask, our clients are people like you and your daughter arriving in Canada for the first time. We help them find work, school, make friends, and form the connections necessary for settling down quickly and nicely in the city. We recognize that these people have just left their homes to begin a new life here in

Saskatchewan, so we do our best to ensure that Saskatoon can become home for them."

"Wow, that's really nice. How do we get to become one of your clients?"

"Let me give you my business card," Isabella reached into her purse, found what she was looking for and handed it over to Owoicho. "It has my name, office and email addresses in front. My work phone number is on the back of the card should you wish to call for an appointment."

"God bless you for this. I'm really grateful for this chance encounter," Owoicho thanked her and her husband profusely again.

"Don't thank me, thank the government and people of Canada. We are merely providing the services they fund us to provide. If you wish, you can come to our office as early as tomorrow, and I can start you off with some of the tools you need to begin your life here, such as language classes for people who can't speak English fluently and special programs for men, women, and children, so no group feels left out. And even before all that, we help with processing health insurance with the Health Authority. We process and set up welfare benefits for newcomers and teach those needing work how to prepare resumes and write cover letters. We do so many things, if you know what I mean."

"Awesome! I'll definitely be in your office tomorrow," Owoicho declared.

"That would be nice," Isabella replied, smiling. "Is it okay to ask what job you did back in Nigeria?"

"I worked in television as a news anchor."

"Oh, that's fancy. That means you're some kind of celebrity."

"Babe, you should let the man be. This is his first day in Saskatoon; I'm sure he'd rather look out the window and enjoy the view instead of being quizzed like he was interviewing for a job," Miguel said to his wife. "I'm going to turn up the radio volume to discourage this from turning into a question-and-answer session, if that is fine with you, my good man."

Miguel didn't wait for Owoicho's response. He increased the volume of the radio just as the sultry voice of a female presenter introduced the next song by an English rock band called Def Leppard. It was from their album Hysteria, and the track had a catchy refrain of the words Pour Some Sugar on me. Though he wasn't exactly a fan of rock music, and it was his first time hearing the 1987 hit song, at that moment, Owoicho fell in love with the tune.

In the coming months, Pour Some Sugar on Me would be the soundtrack in his head whenever he remembered riding with Isabella and Miguel through the beautiful streets of Saskatoon. He listened to it in his car, on his phone, and on every smart device he owned. He listened to the song when he was happy or sad, feeling high or low. He listened to it when his resolve was failing and he needed uplifting. Owoicho listened to Def Leppard repeatedly, especially when he missed Nigeria and the people he left behind. Whenever he heard that song, it made him happy again.

31.

"I can't believe my eyes. Ochanya, if I'd seen you in the mall, I would have walked right past you, honestly. You're all grown up now. Let me see, the last time I saw you, you must have been eleven or twelve years old, and you weren't this tall. What has your dad been feeding you, child?"

"Haba, Aunty Bimpe, I've been this tall since I was ten."

"That's not true jor. Ochanya, tell me what your father has been making you eat so I can force my son, Jason, to eat it too."

"Aunty Bimpe, I'm not lying. It's like you don't even know my dad. The man can't boil water without forgetting that he put the kettle on the fire."

Bimpe laughed at Ochanya's joke, and then she got serious again. "Okay, big girl, a couple of quick things. Here we don't say fire or cooker. We say stove. Another thing you must remember is that here in Canada, no one calls anyone aunty or uncle. People are addressed by their first name only, so please remove that aunty you say whenever you call me. I am not that old. Finally, and this is very, very, very important, you and your father have been calling me 'Bimpe, Bimpe.' My name is no longer Bimpe but Bree. That is what everyone calls me now, and I would appreciate it if you both did the same."

"Bree? Why Bree, Aunty Bimpe?"

"It's short for Briana, a name I gave myself when I got here and realized Bimpe wasn't doing it for me."

"Okay, I'm not sure I get that completely, but what I was really asking is why you have to change your name from Bimpe to Bree or Briana in the first place? Why did you feel like Bimpe isn't a good name anymore because you are in a new country?" Ochanya asked her late mother's friend.

The two of them were in Bimpe's spacious state-of-the-art kitchen making dinner. Jason, his father, and Owoicho were in the living room having their own conversation. There was an old English premier league game on TV, but none of them was watching it.

"I don't have an answer to that question, Ochanya. But don't worry, shebi, you'll soon start school here, and your dad too will be going out to look for work, abi? When that time comes, you'll both understand how important it is that Canadians can pronounce your names easily, or better still, that you have English names that can at least open the door for you until you walk in and they realize you're not white like them but Black."

"Are you saying that the people here are racists?"

"Ochanya, I'm not calling anyone racist. All I'm saying is that Bree is a simple, sweet name that gets me into places Oluwabimipe cannot. Bree good, Bimpe bad. You get?" Bimpe mimicked something she saw on TV a while back, even though she couldn't remember who exactly made the hilarious remark.

"Aunty, that is racism."

"I wonder what a fifteen-year-old girl who has lived a sheltered life in Nigeria knows about racism."

"Enough to worry if someone makes me feel ashamed of my name when they are the ones who should be feeling ashamed for not being able to pronounce it. Bimpe is a good name, if you ask me, and I don't think it is that hard to say either."

"Sometimes I forget how powerful the internet is and how it has made kids all over the world woke all of a sudden. Ochanya, my name is now Bree. I chose the name for myself, and I like it. End of story."

"But this isn't about being woke, aunty. We learnt about slavery, colonialism, and neo-colonialism in our Government class in school. And because our teacher is quite an activist, he tells us about things happening in other parts of the world, particularly in America. You know, like the targeting of Asians, police brutality, racial profiling of people of colour, the killing of George Floyd, and other similar incidences involving white and Black people and how things may not really have changed from when Blacks were captured and sold into slavery and considered less than human by their owners. Our teacher taught us some things that have a racist undertone, like people telling you that your culture is bad, backward or inferior, or that your language wasn't acceptable and so you have to switch to either French or English to be recognized or taken seriously. With clothing, you are told that what you wear is a costume and not a dress or an everyday outfit, and if you insist on wearing it, people start to stare at you in a funny way."

"I wear what I like and no one in Saskatoon has looked at me funny."

"But you changed your name, aunty. You chose acceptance over identity."

"How old are you again?"

"Fifteen, but I'll be turning sixteen next week."

"You are too smart for your age, Ochanya, aka Miss Rosa-Parks-in-the-making. We will have this conversation, but today isn't the day to discuss racism in Canada and the world. Today is for being happy that you and your dad made it here against all odds. So, my dear Ochanya, because you just got here this afternoon, please relax and help me carry this bowl of jollof rice to the dining table. I'll bring the other things."

Ochanya did as she was instructed. Bimpe followed seconds later with the bowl of chicken and salad while her husband Damiete brought out orange juice and water from the refrigerator.

When the table was set, Bimpe invited everyone to dinner. She, her husband and Jason, their seven-year-old son, sat together on one side of the eight-seater dining table while Owoicho and Ochanya sat on the other side across from them.

"I'm sorry neither Damiete nor I could pick you guys up from the airport when you arrived this afternoon. You don't know the crazy hours some of us here have to work," Bimpe began as soon as everyone had something on their plate. "I know you and Damiete have been chatting for a while. I wonder if he has had the chance to tell you what life is like for a newcomer to this country."

"I don't think we got that far in our conversation yet. I've been filling him in on all of the madness happening in Nigeria right now," Owoicho said, pausing to speak before taking his first bite of the chicken on his plate. "He did tell me about the weather, though, and how cold it gets during winter."

"Well, he needs to tell you about work and the kind of jobs we do here," Bimpe said. "I know I didn't say this to you when you were still in Nigeria, but I work in a care home for the elderly. To put it simply, I bathe, wash, clean and feed the aged. Damiete works as a security guard in an apartment building in the city. It pays our bills, and we are happy doing these jobs here in Canada, but it isn't something we talk about with people back home in Nigeria. We just don't think they will understand why we accept to do these menial jobs, so we prefer not to talk about it unless they come over here and see things for themselves, and then we don't have to hide anymore."

Owoicho put down his fork and knife, like he needed some time to let Bimpe's revelation sink in. "I suspected you don't teach in a school, which was the job you did back in Nigeria. Ene told me that much. But I had no clue you work as a caregiver. Again, with Damiete, even though he was here to welcome us when the lady from the settlement agency and her husband dropped us off, we never got round to discussing jobs or anything serious because he was more preoccupied with making sure we were set up nicely in your basement. And then you came back from work and started preparing dinner, and here we are."

"You're very correct, Owoicho. We were busy with the basement and didn't have time for a serious conversation about working in Canada," Damiete chirped in. "I worked all night at my job and only got home around seven this morning. I was tired and needed to sleep, but I couldn't because Bree picked up a shift that opened up in her place of work, so I had to force myself to stay awake and watch Jason."

"Sorry, Damiete, I don't mean to interrupt you, but did I hear you say Breeze? who's Breeze?" Owoicho asked in confusion.

"Dad, Uncle Damiete didn't say Breeze. He said Bree, and that's aunty Bimpe's new name. She says everyone here calls her that and we must do the same. No aunty, no Bimpe, just Bree," Ochanya rushed an explanation to her dad.

"Bree?" Owoicho repeated what he thought he heard his daughter say.

"Yes, Bree. That's my new name now. I left Bimpe in Nigeria; I'm now Bree. Bree Brown or Briana Brown. And if that doesn't sound white enough, then my people, nothing else will."

Everyone at the table laughed.

"You prefer a white-sounding name?" Owoicho asked after the laughter died down.

"Please, Damiete, can you continue what you were saying?" Bimpe ignored Owoicho's question.

"Yes, I was saying how tired I was, but I couldn't afford to sleep too deeply because I had to keep an eye on Jason. I know I should quit this job and look for something in engineering, which is my field, but employers here don't recognize my non-Canadian qualification and experience. Someday, I hope to get an engineering certification or something, or even branch off into another field entirely, but I keep procrastinating. That is why for now, Owoicho, I have to take what I can get so we can pay the bills."

🍁

The more Bimpe and Damiete spoke about their gruelling jobs and crazy schedules that paid a little above minimum wage, the more Owoicho wondered about their big five-bedroom house in what Isabella described as one of the more affluent and newer neighbourhoods in the city. He also noticed the clean GMC Buick parked in their three-car garage and the even cleaner Lexus SUV Bimpe rode in when she returned from work that evening.

Knowing a little about their middle-class background back in Nigeria and how they barely made it to Canada because the person they sold their house to refused to pay for the property at the agreed time, Owoicho was tempted to ask how they could afford so much luxury in the short period they had been in Saskatoon. Even more shocking to him was the claim that their jobs didn't pay well and that their salaries were essentially minimum wage.

Owoicho wanted them to shed light on how they managed to settle down so fast, but he thought against it. After all, he knew a little about their ordeal back in Nigeria, so the last thing he wanted to do was pry or come across as envious of their apparent stability and newly found upper-class status in Canada. He thought asking too many questions on the first day of reuniting with the Browns would be highly inappropriate. The family had done so much for them already by taking him and his daughter in, and it was best not to do anything to upset them or make them give away their survival strategy until they felt comfortable to share and talk about it. However, even though he refrained from asking, Damiete still went ahead to shed light on ways people paid for things they really couldn't afford.

"The good thing about this country is that once you have a steady source of income, you can get loans from financial institutions quite easily. People buy good cars through dealerships, and when you are ready to purchase your own home, there are always opportunities to secure a mortgage, which was what we did for this house."

Before Owoicho could decide whether or not to probe further, Bimpe jumped in with something about the food. It was obvious her husband had broached uncomfortable territory.

"I hope the jollof rice is okay. Damiete always complains that he wants it to be more spicy, but because of Jason, I've had to reduce the amount of pepper I use when cooking. You know these our Nigerian-Canadian children, they only want to eat cheese and burger," Bimpe said.

"And chocolate," Jason added.

"Yes, Jason. And chocolate, too," His mother concurred. "I can't cook with our local pepper anymore because of his allergies."

"Jason is allergic to pepper?" Ochanya asked, smiling. "I'm allergic to pepper too, but my parents wouldn't believe me."

"In that case, welcome to Canada," Bimpe teased. "As for Jason, it's not just pepper. He is allergic to peanuts, broccoli, and mushrooms, plus he's now lactose intolerant."

"Was he like that in Nigeria?" Owoicho asked.

"In Nigeria, he ate everything and anything," Damiete said. "These allergies started when we got here. It is like my wife said, 'Welcome to Canada.'"

32.

THEIR CONVERSATION ABOUT EMPLOYMENT AND LIFE IN Canada continued well into the night. It could have gone on for much longer, but Owoicho noticed Bimpe and Damiete yawning and stretching, and watching the clock on the wall, so he motioned to Ochanya that they both called it a night.

Considering how long they were in transit and how sleep-deprived he felt, Owoicho thought he'd fall asleep as soon as his head hit the pillow, but that didn't happen. One hour after he said goodnight to his daughter and turned off the light in their tiny new living room, he was tossing and turning on the couch like someone whose mind was troubled. Only he wasn't bothered. If anything, his mind was at peace.

For the first time in months, he didn't have to get out of bed at the slightest sound from inside or outside the house. Back home in Nigeria, there were nights it felt like it was the finale of the loudest-generator-in-the-neighbourhood tournament. Those were the good nights. The bad nights were a combination of noisy generators and the relentless sound of water splashing hard on the ground because some neighbours forgot to turn off their water pumping machine.

On his first night in Saskatoon, Owoicho didn't hear any of those sounds, and the silence kept him awake. He felt an uncontrollable wave of emotion in a strange and completely unexpected way. The emotion stemmed from not having to wake up angry in the middle of the night because the security guard had drunk too much alcohol and didn't remember to turn off the generator when he was supposed to. No one wanted to waste money on petrol or diesel on the rare occasions the electricity supply companies left the power on and there was no problem with the transformers in the street.

Owoicho noticed that the Browns didn't have to barricade their windows and doors with iron and metal protectors. They were confident no one was going to break in to steal from them or attack and kidnap anyone in the dead of night. He would never forget the story his colleague had told him about how his uncle's house was invaded by armed robbers. When they tried without success to bring down the bulletproof front and back entrance doors to the man's palatial mansion somewhere on the outskirts of the Federal Capital Territory, they used some kind of explosive device to knock down the walls of the building. That night, the armed men went away with two million naira the man had brought back home from the bank. They also stole expensive jewellery belonging to his wife and all of the phones and laptops in the house.

Most unfortunately, the man's wife and their grownup daughter, who was home because university lecturers were on strike, a niece visiting from America, and their house help were gang-raped by the heartless night lords. After violating them, the leader of the group matched the women into the kitchen, where he commanded that they make eba and vegetable soup for him and his men. He was specific about the number of meat he wanted in his soup. According to Owoicho's colleague, the operation lasted well over two hours, and the police didn't show up until the robbers left, even though a neighbour who suspected there were armed robbers in the house had called for help.

It was hard for Owoicho to take it all in that first night. It was hard believing that whenever sleep finally came, he would succumb to it with his two eyes closed, and he needn't ever have to worry again about people scaling his fence and his daughter being kidnapped or killed by bandits.

Save for the intermittent humming sound made by the single-door refrigerator in the kitchen area, everywhere was quiet. And because in Nigeria, he might have spent a quiet night like that beside his beautiful wife, talking and laughing about random stuff and discussing the children's performance in school or their future when they finished school, Owoicho missed Ene. He really missed her, Inalegwu, and the twins. Canada was her dream, and he felt like an impostor living in it without her by his side, laughing and talking like he knew they would have been doing on this first night in Saskatoon.

But he was in a place of rest, and his mind was at peace. His only prayer that night, in addition to begging for sleep, was that things would happen for him and Ochanya like it did for Bimpe and Damiete, and in three years or maybe even less, they too would be able to say, like his hosts said to them during dinner, that Saskatchewan was home.

33.

STILL UNABLE TO SLEEP, OWOICHO'S MIND WANDERED BACK TO two days earlier when his friend Alegwu saw him and Ochanya off to the airport. He didn't voice out his thoughts, but he was impressed that Alegwu would come all the way from Lagos to Abuja for one last visit with him and Ochanya before their Saturday morning departure.

Despite his insistence that the previous visit and the money Alegwu lent him for their travels was more than enough show of support, his best friend wouldn't have any of it. That Friday evening, they hung out by the poolside of Sheraton Hotel. They had food and drinks and reminisced about their undergraduate days when they were utterly clueless about the real world and what it had in store for them or the trajectories their lives would take. Despite years of childlessness in Alegwu's case and the recent deaths Owoicho suffered in his family, they concluded God had been kind to them.

"Call me the moment you land," Alegwu had said when they got to the second passport and boarding pass check at the international wing of the Abuja airport the next morning. It was the farthest the tip he gave to the airport officials to look the other way and allow him to spend some time with the travelling party could take him. "I think Airtel connects directly from almost anywhere in the world. That is the network provider you use, right?"

"Yes, that's what I use, Airtel."

"You said there are many Nigerians there?" Even Alegwu knew that his questions were becoming arbitrary at this point, but he didn't care. He just wanted to keep the conversation going for as long as possible.

"Yes. I believe there are," Owoicho replied. "That's what Bimpe said when I asked her about the Nigerian community."

"Good. It means making new friends won't be difficult for you and Ochanya. And please, when you get there, don't dull. You know say Naija no dey carry last, right?"

"Alegwu, you've said that a million times already. No worry. I won't go there and dull myself and I no go carry last," Owoicho reassured his friend.

"That's my guy. I know things will work out for you in that country and your star will shine."

Owoicho was tempted to say Amen, but he didn't because it was hard to tell if Alegwu was praying for him or just making conversation.

"By the time one or two people realize how talented you are as a broadcaster and they know the number of years you have put into this television thing, I swear, they will rush you like today's bread."

'Thank you, Alegwu."

Owoicho recalled that last conversation and his promise to his friend to stay in touch.

Thinking about it made him remember that he was yet to inform his in-laws and Alegwu of their safe arrival. Since sleep, the one thing he needed to recalibrate and immerse himself in his new environment, eluded him, he decided to call Nigeria. Owoicho disconnected his phone from the socket where it had been charging for hours and headed back to his spot on the couch. While scrolling through his contact list for his father-in-law's number, he made a mental note not to plug in his phone all the time now that he was in a place where power supply wasn't a problem.

His in-laws were happy to hear from him. After responding to their questions about their flight and what Saskatoon looked like, they prayed for him and Ochanya. This took about fifteen minutes. Owoicho ended the call after another fifteen minutes of more questions, prayers, and a litany of complaints about the president and his recent decision on fuel subsidy.

Next, Owoicho called Alegwu.

"Haba, Owoicho, I've been worried sick about you guys." Those were Alegwu's first words to his friend after waiting hours for his call.

"Baba, sorry. I should have called earlier, but we've been trying to settle in since we arrived. And your Airtel thing didn't work. I guess it's my phone, though. Anyway, because of that, I had to wait until we got to the house and I could connect to the Wi-Fi," Owoicho explained.

"I see. So, this Bimpe woman rented a place for you like she said she would?"

"Well, you can say that, though technically, we live with her in her basement. I know you don't know what that means, but a basement is like what you will refer to as a boys' quarters in Nigeria. The difference is that instead of being detached, it is in the underground of the main house. They say it can be cold in the winter and extremely hot in the summer."

"Jehovah, I don suffer. So, person when never go Canada before no go fit sabi wetin basement be again, shebi?"

They both laughed at Alegwu's funny reply.

"Anyway, I think your friend did well letting you stay in her basement. I think it's really kind of her. You're staying rent-free, right"

"It isn't free, oh! We pay rent. Bimpe says a basement the size of this one goes for about one thousand five hundred dollars monthly, but she is letting us have it for one thousand. Plus, we don't have to pay for power, internet, and other utilities. And she gets to cook for us occasionally."

"It's not a bad deal then."

"Yeah, I think so too."

"But are you comfortable living in the same building as your friend and her family? Why didn't she just look for a house somewhere else for you? I hope she doesn't tire of you soon."

"Why would she tire of me?"

"Is it not you again? Small time you go begin carry woman come the house, and that one fit cause wahala between you and her because she no go want make you come be bad influence to her children."

"For your information, she has just one child, and he's seven. And if you must know, I didn't come to Canada to carry women. I came to give my daughter a better life, give her the best education possible and expand her horizon so she has a global perspective on things and issues. But to answer your question, honestly, I don't know why Bimpe decided to bring us here. I thought we'd have our own place, but it is what it is. I figure she thinks we'd be more comfortable here, but we'd wing it for now and see how things go. As it stands, she and her husband have been really nice and welcoming to us."

"And this basement, does it come with furnishing or not?" Alegwu asked.

"Actually, it does. They only recently moved into this place, like a month ago. Since it's a much bigger and nicer place than their last rented apartment, they had to get new furniture, so some of their old stuff were moved in here. The bedroom has a queen-size bed, a very nice couch and a TV in the family room, and the kitchen seems reasonably functional. There are pots and pans and most of what we would need to start our life here. In all, I would say it's a small but comfortable space for Ochanya and me."

"That's good. I'm happy you are comfortable and settling in nicely. By the way, how's our Ochanya doing?"

"She's doing great. She's sleeping in the room, and I am out here in the tiny parlour struggling to find sleep. Looks like I'm going to have to get used to sleeping on the couch from now on."

"From bed to chair," Alegwu joked. "Anyway, I'm sure being awake has nothing to do with your new sleeping arrangement but more with jet lag and maybe the change of environment. In a few days, I bet you'd be sleeping and snoring like you used to do back then in the university."

"You just had to bring in my snoring,"

"No vex, I couldn't resist the temptation of yabbing you small," Alegwu laughed. "But seriously, buddy, I'm glad everything is working out for you and Ochanya. Please, greet her for me when she wakes up."

"Sure thing, I will."

"Awesome. So, I guess your countdown to becoming Canadian citizens has begun. One day gone, one thousand and ninety-four days to go."

"Men, we're talking three years o! Three years before I become eligible to hold a Canadian passport."

"See as you dey talk like say three years dey tey. Before you know it, three years don waka. It's just a matter of time. Once you begin work like this, na so time go dey fly," Alegwu said. "By the way, when do you start looking for work?"

"In the morning, I guess. There was this lady on the flight from Toronto to Saskatoon whom Ochanya and I became friends with yesterday. Incidentally, she works with an employment agency with a track record of helping newcomers settle in quickly. She wants me to see her about work, government welfare, and all that."

"Oh, nice."

"Yes, it is. Damiete, that's Bimpe's husband, will take us out in the morning to shop for a couple of things we need in the house. We want to get groceries and sort out some of the paperwork the government still requires from us, and Damiete has offered to be our chaperon for the day. He also said he'd accompany me to this woman's office. I'm optimistic that something positive will come out of it and we'd have a smooth and successful transition, or should I say integration?" Owoicho laughed.

"Who knows, when we are settled, maybe you and your family can even come and spend your holiday with us. It will be fun," Owoicho continued.

"That isn't a bad idea at all. I'm already looking forward to it. All the best, bro. Let me allow you to rest then. We'll talk again soon."

"Yes, soon." Owoicho hung up the phone. This time, sleep came when he closed his eyes.

34.

DAMIETE COULDN'T MAKE IT IN THE MORNING. HE CAME down hard with the flu and had to sleep in so he didn't pass it on to anyone else in the house. Thankfully, Bimpe had the next three days off from work, so she offered to drive Owoicho and Ochanya out. She figured the prospect of allowing two people, who were fresh off the boat, to navigate the city's public transportation system by themselves might be too much for them to handle. The way Bimpe saw it, they would have to decipher the fares, study maps, understand transfers and memorize bus numbers and routes–confusing things she didn't understand. Because she didn't have to do any of those things herself when she first arrived in Saskatoon, there was no way she could explain it to someone else.

When her family arrived four years earlier, they were fortunate to have been given a car by the pastor of the Nigerian church they attended. That car served them until they bought their own vehicle five months later. They would later fall out with the pastor and his wife when word got to them that Bimpe and Damiete lied about being members of the Abuja branch of their church. The truth was that they weren't churchgoers in Nigeria. In Canada, they opted for a particular Pentecostal church with predominantly white members. The church was extremely popular within the Nigerian immigrant community in Saskatoon based on a widespread belief that the more Caucasians there were in a church, the greater the potential for networking and securing employment through that connection.

"And did this church help you find work?" Owoicho asked, interjecting Bimpe's story.

"I would say so. My first job serving and washing dishes in a Nigerian restaurant came through a friend I made there. Even after I got my current job, I was still combining both until this foolish woman made some stupid, baseless accusation about her husband and me just because he confided in me about some things going on in their marriage. Anyway, I was fired from the job because she was close to the owner of the place and in annoyance, I stopped going to church completely."

🍁

Owoicho was surprised that Bimpe would open up to him about things that were borderline scandalous. Things he might never have known if she hadn't brought them up herself. Things that happened to the Browns back when he and Ene were still contemplating whether or not they should even commit to migrating to Canada. Things that raised questions in his head and made him want to find out more about the scandals she spoke about. However, being the uneffusive person he was, Owoicho chose not to question her further or dig deeper for more stories. That morning, he was so happy and relieved that she volunteered to drive them around, which made things much easier for him and his daughter.

First, Bimpe took them to a Bell sales and service centre to get SIM cards, then she drove them to a branch of RBC so Owoicho could open a bank account for his salary when he got a job and for all the other financial transactions he would have to do going forward. After the bank, Bimpe said their next stop would be at the Service Canada office to properly document their Social Insurance Number.

With that done, Bimpe took them downtown to the offices of the Greater Saskatoon Catholic Schools division to get Ochanya enrolled in school. The choice was between a public or Catholic high school; Owoicho chose the latter because, as a child, he attended catechism with his neighbours even though he wasn't born or raised catholic. The adults in his life at the time didn't care very much about church and religion, and as he grew older and could reason for himself, he took sides with them. In later years, he would go to church because of Ene and the children, but he never joined any unit in the church or put himself out there for special recognition, seeing as he was a popular face on television.

When they got back to the car, Bimpe asked if they were hungry so she could take them somewhere fancy for a sandwich or maybe some burger and fries, but Owoicho, speaking on behalf of Ochanya, said they would pass. For him, the most important item on the day's itinerary was finding work. Lunch could wait.

"Do you remember Isabella, the lady who called you from the airport yesterday?" Owoicho asked Bimpe.

"Of course, I do. How can I forget so soon that she and her husband saved you from being stranded at the airport?"

"That is true," Owoicho agreed. "She works as a settlement advisor with the Newcomers Outreach Network of Saskatoon. She gave me her call card yesterday and asked that I see her in her office. She wants to discuss work and other things we need to know about settling. I'm thinking we can go there now. You were in the kitchen cleaning up after dinner, so I might have mentioned it to your husband alone. I'm sorry. Damiete thinks it is something we should do immediately. You know, strike while she still remembers me and what I look like."

Bimpe paused to think for a bit. "Owoicho, if you ask me, I'll say there are so many ways you can get a job here in Canada. You don't have to enrol or give your SIN, health insurance number, and other confidential information about yourself and Ochanya to just anyone. These people in this settlement work are just looking for people to help them meet their target so they can continue being funded by the government."

"Are you saying they are not genuine?"

"I am saying many people come to this country, and they find work without subjecting themselves anecdotally or statistically to these government-funded agencies and their propaganda."

"How then do they find work?"

"There are countless sites online that advertise job postings. All you have to do is sign up for one of them. Dami is quite good with writing resumes and cover letters Canadian style. He can teach you if you want. The mistake some of us make when we come here is that we quickly tie ourselves down for weeks and weeks when we really should be out there knocking on doors and searching for work by ourselves. I personally consider them a waste of valuable four to eight weeks in the life of a newcomer."

"How then do I find work? I need to get something immediately," Owoicho told Bimpe. He deliberately left out his indebtedness to his friend Alegwu. He didn't like that he owed so much, so the earlier he started working and could be debt-free, the better for him.

"No, I don't think you should be in such a hurry to find work. Do you know what my advice to you would be? I would say don't even worry about it for the next two weeks. You only just got here. Consider the next fourteen days a well-deserved holiday. You and your daughter survived Nigeria; give yourself a break and just celebrate that. After these two weeks, you can then start the process of getting your driver's licence and looking for work. That's what Dami and I did."

"Really?"

"Yes, that's what we did. Look, you guys will be fine. I've had at least one very serious conversation with Ochanya. She's very smart, wise beyond her years, and that's what they like here in this country–intelligent and inquisitive kids. Your daughter will do very well here, and so will you. Seriously, I don't see you having such a hard time finding work in television or radio. The key is being strategic in your search."

"But when I'm ready, how do I begin?"

"Just so you don't put yourself under undue pressure, I'd say start with a survival job. It can be exhausting, depending on what you get, and it won't be in your field, but it will pay the bill. And trust me, my brother, dem no dey joke with bills for this country.

You must pay; otherwise, you could die of cold or heat if your utilities are cut off."

"A survival job?"

"Yes. You need it for rent, groceries, and to save up for a car. I don't know how much money you came with from Nigeria, but trust me, if you don't start earning Canadian dollars within the first three months of your arrival, you will watch that money deplete like the ozone layer in no time. As e dey happen, I swear your medulla oblongata go start to touch."

"Bree, why are you telling me this now? Why didn't you tell me about survival jobs and all these scary things when I was still in Nigeria?"

"Would it have made any difference if I did? You are here now with your daughter; that's the most important thing. I told you about washing plates in the Nigerian restaurant downtown, didn't I?"

"Yes, you did."

"When we first got here, Dami worked in a gas station, filling up people's cars and cleaning their windscreens in -50°C temperature. It was brutal. He has also worked in a fast-food restaurant, flipping burgers and cleaning up at the close of business. Some people have one job; others juggle two or even three jobs at a time. It is what people do here to survive, pay their bills, and send money home. We start that way and then luckily find our feet."

"Isn't this why I should see Isabella?"

"Owoicho, forget her. Like I said earlier, she just wants to use you to get her numbers up and maybe even get a promotion at work. I'll take you to another settlement agency not too far from here. It's a one-stop-shop for everything you are looking for and maybe even more."

Owoicho didn't speak anymore. He didn't know what to think or feel. It was his early days in Saskatchewan, yet he wondered if he was not making a mistake. He was under pressure to find work; nevertheless, he agreed that he needed to pass the driving test to make things easier for him and his daughter. He could only use his Nigerian driver's licence for three months, and getting around was very important, especially during winter. So, he decided to hold on his desperation to get a job and concentrate on passing his driving test.

The first time he did the road test, pedestrians kept appearing from nowhere at every intersection as if they were on a mission to destroy his destiny. That movement unsettled him greatly, and he didn't have to be told he'd need a better score to qualify as a driver in Saskatoon. His second attempt was even worse. On that occasion, he had chosen 8:30am for the test; meanwhile, sunrise was forecasted for 8:45am. Needless to say, he failed woefully because it was still dark and he couldn't see any of the dividing lines on the road.

Luckily for him, the third time was a charm. This time he didn't forget his shoulder checks. There were no pedestrians on the road; he didn't turn right when the instructor said left; he remembered to count to three before continuing on when he got to a stop sign, and he nailed his parallel parking.

Owoicho knew that getting his driver's license would open up fresh employment opportunities for him. And, if nothing came up soon in his area of interest, becoming a cab driver or working for any of the food pickup services as a deliveryman were options he could now explore. He had seen so many responsible and comfortable-looking immigrant men and women with really good cars doing it, so potentially it couldn't be that bad or stressful. Plus, he got to stay in his car and stay warm instead of being out in the cold.

🍁

Owoicho's conscience wouldn't allow him rest or sleep comfortably until he made the call he should have made the first chance he had to speak to anyone back in Nigeria. He didn't know how the conversation would go, and he didn't want Ochanya to overhear him in case things became tense, so he left her in the living room and went into the bathroom. He brought out his phone from his pocket, scrolled until he found the name he was looking for, took a deep breath, and pressed the call sign.

"Onjefu?"

"Owoicho? Owoicho, is that you? I don't know this number. It looks like you're not in the country."

"I'm in Canada. Ochanya and I arrived yesterday. We relocated."

"Wow, Brother! And you're just telling me now?"

"I'm so sorry, Onjefu. I know I should have told you, but the whole thing happened somehow. You know now, after what happened to Ene and the children. I don't even know what to say, but it was a very confusing time for Ochanya and me. I had so much in my head and was worrying about many things; I just thought it was best we left for somewhere safe. But you are right. I should have told you earlier. I wanted to, but there were just too many things in my head. That is why I am doing it now. I don't want you to hear it from someone else. In fact, you are the first person I am speaking to since we got here."

"Oh, please. Don't give me that crap, Owoicho. Just say you didn't want me to know because you think I am a bad person and my bad energy might have negatively affected your travelling and maybe even brought down the plane."

"Onjefu, I'm sorry."

"You don't trust me, Owoicho. You don't trust me. How could you keep such a thing away from your own blood brother?"

"To be honest, I didn't tell anyone. Okay, maybe one or two people knew, but that was it. It had to be hush-hush."

"Look, Owoicho, I've got to go. I've got an important call coming in from Malaysia. I'll talk to you later."

Owoicho wasn't exactly shocked at his brother's reaction. He would have also felt bad if he had been kept in the dark. However, a part of him had hoped that Onjefu, of all people, Onjefu, the internet fraudster, would have understood that some things were not discussed until they came to fruition. Some dreams should not be shared until they become a reality.

35.

"I DON'T BELIEVE YOU'RE STILL MAD AT ME AFTER ALL THIS time," Ratamma said when Oroma eventually answered the phone.

"I'm not mad at you, Ratamma. I've just been keeping to myself, that's all."

"But it's obvious you still blame me for what happened between you and Chike. That's what mummy told me."

"Well, I don't know where she heard that from."

"She said both of you talked last week."

"We talked about my new job. I don't recall Chike's name coming up at any point during that conversation."

"Oroma, you don't call me unless I call you. If I did something wrong or you feel I offended you, why don't you just say it so we can trash it out once and for all?"

"I've had a busy day, Ratamma; I just came back from work. Can we do this some other time, please?"

"Oroma, you are not the only busy person in this world. You know the businesses I run in Nigeria and the number of people who work under me. Still, I find time to call and check up on you. Many times, I've stayed up till very late at night here, so we can catch up on things, only for you to tell me that you want to study or that you're tired. I call you, Oroma. I call you. But you, if you don't hear from me, you don't bother calling, and that's not fair at all. I know you are not happy with me, but you should know that whatever I suggested to you two years ago came from a place of love and concern."

"Ratamma, I don't blame you for anything. I've told you this a million times. Whatever actions I took, I took them because I wanted to. No one forced me to come to Canada. It was my choice."

"But I put the idea in your head."

"You told me to follow my heart, and I did. It is not as if you gave me kayanmata to come and use to trap somebody and it didn't work. Yes, you said I should come and meet him. I also felt it was the right thing to do. If Chike hadn't-- look, I don't want to talk about Chike or anything else from the past. I'm finally in a good space. I have a new life and a new job, and that is all that matters to me right now. My focus is on me, my job, the present, and what the future holds for me here in Saskatoon."

"I'm glad to hear that. I am really happy that you are doing fine. Mummy told me about the job. Congratulations."

"Thank you."

"Do you want to talk about it?"

"Talk about what?"

"This new job you got. Is it with a pharmacy or a hospital?"

"No, it's not with a pharmacy or a hospital. I work for a CBO–a community-based organization that focuses on mental health and substance abuse. I'm one of three programme advisors in my unit. We facilitate sensitization workshops in schools and youth groups in the city and advise other not-for-profit organizations on ways to help at-risk youth and other vulnerable people in the community who are dealing with addiction issues."

"Wow! This is great news. I'm really happy for you, Oroma. You don't know how sad I was when mummy told me a while back that you were still serving drinks in a bar or something."

"It was a café, and I don't work there anymore."

"Thank God! It brought me to tears when she told me you were doing that kind of job. Ha! A whole you serving tea and coffee to people you would have been paying salary to if you were still in Nigeria. God forbid!"

"Ratamma, this country is different. Those things don't matter here. Nobody cares what you do as long as it is legitimate and pays your bills. Besides, if I didn't have experience working in the café and in all the other places I volunteered and put in long hours without collecting a kobo, I doubt I would have this job today. So, I don't see it as a bad thing. Everything happens for a reason. What is important now is that I'm learning something new in a field I never imagined working in. I get to use what I learn on the job to assist people battling personal demons and who, more often than not, are in real danger of harming themselves and destroying their own lives."

"That sounds interesting."

"It is. I come home every evening feeling like I've done something important in the community. I am happy to help these strangers make better choices and decisions about their lives."

Speaking to her sister about choices and decisions reminded Oroma that she had made a few bad calls in the last couple of years. She cringed just thinking about them, like her decision to seek Ratamma's opinion when people began insinuating that Chike might be stringing her along and would most likely marry somebody else if she didn't act fast.

Another poor decision was letting Ratamma convince her to surprise Chike in Saskatoon. She had listened to her sister's counsel and began putting her relocation plan in motion without letting Chike know what she had up her sleeve. From applying and being accepted into the Masters in Public Health programme at the University of Saskatchewan to securing her student visa, purchasing her flight ticket and landing in Saskatoon on the seventh of July of the next year, Chike was completely in the dark. He didn't suspect anything, and she didn't tell him anything either, although they spoke at least four times a week and texted each other even more frequently.

She had his address, so she didn't have to call him from the airport. Oroma took a taxi and prayed her boyfriend was home. Luckily, he was, but he wasn't the one who opened the door when she rang the doorbell. It was his roommate.

"Hi."

"Hi."

Awkward silence. Oroma decided to try again.

"Hi, my name is Oroma."

"Hi. And how may I help you?"
"I hope I'm in the right place. I'm looking for Chike."
"Oh, you're friends with Chike?"
"Yes. Does he live here? Is he home?"
"Yes, he is in. Chike! Chike! He likes the TV really loud."

Hearing a total stranger tell her something about her boyfriend she knew to be true brought back memories of their life together in Nigeria. But the memory was fleeting. It disappeared almost as soon as the thought flashed.

"Just hold on. I'll go and get him."

Oroma's heart was pounding really hard in her chest, and she had to lean on the doorframe to stop herself from falling.

Chike froze when he saw her. He didn't smile, hug, or kiss her. He couldn't even look at her face. His gaze was on the four suitcases in the driveway.

At that moment, Oroma realized she had made a grave mistake by quitting her job and leaving everything she had going on for her in Nigeria because she believed Chike needed her with him in Saskatoon. At thirty-seven, she shouldn't have allowed the ticking of her biological clock, whatever that meant, to becloud her sense of reasoning. She should never have let her sister and friends project their own expectations and insecurities about men, dating and marriage on her. She should never have allowed them to talk her into surprising Chike in Canada the way she did. She should have known better. But she was in love, and love makes people do irrational things.

Oroma couldn't believe how naïve she had been to have trusted Chike all those years. Suddenly, all the pieces came together, making perfect sense. Hinting at marriage without pursuing it further, changing the subject whenever she brought up paying him a visit, and discouraging her from sending money and gifts to his aged parents in Nnewi. It all made sense in that moment.

His roommate, the one he always spoke about but who was never home for her to say hello to whenever she called, wasn't

Pakistani or a bubbly guy studying to become a doctor. His "roommate" was Bailey, a very beautiful pregnant white woman.

"Oroma, what are you doing here? Why are you here?"

She didn't know how to respond to Chike's questions without appearing foolish. And while he fidgeted at the door, Oroma stood there transfixed. If she wanted anything, it was for the ground to open up and consume her whole. Bailey was his pregnant girlfriend, maybe wife even, and the reason he didn't want her in Saskatoon.

"Ratamma, I have to go. Maybe we can talk on Saturday or Sunday when I'm not working."

Oroma didn't wait for her sister's response. She ended the call and went straight to bed. She thought she was fine, but she wasn't. The hurt cut really deep and recalling that horrible experience from two years earlier brought it all back.

She tried to stop it but couldn't, so she let the tears flow freely. The anger and pain of Chike's betrayal still felt fresh like it happened yesterday.

36.

IT WAS MONDAY MORNING, AND OCHANYA COULDN'T BRING herself to get out of bed. She knew she should be excited about returning to school, but her nerves wouldn't allow her to relish the prospect. Between the time she thought she'd be starting school in Makurdi and the commencement of the new academic year in Canada, it had been months since she was last in a classroom with kids her age.

Ordinarily, Ochanya would consider herself a shy teen and starting a new school was definitely a trigger for a bout of panic attacks, but in this particular instance, it was even more nerve-wracking because she was going to be in class with a bunch of kids who looked and sounded nothing like her.

Bimpe, whom she had now gotten used to calling Aunt Bree, had told her so many times that she would do well in St. Joseph's High School because she was just the kind of student high schools and colleges in North America were on the lookout for. She was intelligent, talented, and outspoken when necessary. Most importantly, she checked the diversity box. Aunt Bree and her husband told her that as more schools and organizations in Canada continue their drive towards more inclusiveness and being demonstrably accepting of representation in their composition, admissions, and recruitment, someone like her stood a good chance of becoming a success story for diversity and integration in Canada.

The Browns sounded pretty confident in their assertion that every sector in the country had a Black, indigenous, minority, and people of colour quota that Ochanya was imminently qualified for as long as she stayed focused, had the right amount of extra curriculum activities to her credit, projected the right attitude, and kept her grades up.

In spite of their words of encouragement and belief in her, Ochanya couldn't help wondering if people in her new school – students and teachers alike – would take a liking to her and give her the chance to succeed in this new environment. She wondered if she would thrive, if the system would allow her to grow into herself and flourish.

Ochanya worried about her accent. She feared that its thickness might put a target on her back and make her a laughing stock every time she pronounced a word differently from how her classmates would. She imagined them laughing at her whenever she opened her mouth to speak or asked that a word or sentence be repeated because she didn't understand what they said the first time.

Ochanya worried about the way she looked and the colour of her skin. Again, because she imagined being the only Black girl in the school, she worried about standing out in ways that might make her overtly self-conscious in class. She didn't know what she would do if her classmates asked her about her hair which she insisted on wearing natural and free of chemical products. From the videos she had watched on YouTube, she expected to be asked shocking questions about Nigeria and Africa. She prayed such questions would give her the opportunity to speak about the beauty of her country and continent.

Dragging herself out of bed to begin her day, Ochanya wished she had listened to her father when he advised her to hold on for one more week before starting school. Since she didn't listen, and the day was upon her, she had no choice but to go out there and face her fears. Ochanya also wished she had resisted the urge to respond to Oche's WhatsApp messages after ignoring them for weeks. She knew his reason for reigniting what he extinguished months back was so he could brag to his friends that he had a girlfriend in Canada, but that didn't bother her. All she wanted was a friend, someone her age she could talk to and who would tell her she was brave and amazing and that she would be all right.

37.

As Owoicho dressed up to go out on the first day of his second job in Saskatoon, he couldn't help wondering if he did the right thing by not following up with Isabella. Bimpe and Damiete were persuasive in their argument. They told him point-blank that they were against him enrolling in an eight-week-long newcomer assistance programme when he could just as well register with a manual labour recruiter in the city and start making money immediately. Their argument was that if he was able to secure a job that offered fairly consistent hours and wages, his mind would be at peace, and he wouldn't have to worry too much about his bills in Canada or meeting up with the obligations he might have to family and friends back in Nigeria. They also told him that once he took up unskilled labour employment, finding a skilled job would become easier.

Owoicho heard them quite all right, but his initial reaction was resistance. It was hard for him to wrap his head around the idea of a graduate with one, two, maybe three or even four degrees cleaning floors, wiping old people's butts or delivering dinners to families too lazy to go out or cook their own meals. It didn't make sense to him that highly qualified men and women would accept to work for minimum wage simply because they moved to Canada where the economy was supposedly stronger than where they had come from.

Every time Bimpe and her husband brought up the issue of work, Owoicho looked them straight in the eye, and he'd say something like, "Thank you, but no thanks. I'll skip the survival job and just wait until I get a call back from a radio or television station I applied to."

However, reality came knocking really fast and hard. It hit him when he checked his bank balance at the end of their first week in Canada and saw that the money he brought from Nigeria was almost gone.

No doubt, he knew the Nigerian currency was weak compared to the Canadian dollar, but seeing how little he got for the naira he exchanged for dollars made him rethink his earlier stance on survival jobs. If all his savings, proceeds from the sale of assets, and the money he borrowed from Alegwu combined could only afford him a rickety 2004 Honda CRV from the auctions, then he was in serious trouble. Of course, the money got him more than a car. Some went to Bimpe and her husband to cover three months' rent. He replaced some of the old furniture in the basement with new ones, bought clothes, and paid for Ochanya's school supplies.

At the end of the two weeks he spent pretending he was vacationing in the prairies, Owoicho approached Damiete for help. His new friend told him what he must do, then back in the basement, the mental struggle and psychological torture continued. Damiete wanted him to get a job as a security guard because it was what he did. And if Owoicho was able to complete the one-week in-person security course successfully, he might pull some strings in the company he worked for and maybe find him a spot there.

Still, Owoicho struggled with the idea of dressing up in a uniform and working as a guard when only a few weeks back, he had security guards he paid from his salary. It was hard, really hard for him to process.

Owoicho worried how his Nigerian fans would respond if they saw him disguised as a security guard because he was on national TV practically every night, and people knew him and recognized his face when he went out. He wondered what his family and friends would say if they got to know he was attending to cars in a gas station or stacking shelves in a grocery store, or harvesting granola seeds on a farm. While asking himself these questions, a solution came.

His first job in Canada didn't come from Miller Services, a third-party recruiting company Damiete had initially suggested he register with. It also wasn't as a security guard because the Browns could see how much he detested that option. He got a job as a deliveryman in one of the biggest furniture companies in the city, Pope and Buchannan Homes. Damiete had a hand in making it happen. One of Damiete's friends, Segun, had worked there for a number of years but was leaving to begin a Masters' programme in Social Services in another city after spending eight years in Saskatoon. Since Owoicho had a heads-up, he applied early.

Getting the job wasn't difficult. The only thing the manager who interviewed him wanted to know was if he had experience lifting heavy things, and Owoicho said he did. In fact, in the resume he submitted to the company, nothing was mentioned of his university education or his years in broadcasting. Instead, he stopped at his secondary school qualification and fabricated a position as a furniture carrier in a non-existent furniture company in Abuja.

The job entailed loading furniture from the warehouse into a truck driven by another employee he was paired with and then dropping off the items at the buyer's home or office. He was given one day for his paperwork, and the second day was dedicated to training and orientation about his role and the company's policies and rules.

Owoicho quit after three days of heavy lifting because his back hurt and he couldn't walk straight. His entire body felt like he was flogged with a two-by-four wood and left for dead. The Advil from the pharmacist helped, but his family doctor thought it was best he stayed away from doing anything strenuous for a while.

His second job came through the same Miller Services. It was a temporary assignment to fill up an opening for only two weeks. The job was to stack boxes of frozen chicken onto pallets and then position the pallets to make it easy for the forklift drivers to lift them into waiting trucks that then delivered them to shops in Saskatoon, Regina, and Prince Albert.

Bob, his scheduler from Miller Services, had called ahead of the email to ask if he was up to the task because the guy who had the job originally had called in sick at the last minute. And because he had been home and idle since quitting his first job, Owoicho was more than happy to stand in for this person, so the job was reassigned to him.

Driving to the location, a cold room on the east side called Farmfresh Delite, Owoicho didn't know what to expect. The job instruction emailed to him the day before asked that he come along with warm clothing, preferably layers of it, and a pair of steel-toe boots.

His silent prayer as he pulled up into the company's parking lot was that he wouldn't be asked to lift anything heavier than twenty kilograms. After his experience with the furniture company, he was scared for his back, but he needed work to stay active and not lose his mind. He needed to prove to them at Miller Services that he was strong and ready to work. He also needed the money, more than he cared to admit.

38.

The contact person from Miller Services had left his name with the pretty lady at the front desk of the cold storage company. She introduced herself as Pattie. After getting him to write down his name and the exact time he clocked in, she showed him where to hang his jacket if he wanted to take it off, but he chose not to. She also got him to sign for a company toque, hand gloves, and a safety vest with Farmfresh Delite monogrammed on it.

Before allowing him through the door marked "Staff Only," another employee of the company, this time a burly redhead with dark brown eyes and a great big smile, read out loud to him some important safety guidelines and procedures to follow in the event of a fire outbreak or any other emergency that required evacuating the building. When the fellow was done reading, he made Owoicho confirm in writing that he understood the instructions in the paper he read from and was ready to abide by all of them.

Even though he was fifteen minutes early, Owoicho was surprised to see that every available seat in the staff common room was taken. There were five Blacks, two Asians, and one Caucasian. The Caucasian guy looked really young and frail, though, for the kind of work described in the job notes. Owoicho learned later during one of the breaks that he was a college student taking a break from the University of Regina to discover himself before deciding what he wanted to do for the rest of his life. Like Owoicho, all eight men were casual hands from Miller Services, and none of them looked like they had had a good night's sleep.

Instinctively, Owoicho walked towards the section of the room where the Black guys were huddled together and perched himself at the edge of where one of them sat. He said hello, but they barely acknowledged his presence. If anything, they were cold towards him, and it was hardly the reception he expected from his fellow dark-skinned brothers. Despite their seeming standoffishness, he chose not to take offence.

Though he had only been in Saskatchewan for a short while and this was his first time out on a job site of this nature, he was a fast learner. While he may never have had any experience with immigrant workers compelled to show up for work in a cold room so early in the morning, he had seen and heard enough from others to conclude that Canada humbles people.

From what Owoicho gathered in the email from Bob, he was supposed to be there from seven in the morning until three o'clock in the afternoon. The email stated that he should brace himself for some tough work. It affirmed eight hours of hard labour with two fifteen-minute breaks in between. There was another thirty minutes for lunch, even though he forgot to pack a proper lunch for himself because he didn't want to be late to the address if the GPS in his phone acted up and he missed his way.

At exactly five minutes past seven, the cheerful redhead, who told them to call him Kirk, walked briskly into the staff room with three other white men he introduced as Maurice, Langley, and Ivan. They were the forklift operators for the day and perhaps for the remainder of the two-week duration of this particular assignment. Owoicho and the eight other guys stood up and followed the forklift operators through a giant iron-like door that resembled something that should be in prison. A white and red sign on the door read, "Restricted Area." The door also had several caution stickers pasted on it.

From the moment they were escorted into the cold room by Kirk and his friends, and Owoicho experienced the first gust of chill from the cooling system in the room, he knew he had walked into trouble. It was -16°C and freezing inside the warehouse. Within minutes of getting himself organized and acclimatizing to the task and the sub-zero temperature in the room, his entire body began to shake. He showed up for the assignment layered as advised, but it didn't help much.

Owoicho didn't know how he did it, but he survived the first two coffee breaks without throwing in the towel and going back home. But during lunch, he cried out to Obinna, the Nigerian guy he was paired with and with whom he shared a table at lunch, although he didn't come out with any food to eat.

"Bro, this work hard o, I no go lie."

"This work hard? E be like say you never see anything," Obinna replied, munching on his sandwich.

"For sure, it's hard work. Plus, it's freezing in there, or am I the only one who can't feel my face and the rest of my body?"

"You're not the only one, trust me. It is cold and freezing in there. But the truth is that I've been through worse."

"What can be worse than this?" Owoicho was shocked at Obinna's response.

"Do you want to know my first job when my family and I got here two years ago?" Obinna asked.

"Please go ahead and tell me."

"We arrived in the fall, and that same week I got a job clearing out some fields owned by the U of S for research being carried out by their Faculty of Agriculture. Not only was it cold and windy, because we were outdoors all the time, but there was a lot of bending and pulling involved, and I don't even want to talk about all the dirt that got into my shoes and clothes throughout the task. We were there for eight hours, Monday to Friday, until all the crops and markers were gone two weeks later. I still remember my first day there. When we were done for the day and they dropped us off at a central point in University Heights, where people packed their cars or waited for the bus, this Yoruba guy with us on the farm offered to drive me home. As soon as I got home, I ignored my wife and kids and headed straight into the bathroom. I locked myself in there, got under the hot shower to wash off the dirt from my body, and actually cried for more than half an hour. That was one of the worst days of my life."

"Wow, that must have been tough," Owoicho said, unsure what impact his sympathy would have now.

"My brother, it was o. But something good came out of that agonizing experience. I became friends with another Nigerian guy who told me about this opportunity of making good money planting trees all over Canada."

"Planting trees?"

"Yes, planting trees. Last year we went up North to the City of Grande Prairie, somewhere between British Columbia and Yukon. We were there for four months planting trees as part of a government initiative to grow millions of them all over the country. There were people from all over Canada and every imaginable ethnicity camped together in the wild with one purpose in mind."

"To make money?" Owoicho interjected.

"Yes. We were all there to make money. College students, young and not-so-young people, men and women, immigrants and non-immigrants, white, black and brown, worked from sunup to sundown because we couldn't afford to stay idle. Again, the work was gruelling and repetitive, but it paid really well. I made more money in those four months than I would have made doing this job for the whole year in Saskatoon. The downside was that I was useless for nearly a month when we got back. My body ached, and moving around was a struggle. I could barely use my hands for weeks, and my fingers were sore. When I saw our doctor, he recommended some medication and a lot of rest, and because his prescription worked, I went back there this year and only got back a month again."

"When you say a lot of money, how much are we talking about here?"

Obinna paused to think for a minute, and then he said, "We are talking between ten to fifty thousand dollars, depending on how long you stay, how much time you put into the work and how many trees you planted in that time."

Owoicho's jaw dropped when he heard the amount of money people made planting trees for a few months. "If you ask me, I would say that is plenty of money in every currency of the world you can think of, especially our naira. So Obinna, if you have already made all this money and the year hasn't even ended, what are you still doing here dragging this small work with us that need it to survive?"

"Bro, why you dey talk like this na? Money dey reach person? Now that I am young and still have the strength, I have to work as much as possible so that in a few years, I can open a car dealership in Lagos and send cars from here to my younger brother. You know we can't stay here forever. We must return home one day, and the hustling will continue there."

"That's a very good point," Owoicho agreed. "You know, the more I interact with people, the more it hits me that many of us have come here from Africa and other parts of the world based on an incomplete or false narrative. It really doesn't take long to be astounded by the stark difference between the picture painted for us or what we chose to believe versus the reality on the ground. In my case, I am skilled and highly qualified in my journalism field, yet I can't find a position or a job befitting of my status and accomplishment."

"I know, bro. I used to watch you read the news most nights on TV."

"For real?"

"For real, men. And sorry about your wife and kids. I read about what happened on social media."

"Thank you, bro." Owoicho was silent for a minute. "You do stay on top of what is happening in Nigeria. That's really good."

"You think you are running away from your country, and then you arrive here and news about home suddenly become your oxygen."

"That's really true. It's the same for me too. I watch Arise News, TVC, and even Nollywood movies as if I'm still in Abuja."

"To be honest, bro, I was shocked when I saw you come in through the door. I felt you'd be embarrassed meeting people from back home who know you and what you used to do there.

That was why I didn't say hello. I thought it might make you feel uncomfortable because I can relate. I used to be a big shot in one of the big banks in Nigeria. Whenever I tell people who I was back home, I see the look in their eyes. They want to know why a bank manager is happy planting trees or working in a cold room."

"What do you tell them?"

"The children, I came because of the children. And I am not the only one. This, right here," Obinna said, pointing to himself, "this is the story of so many immigrants you will come across in this country."

Owoicho took a deep breath. "At least we have work, and we don't have to beg anyone for money."

"I don't disagree with you on that point; there's work to do and someone has to do it. My only problem is that if a big retail company is looking for store clerks, why do they have to hire a lawyer from Nigeria for that? If their agricultural sector is short of farmhands, they don't need a pharmacist from Iran to harvest crops from the fields, and if Saskatoon needs more taxi drivers, why should a tech guru from India or an engineer from Burundi be the one to do the job?"

Redhead Kirk chose that moment to announce the end of the lunch break so Owoicho didn't have to answer the question posed by his new friend. They went back to work and neither of them spoke about their challenging experiences and the trauma of settling down until the day was over. Before leaving the building, both men exchanged phone numbers. Owoicho wanted to stay in touch to find out more about the tree-planting gig. He was already thinking about next year and wanted to keep his options open.

When Owoicho got home that afternoon, his fingers were ashen and almost numb from the freezing temperature in the cold room. He looked at his hands and then thought about the pay and how it will help with his bills. He wanted to be strong and endure the pain and discomfort because of his daughter and the bright future he wanted her to have in Canada. That was what he did, and a lot of men, immigrants and non-immigrants, did it every day. But it was hard.

Back home, while nursing another terrible ache all over his body, he thought about it long and hard. Should he or shouldn't he go back? In the end, he decided he wasn't going back to Farmfresh Delite. It just wasn't for him. He tried, but all that bending and lifting and exposure to extreme cold conditions, all in the name of survival, wasn't him. It wasn't worth it. If he got pneumonia and died, his daughter would be an orphan, and he would never forgive himself, even in death, if that happened.

Owoicho wasn't comfortable continuing with the job. He didn't see himself getting used to it. Not now, not ever.

39.

Oroma had another bad day. It all started with a call from her mother at 3 a.m. her phone's relentless vibration on the nightstand woke her up from the crazy dream she was having about being pregnant for Naira Marley. Because she didn't know if it was a good or bad thing, she was happy at first that she didn't have to find out what became of the baby in her belly. Even in the dream, it was a mixed bag of emotions and all so very confusing to her because, on the one hand, she was Mrs. Marley, and on the other hand, the Afro-rap artist made her smoke marijuana laced with tons of ecstasy on the night the baby was expected. The drugs came from a stash they confiscated from kids at a rehabilitation facility they were both supposed to oversee, and the cops were after them. The relief Oroma felt when she realized it was a nightmare was immediately followed by fear.

"Mummy, it's the middle of the night here. Is everyone all right? Did something bad happen?"

Even though she was only half awake, she knew her mother wouldn't have called when she did unless there was an emergency and someone in the family was in danger. "Mummy, please say something."

"Oroma, there is a problem. We have a big problem." Her mother was breathing heavily. "It is Ratamma. She is in the hospital."

"Hospital? Where? When? What happened?"

The way her mother explained it, her sister had been in a fight with one of her customers. Only it wasn't a fight as such. A fight was something that happened between equals. This was a mauling. An ambush by an angry mob. Ratamma had sold a lotion from her newest product line to a Lagos-based socialite, who paid five hundred thousand naira for this product. Called

The V-Sweetener Series or VSS, it was advertised as having the special ability to make anyone, including governors and presidents, malleable to the wishes and dictates of the user. As instructed, the woman applied the cream to her private part before and after sex with her target. By the third encounter, when the desired result was expected to manifest, her maintenance allowance was slashed from half a million naira monthly to a miserly one hundred and fifty thousand naira by her sugar daddy.

The same day her upkeep was reduced without explanation, her business mogul boyfriend and husband of three was seen with another woman at a hotel in Abuja. The person who saw them said it was their third night together. So essentially, instead of the Sweetener making her irresistible to her man, it ended up having the opposite effect on him.

To make matters worse, when pictures of the philanderer and his new love interest surfaced online, Jaruma Empire, sex therapist and Ratamma's biggest business rival, immediately made a cryptic post on Instagram about Panadol and how if it wasn't the real pain-relieving medication, it couldn't have the same effect as the original. Her competitor's simple but targeted post went viral, and before long, more users of the cream popped out of the woodwork with stories of how they had also used it on their partners without success.

Feeling like she had been scammed, the woman and some of her friends drove to Ratamma's office for a pound of flesh and also to get her money back. Needless to say, Ratamma wouldn't be selling kayanmata to anyone anytime soon.

"Right now, she is very weak. One of the nurses told me in confidence that she might slip into a coma any moment now if we don't act fast. The doctors are ready to operate on her, but we can't reach Wabiye."

"I don't understand. What do you need Wabiye for?"

"For the bills and to tell them to go ahead with the operation."

"That her husband sef, he never stays in one place."

"I was told he's in Turkey for business, and his phone has been switched off all day. I don't know who else to call or speak to for help because the hospital won't do anything until they get their deposit or Wabiye's consent."

"Don't worry, mummy. Just let me know how much you need, and I will immediately transfer it to your account. I'll be in meetings and presentations all day, but please let me know as soon as she is out of the theatre."

That was at 3 a.m. And as if her day wasn't already off to a bad start, Oroma got to the office at nine, and it got even worse. Her phone rang just as she was settling in for the morning. While scrambling to answer it before the caller hung up, she mistakenly knocked down the large Tim Hortons cup of coffee she got for herself on her way to work, spilling its content on her laptop.

Reporting the incident to HR and IT was one of the most humiliating experiences of her life. It reminded her of one time as a kid when her mother asked her to iron a dress she wanted to wear to a party. Oroma wanted to quickly get back to the soap opera showing on TV, so she got distracted and burnt the dress beyond fixing. She expected to get a good hiding from her mother for being careless and destructive, and the woman didn't disappoint.

The final straw was running into Obinna Achinike at Red Pepper during her lunch break. He waved when he saw her walk into the restaurant, and she waved back at him. Their brief hug was awkward and totally unexpected, but Oroma gave in to it anyway because they hadn't seen each other in such a long time.

Considering the day she was having, with her elder sister still hospitalized and her work laptop refusing to come on, she needed the hug, but she couldn't tell Obinna that. Instead, she told him that he abandoned her because of his friend, and she was still unhappy with him and his wife.

To mask his guilt and embarrassment, knowing she spoke the truth, Obinna laughed at her accusation. And then he asked her to join his table if she wasn't meeting with anyone. She wasn't, so she did.

"What brings you here? Do you work in downtown now or something?"

"Yes, I do. My office is only a couple of blocks away. I work with Sisters of Kindness Foundation as a Programme Advisor."

"Wow! That's a really good position and a great place to work. Congrats, Oroma. I am happy for you."

"Thank you."

""Oroms, Oroms. I no know say you still dey Saskatoon, true."

"Where I for come go if I no dey Saskatoon? How we dey take talk am again for Naija? No leave, no transfer, abi no be so?"

"Na so, my sister. And by the way, you look really, really good. The last time I saw you, your hair was short. Now you're wearing dreads, and it suits you."

"Thank you. It looks like you've been busy at the gym. You look good yourself," Oroma returned the compliment. "Although you had some hair the last time I saw you too. Now you are bald. Where did all your hair go?"

"Leave that hair matter," Obinna laughed. "Wetin man go do? My doctor says I must stay healthy, so I've been working out more, enjoying the outdoors, and generally taking things easy before winter starts again. We have to keep ourselves happy in this country, abi how you see am? That's why I even drove out here to treat myself to a nice lunch. I can't come and kill myself for obodoyibo."

"But would your wife be happy when she finds out you're eating out instead of bringing the money home?" Oroma asked seriously.

"You're acting as if you don't know Nkechi. That one would be happy that she doesn't have to cook." Obinna chuckled. "Speaking of cooking. My madam is feeling very patriotic this year, and she wants to host a few of our friends to a Nigerian dinner on Independence Day."

"October first?"

"Yes. I think you should come. Nkechi would love to see you again, I'm sure. The last time you visited, you and--"

He didn't want to mention his friend's name, and Oroma understood. She also didn't want him to think she hadn't recovered from the betrayal and heartbreak, so she accepted his invitation even though she knew some of the people she had succeeded in avoiding for months would be there.

"Oroma, I hope you know that Nkechi and I didn't take sides. We stayed neutral through it all, and even on the occasions we were forced to speak, we let Chike know that what he did was wrong."

"Can we not talk about him, please?"

"Maybe we should. Maybe it will help all of us get past what happened, and then we wouldn't feel awkward around each other anymore. Like I said earlier, Oroma, Nkechi and I never took sides."

"I never asked anyone to take sides. I was just surprised that people would avoid me when I needed them the most. Up to the people in Alabaster."

"Do you want to know the truth? Half the time, people, including Nkechi and I, didn't know what to say to you. And the other half, we didn't want to come across as meddlesome or interfering when you might prefer that your private affairs stayed private. This country has taught us to respect boundaries."

"And half the time, I thought you were his closest friend in Saskatoon, so you would support him anyway." Oroma said that because she met Obinna through Chike.

The two men had met in Saskatoon and quickly became friends when they discovered they were both from the same local government area in Anambra State and even had some mutual friends back in Nigeria. When she eventually made it to Canada, apart from church and grocery stores, the Achinike's home in Brighton was the only other place in Saskatoon they visited together, and they could visit at any time without calling ahead. He had other Nigerian friends who came to the house occasionally, but Oroma always received good advice from Obinna, especially in the early days of her arrival. And his wife, Nkechi, treated Oroma like a sister and told her where to get the prizes.

Recalling those visits brought back memories of the nine horrible months she stayed with Chike in Saskatoon. She went to church with him every Sunday. She fasted and prayed in secret that things would get better and she wouldn't be put to shame. She forgave him.

Bailey had left the night she arrived. Apparently, Chike had also lied to her about his relationship status, and she wasn't having it. Not minding how far gone her pregnancy was, she left for British Columbia, where her parents resided, to heal and to have her baby. Oroma later heard that she transferred from the U of S to a medical school in Vancouver after the birth of her son.

Chike made her believe he chose her over Bailey and was ready to make things work. He apologized, and she accepted him. At that point, she had no options. The alternative was to go back to Nigeria, and then everyone would know what a fool she was to have been waiting for a man who had stayed all by himself for so long in a cold country. She didn't want that. She couldn't stand people laughing at her. Of course, her mother and siblings knew everything, but she begged them not to tell anyone because Chike gave her a ring and promised to commence the formal process of asking for her hand in marriage as soon as she settled down in her new school.

But there were red flags everywhere. She just chose to ignore them. The phone calls he would end whenever she appeared, the annoying and narcissistic way he referred to himself in the third person when he spoke, and how he spent time in the bathroom shaving his chest hair were signs that all was still not well. Many times, he wouldn't eat after she had spent hours making him Nigerian dishes she knew he liked, and whenever they got into an argument, no matter how slight, he would end by saying that her sister's kayanmata wouldn't work on him. But she was new to Canada and dealing with settlement and culture shock issues; with everything going on at the university and adjusting to life in Canada, the last thing she wanted was to compound those problems with Chike's lies and suspicious behaviour.

And then, nine months after she arrived, he dropped the bombshell. He got a job in Vancouver, and he was moving. He told her it was an offer he couldn't resist and that it had nothing to do with Bailey and their child.

But Chike lied. Again.

"And the other half? Obinna asked, bringing Oroma back to the present.

"The other half, I was blank. I didn't know what to think."

"I am so sorry, Oroma. I truly am. I should have looked out for you no matter what. I should have called. Even texted."

"Maybe I wouldn't have answered you because I was in a dark place at the time. I gave up everything for him, yet I was the one made to feel ashamed. I was made to run and ride when he should have been the one hiding for calling off our engagement over the phone when he got to BC. He didn't even have the courage or courtesy of doing it in person."

"I told him he shouldn't have done that. Not after everything you guys had been through and how you supported his move to Canada and stood by him despite everything. You are strong, Oroma, very strong. Not many women, even men, would have survived what you endured."

"I was heartbroken and isolated, but what could I do? Suddenly, I found myself alone, and there were all kinds of problems to deal with–rent, food, transportation, and utilities. I didn't have a job; I was despondent and losing focus. But God helped me. I buried myself in my academics and concentrated on volunteering until I got a job at a café. By this time, the money I brought from Nigeria had almost finished and I was getting frantic. Honestly, God saved me."

"Honestly, I wish you had called."

"Your friend stabbed me in many places, not just in the back, and no one, none of you, called him out. Like I said before, I was the outsider. He was your friend long before I showed up. I guess it's what they call the bro code."

"Bro code? For what it's worth, Oroma, he asked me to be his best man, and I said no. Nkechi and I didn't even attend the wedding."

"Can we change the subject, please? I'm good now, I really am. I am happy."

"I can see that." Obinna hesitated. "There's something I feel I should tell you, though, before we change the subject. It's possible you already know about it, but since we're discussing Chike and his family, I feel at this point I shouldn't keep anything away from you."

"What is it this time?"

"He called me two nights ago. He and Bailey just welcomed their second child. Another boy."

After that, Oroma didn't know how she survived another half an hour of eating and conversing with Obinna without bursting into tears. The evil Chike now had a wife and two children, and she was still single. She didn't even have a cat. The same Chike that wouldn't make love without protection and would always ask her about contraceptives was now a baby-making factory while she was almost certain she'd leave this world childless.

Oroma couldn't believe the injustice. She could hardly believe the wickedness, but she sucked it all in. After all, she was already having a bad day.

40.

"So, how was school today, Ochanya?" Oche asked.

"Not bad, not bad. And how was yours?"

"It wasn't too bad either. You know it isn't easy being in SS3. The teachers don't want to give us any breathing space at all. They keep bombarding us with tests and assignments every day as if we are already in the university. I wish they'd take it easy with us, though. It's really frustrating."

"How is it frustrating? If you ask me, I would say you're lucky because all they do is try to bring out the best in you."

"How are they bringing out the best in me when all they do is infringe on my right to be young and reckless?"

"Oche, college is intense."

"College?"

"That's what universities here are called. Secondary schools are called high school. I thought I told you this the last time we spoke?"

"Yes, you did. And sorry, I forgot."

"You bet. Anyway, I was saying that the workload at that level of education must be pretty intense, and I really don't see any harm in your teachers making you put in some extra work into your study now as a form of training so that you can get used to the pressure when you're in the university. I would be happy if my teachers here did the same thing. We seem to have too much time on our hands, and it's nothing like schooling in Nigeria, where the focus is more on academics and less on extracurricular activities."

"I thought you'd be happy about that because of your love for painting and creating art."

"You are right. Being a member of my school's art society sort of made me popular really fast, and I've been able to make friends and form genuine connections. I would have probably had difficulty making friends if God didn't bless me with this talent. Our art teacher, Ms. Riley, says that if I continue doing well in my art class and other subjects, I might be eligible for a scholarship when it is time for me to get into college."

"But that's not going to happen until next year or maybe even the year after, right?"

"You're right. I still have two years before I'm done with high school. I told you students here are placed in grades based on their age. That's how it works here. Everyone in your class is the same age as you, and you are just older or younger depending on the month you were born. I'm in grade ten because I turned sixteen when we got here."

"It's like you lost two years then. If you had started in my school like your grandparents had wanted you to, you'd have been in SS3 right now, preparing to enter university; sorry, college."

"The good thing is that when I get into college, there won't be any strikes, lockdowns, or protests, and I can decide to take extra credits, so I graduate after three years instead of four."

"That means we might still finish university the same year."

"For sure. That's very possible."

"Speaking of possible and impossible things, I was just wondering about your accent and if you have any plans of changing it so people in your school won't have to struggle to understand you when you speak."

"If I change my accent so they understand me when I speak, will they be changing theirs so I understand them when they speak? Having an accent simply implies that I know a second language that they don't. Then, how can my accent change when we only just got here? I know with time, it will happen; I'm just not forcing it. Maybe in another one or two years, I'd have mastered the Canadian accent to a T, and maybe even I won't understand myself when I speak, but for now, I have to accept that I sound different and take pride in it."

"And your name, how have they managed to pronounce it?"

"Initially, I was going to make them call me Cha, Chacha, or even Chanie, but during introductions on my first day, this guy in front of me gave his last name as Abeysirigunawardena, and no one laughed or suggested to him that he shortened it to Abey or Siri or Dena. That in itself gave me the courage to remain Ochanya. Some people still don't get the pronunciation right, and I don't fight. The most I do is encourage them to say it slowly. But I'm not changing my name for anyone or anything like my Aunt Bree did."

"Ochanya, you've become fierce. How come I didn't see this side of you when you were here in Makurdi and we hung out together? You've changed. Canada has matured you."

"Losing my mother and siblings matured me. That was what changed me, not moving to Canada. I must admit that children have more rights here, so maybe I am more vocal and able to express my thoughts more freely than I did in Nigeria, but that's it. I'm the same old Ochanya who took walks with you to RecDC during our evening hangouts. And let's not forget that I am sixteen now."

"Sweet sixteen, duh! But tell me, has anyone ever treated you a certain way?"

"No, no one has. On the contrary, my classmates have been super nice and welcoming from the get-go. Since I started school, no one has made me feel like I'm different or that I don't belong. That doesn't mean some people aren't curious about Africa. They are. And whenever I sense a genuine interest in my culture and where I'm from, I'm more than happy to explain things to people and help dispel whatever notions of falsehood the press and television have forced down their throats. Sometimes, it is a challenge, but in the end, I believe it is the best way to develop lasting friendships and share each other's stories."

"But you aren't the only Black person in the school now, are you?"

"Oh, there're lots of us. In my class alone, we are three Nigerians, a South African, and one Kenyan. There're also other immigrants from Asia, Latin America, and pretty much everywhere in the world you can think about, and we all get along really well. You are more likely to see white girls hanging out together. Black and brown girls do the same thing. It's like an unspoken rule that like gravitates towards like, but there's no discrimination in my school. At least I haven't witnessed it."

"Are you saying racism doesn't exist there?"

"I've heard things, but I haven't witnessed anything personally. Maybe I just haven't lived here long enough. For now, I would say that the people I interact with treat me with the utmost respect based on who I am, my contributions in class, and my talent."

"People like your boyfriend?"

"Oche, I've told you Cheyenne isn't my boyfriend. He's just a guy in my class with whom I was paired for a project for the art society."

"The same project you're supposed to come up with a piece of art about Native American people?"

"Indigenous people, they are called Indigenous people and not Native Americans because they are the original owners of this land, and they have lived on it from time immemorial. They lived here long before the European colonizers came. The sad thing is that this country hasn't treated them nicely, to the extent that Canada had to set up a reconciliation panel to make things right after many years of oppression and inhuman treatment."

"This is kind of similar to what they did to us in Nigeria."

"Except that in the case of Nigeria, they came to trade and give us a new religion. They never intended to stay. I guess they were happy taking us away from our land and using us as slaves on their own land. Here, they stayed and forcefully made the land their own."

"Fascinating stuff. So, how will you and your boyfriend capture this through art?"

"Dude, calm down. Cheyenne isn't my boyfriend. Anyway, as I was saying before you rudely interrupted me, we are done with that first assignment, and now we are on to something even bigger. In the last couple of months, unmarked graves have been discovered in old residential school compounds across the country."

"Residential schools? What are residential schools?"

"They were Catholic-run schools used by the Canadian government years ago to convert Indigenous children to Christianity by forcing them to forget their religion, languages, culture, and even their parents. Ms. Riley told us that it is the most shameful part of Canadian history, and the government and some people don't like talking about it. So, back to my story. When the graves were dug up, they discovered the bodies of several indigenous children and adults buried in the ground. Now the entire nation is in mourning because they have now found hundreds of decomposed bodies as at the last count. Just think of how many lives were wasted and what these kids would have been if they were given a chance to live."

"Oh, wow! That's sad."

"It is sad. That is why to help create awareness about the travails of Indigenous people, this popular museum in the city is collaborating with the Saskatchewan provincial government to use arts as a tool for acknowledging the horrors of residential schools and helping survivors find healing. The museum and the province are organizing an art competition for high school students across Saskatchewan. Since Cheyenne and I were the winning pair in our last class assignment, Ms. Riley has asked us to jointly represent our school in this competition. The winning artwork gets to be showcased in the museum here in Saskatoon, while the creator or creators of the winning piece, as in our case, will receive partial funding to participate in any short-term arts-based training program of their choice anywhere within our province."

"Wow, Ochanya, that's really huge!"

"It is huge. Cheyenne and I have decided to collaborate on an acrylic painting we have titled "Bones.""

"Bones? Why bones?"

"Because it was the first thing that came to my mind when Ms. Riley told us the story of the residential schools. Throughout that day, Cheyenne and I discussed the unmarked graves and the secrets buried in them for so many years. We talked about how best to express the emotions evoked in us seeing all those bones buried beneath the earth, then it hit us. There's no black or brown or white in death. It's all bones; we all become bones. Death doesn't see colours, ethnicity, race, or religion. Death sees bones."

"You are so right, Ochanya. When we die, the things that separate us quickly decompose or fade away, and all that is left are our bones. Status, nationality, state of origin, and family name all disappear."

"And just by looking at it, no one can tell if a bone was Jamaican or Canadian, Indigenous or non-Indigenous. We become equal, and we are treated the same way. That's the message in our painting, and that's why we chose "Bones" as the title of our work."

"Is Cheyenne Indigenous?"

"Yes, he is. His full name is Cheyenne EagleFeather, and he is what they refer to here as First Nation. There are different kinds of Indigenous people in Canada, and those called First Nations are just one of them. The others are Inuit and Métis. Unlike the other two, though, Métis people are of mixed Indigenous and European ancestry."

"Well, wherever he's from, I think the two of you have come up with a brilliant idea. I'm rooting for you, and I sincerely hope you and your boyfriend win this thing."

"Cheyenne isn't my--"

"I hear you, Ochanya. I've heard you. Cheyenne isn't your boyfriend."

"Oche, don't tell me you are jealous."

"What if I am?"

"But I've told you several times not to be. There's nothing going on between Cheyenne and me."

"I know you said that, but you know what you can do if you don't want me to be jealous of him?"

"What?"

"Send me the pictures I've been begging you for."

"Oche, but you know--"

"Please, Ochanya, please. I can even send mine to you if you want. And you don't have to take off everything. Please, Ochanya, I'm begging you."

"And if I refuse?"

"Nothing, I will just be very unhappy, and I don't know why you want me to be unhappy. If you can't do it today, please, Ochanya, promise me you will give it some thought."

A week ago, her answer to his plea was a definite no, but now she wasn't so sure.

41.

OWOICHO DIDN'T EXACTLY QUIT HIS THIRD JOB. HE WAS FIRED. He was told to leave by the General Manager because he refused to clean up the human excreta that mysteriously appeared in the hallway of the Fifth Knight Hotel on Idylwyld. Obinna, the connection he made when he worked with Farmfresh Delite for a day, was the one who told him about the opening for the position because his cousin's wife was one of the breakfast ladies in the hotel. He applied, aced the interview, and was told he could start immediately. The job was as a night cleaning person.

After staying at home for nearly two weeks without the prospect of finding work of any kind, Owoicho was ready to accept anything. But he was particularly jubilant about this one because it was mostly sweeping, dusting, mopping, and taking out the garbage. If he had second thoughts about taking the job, all doubts went out the window when he discovered he only had to work at night, so hopefully, no one he knew would see him dress up in the dreary uniform given to him. Plus, the hotel was prepared to give him five nights a week even though it wasn't a permanent position. At the time, it felt like a well-deserved break, and he embraced it.

Owoicho was prepared to do anything to keep the job, but he wasn't prepared to handle adult human poop that had no business being in the area of the building it was found. For sure, the discovery of human waste in the hallway at one o'clock in the morning caused a commotion amongst the hotel staff on duty that night, but he wasn't perturbed. He just knew he wasn't going to clean it.

When the Front Desk Agent called the General Manager that night to inform him that the new cleaner had refused to do his job, the GM, an elderly man from India who always looked like he had heard bad news from home, asked to speak to him. Owoicho tried explaining to his boss that touching a grown person's shit when they weren't ill or hospitalized was a taboo where he was from, but the man would have none of it. In the end, when he realized that Owoicho wasn't going to budge, he asked him to leave and never come back. It was his second day on the job. Once more, Owoicho was out of work, but this time it felt different.

As if the gods knew he needed cheering up when he got into his car and started the engine, the radio station was playing that song he liked, Pour Some Sugar on Me. Owoicho bopped his head to the song as he sped off into the night. For the first time in Saskatoon, he didn't care about street cameras or being caught and pulled over by the cops for exceeding the speed limit. He just wanted to go home, take his clothes off, jump on the couch, cover himself up with a thick blanket, and fall asleep to the voice of Def Leppard.

He woke up in the morning to a text message from Obinna inviting him to a party at his house on the first of October. After losing his job, the last thing he wanted to do was party, but he saved the date and address on his phone anyway. Perhaps he would change his mind later. Obinna had been good to him.

42.

Owoicho didn't get the sleep he craved when he got home that night. Bimpe didn't tell him whether or not it was intentional, but she was still up when he pulled up into the garage and parked his Honda in the third spot reserved for him. He noticed the two cars in the garage, which meant that Damiete was home too, but the silhouette by the door leading into the main house was that of a woman. It was that of Bree

For a split second, his mind told him she must have made something special for dinner and seeing him come in that late, she wanted to catch him while he was still in the garage and hand him some of the leftovers so it didn't go to waste. But when she switched on the light, she was not carrying anything. Bimpe walked up to him, and that got him even more confused. This catching him in the garage before he escaped to his part of the property had never happened before.

"How was work? You're home early," she smiled at him. "I thought you don't get back until about six in the morning. Or did something happen?"

"Nothing happened," Owoicho answered under his breath, but just loud enough for her to hear him. "Everything is fine." He didn't think he was ready to talk about what happened at the hotel, so he lied.

"I know how tired you must be right now, but if you have a few minutes, there's something very important we must discuss. I don't think it can wait because I will be busy at work later today and probably for the next couple of days, so we might not see each other."

"Are you sure this can't wait until we are all up and about later in the day?" a still-confused Owoicho asked.

"Something else kept me up, but when I noticed you come in, I was glad I hadn't gone to bed yet. Owoicho, we need to talk. And no, it can't wait because it is about Ochanya."

Immediately he heard her say his daughter's name, sleep disappeared from his eyes, and Owoicho became automatically attentive.

"What happened to my daughter? Is she all right? Was she in an accident? Did she get into trouble at school?"

"She almost did. Ochanya almost got herself in trouble, but fortunately, God guided my steps, and I intervened before any damage was done."

"Please, what happened?" Now he was breathing really fast, and his chest was pounding too. "She didn't get suspended from school, did she?"

"No, it wasn't anything that happened in her school or even around the neighbourhood. It was something she did here in the house yesterday. She begged me not to tell you, but I don't know…I don't think I'll be doing right by you and her late mother, God rest her soul, if I kept it away from you."

"Please, Bree, tell me already." Owoicho was on the verge of losing it, but he kept his anxiety in check.

"Well, the thing is that yesterday when you were out for your evening run, something came up involving a very close friend and her husband. I had to go out to help with that situation, so I thought I might plead with Ochanya to help babysit Jason since I didn't know when I'd be back and Dami wasn't home."

"This suspense is killing me, Bree."

"Because I knew you weren't home, I didn't bother knocking before entering your place. I got into the basement, and what did I see? I saw Ochanya taking a topless picture of herself. The girl had nothing on but her panties."

"My God! My God! Jehovah! Where is she?"

"Owoicho, please calm down. I'm begging you to take it easy. I have spoken to her, and she will not do it again."

"Ha! No, oh, no. My daughter, my own child. Ha, Bree, I must handle this myself."

"What do you want to do? Flog her, shout at her? You know this is Canada and not Nigeria. You don't just shout at your children anyhow o. You will get into trouble. In fact, the worst thing you can do here is touch a child or dare get physical with even your own pikin. You may land yourself in a big problem."

"What kind of problem, Bree? Do you want me to fold my hands and watch Ochanya destroy the good life I am working so hard to build for her? She is going to get it hot from me tonight."

"No, Owoicho. You can't hit her or scream at her or something like that. Here, you talk to them. It is called negotiating. You have a conversation."

"Who conversation help?"

"You are in Rome, Owoicho; please behave like the Romans."

"Bree, have you forgotten how our parents brought us up? The old people will say, 'Spare the rod and spoil the child.' Can't you see how we turned out? Or do you think we didn't turn out fine?"

"We can talk about that another day. For now, we have to think of giving her all the love and encouragement she needs so she wouldn't be tempted to try something like that again."

"Lord, what did I do wrong? What was she thinking, taking a nude picture? Did someone make her do it? Is it a boy in her school?"

"No, it is a boy in Nigeria."

"Nigeria? My God!"

"Owoicho, your daughter is a very smart girl. That's why you have to handle this matter delicately so you don't push her over the edge. You should have a conversation with her, then we should think about how to guide her in the future. Your daughter is intelligent; I have told you this before. This girl you are seeing so, she has the potential of being another Greta Thunberg or even Malala Yousafzai. Have you heard her discussing politics with Damiete and analyzing things happening in Nigeria and here in Canada? You should be proud of her. She was about to make a potentially costly mistake, but God saved her in the nick of time."

"What if you hadn't walked in and stopped her? She would have sent her naked picture to a boy in Nigeria who thinks her father is making dollars in Canada. Before you know it, someone is blackmailing you, and the girl might take her own life because of the shame."

"God forbid bad thing."

"After talking to her, what next? See me that came to Canada to hustle. Will I now stay at home to monitor a teenage girl when I should be out there working?"

"That is the other thing I was going to discuss with you. I think Ochanya should move into the main house with Damiete and me so we can help keep a closer eye on her."

"Do you think that is a good idea? I wouldn't want her to inconvenience you and your husband."

"It won't be an inconvenience at all. I have thought about it. I even discussed it with Dami. If she moves upstairs, she will not just be living with us; she will be helping us babysit Jason whenever we are out and getting paid for it. She can also do other chores, and we will pay her well."

"I don't know."

"Owoicho, it's a win-win. We keep an eye on her, she gets to earn money, and before long, she is buying a car like all the children her age here are doing because now that she has turned sixteen, they will teach her how to drive in the school whether you like it or not. And the government is paying for all that."

"Let me think about it."

"Okay. Think about it. I just want to help because if Ene was around, and the tables were turned, she would do the same for me. She would take care of my son as if he was her own. You know her."

"Let me give it some thought. Please, give me a day or two, and I will let you know what I decide."

43.

When his phone rang in the middle of the night, Owoicho knew it was a call from someone back home who was obviously in denial of the science of the equator or oblivious to the time difference between Nigeria and Canada. His initial reaction as he struggled to find his bearing was to ignore the call, but its persistence bothered him. For all he knew, someone close to him may have died or was dealing with an emergency, so he grudgingly stretched his hands toward the nightstand and hit the green sign on his cell phone. It was quiet on the other end, but he was determined not to speak first.

"Hello." When the furtive caller eventually spoke, his voice was gruff and unfamiliar.

"Hello," Owoicho's voice was barely a whisper.

"Mr. Owoicho Adakole?"

"Yes, who is this?"

"My name is Ochulayi, Conrad Ochulayi, and I am the ADC to the governor of Benue State. I am calling from the Government House, Makurdi."

Owoicho promptly jumped out of bed when he heard the name and location of the caller. "His Excellency is right here beside me, and he would like to speak with you about an urgent matter, sir."

Owoicho left the bedroom to sit on the couch in the living room. He was fully awake now.

"Adakole."

"Good morning-- Sorry, good evening-- Good afternoon, Your Excellency." Owoicho had never had problems figuring out the time disparity whenever he called home or when someone in Nigeria called him, no matter how tired or drowsy he was, but this time was different. This time, he fumbled badly

because the call from the governor of his home state in Nigeria was completely unexpected.
"Adakole, can you hear me?" Governor Lazarus Ochepo screamed in his ears.
"I can hear you loud and clear, sir."
"I know it has been some months now, but I don't need anyone to tell me that the death of your wife is still fresh in your mind. So, Adakole, once again, on behalf of my humble self, my family and the good people of Benue State and the entire Nigeria, please accept my deepest condolences on the demise of your amiable wife, Ene."
"Thank you, Your Excellency."
"Good, good. So how are you doing? How is your son?"
"Daughter, Your Excellency. She is doing well by the grace of God."
"Thank God the girl is fine. So, is it true you are no longer in Nigeria?"
"That is correct, sir. My daughter and I now live in Canada."
"I don't even know whether or not I should congratulate you for leaving this our beautiful and sweet country," the governor continued with his loud voice. "Make I tell you something when you nor know. Nigeria is sweet; I hope you know that. It is very sweet. It is just that so many people don't know how to manipulate-- sorry, I meant to say navigate the system. But that is by the way. So, my young man, let me start by apologizing that we did not get to speak when you came to Makurdi for your wife's commemoration service. You were at the burial, right?"
"Yes, Your Excellency, I was there. You sent a plane to fly us to Makurdi, and I was standing beside you when you gave your eulogy."
"Oh, that is true. Now I remember vividly. In fact, the speech I delivered that day was one of the best speeches I have given since I became governor. I even heard it was on CNN."
Owoicho heard a female voice in the background say it wasn't CNN but Arise News, but the governor just went on with his propaganda. "We really have to let the whole world hear us and

see what we are going through in this country. These bandits and terrorists have taken over our country."

At this point, the governor stopped talking to him. Owoicho heard him yell to his ADC to organize a meeting with the Commissioner for Information and his Chief Press Secretary. He wanted them to arrange another world press conference, and this time, in addition to CNN, he wanted Al Jazeera and Sky News present when he lambasted the presidency and those in his kitchen cabinet.

"Yes, where were we again?"

"You were talking about bandits and terrorists, sir."

"Yes, those wicked criminals and murderers that don't want our children to go to school. Even our men and women in the village cannot farm anymore."

"I wish something could be done about them, Your Excellency. Many of us won't be out here struggling if we felt safe in our own country."

"Don't worry, Owoicho. We have a plan. By the time we regain power at the centre in the next general elections, all this rubbish will stop. Anyway, that will not happen until another two years, so let us leave that one. For now, let us focus on the present. So, tell me again, what are you currently doing there in Canada?"

"Do you mean like work?"

"Yes. Are you in school, or are you working?"

"I-- I-- work in a museum, Your Excellency" Owoicho couldn't think of anything to say, so he lied. He didn't want the governor or anyone who might be listening in on the call to think that he wasn't doing well. Makurdi wasn't such a big place, and the last thing he wanted was for his in-laws to get wind of his fall from grace to grass and how he was struggling to make ends meet in Saskatoon.

"That is good. It gladdens my heart to hear that you are doing well and making us proud over there. Please, keep flying our green-white-green flag high."

"Thank you, sir. I will keep doing my best."

"Yes. There's another extremely important matter I want to discuss with you. In fact, it is the main reason I called you. You know we were just talking about letting the world know what our people are passing through in the hands of bad people and what we are doing as a government to make their lives better?"

Owoicho couldn't recall them discussing the governor's plan for his people, but, all the same, he responded in the affirmative.

"Well, we made a major decision during the Executive Council meeting today. Adakole, the decision we reached concerns you."

"Your Excellency, please can I ask what this decision is about?"

"We want to revamp our state-owned media outfits. The plan is to bring the radio, TV, newspaper, and online platforms under one umbrella and under one management. This new structure will be called Benue Media Agency. As we speak, I have fired the heads of the various establishments as currently constituted. The fools were just embezzling money and running everything down. Now, because of your vast experience as a newsman and your all-round high profile in the media industry in Nigeria, I have made you the General Manager of BMA."

"Me?"

"Yes, you. I want the Commissioner for Information to make the announcement this evening or maybe first thing tomorrow morning. That is why I decided to call you because I want you to hear the good news from me first. Adakole, don't forget, this thing I am doing, I am not doing it for you alone o. I am doing it for your late wife as well."

"Thank you, Your Excellency," Owoicho thanked the governor. He had many more things he wanted to say to Lazarus Ochepo in appreciation for such a lucky break, but no words came.

"How soon can you be in Makurdi to get your appointment letter and do the swearing-in?" the governor asked.

"Your Excellency, I-- I have to settle my daughter in school. She is in the finals of this art competition in the city, and I'd like to be here for her when the winner is announced. Then there's my job--"

"How much time do you need?"

Owoicho didn't want to appear desperate for the job, so he told the governor three months.

"One month. One month or I give the job to someone else. My ADC will arrange your ticket. Call him when you are ready."

Owoicho didn't go back to sleep. He couldn't risk falling asleep and waking up much later in the morning to find out that his conversation with Governor Lazarus Ochepo was all a dream.

44.

THE GET-TOGETHER AT THE ACHINIKES TO CELEBRATE Nigeria's independence was scheduled to begin at four p.m., but guests didn't start arriving until five. When Obinna chided them for being late, some quickly reminded him that it was a Nigerian party, so they should be pardoned for following African time. Three families came with packs of soft drinks and hors d'oeuvres he was familiar with from back home, and he thanked them for the surprise. Those who didn't come with food or snacks brought at least a bottle of red or white wine for their hosts. There were peppered snails, bole and roasted fish, garden eggs and groundnut paste, puff-puff, chin-chin, meat pie, asun, suya, nkwobi and isi-ewu. The aroma from the trays reminded Obinna of a typical Lagos owambe party, and he didn't have to taste anything on them to know they'd be extra "water-running-down-the-eyes-and-nose" spicy and delicious. There were also pots and coolers filled with grilled and fried chicken, egusi soup, fried fish, moin-moin, salad, dodo, eba, semovita, goat-meat pepper soup, pounded yam, oha soup, and jollof rice. The Achinikes pulled out all the stops to commemorate the day in 1960 when their beloved country gained its sovereignty from British colonial rule.

Seeing all the food laid out on the island, Obinna questioned why they spent so much money entertaining people who were more than capable of preparing whatever they wanted to eat in their own homes. But his wife, Nkechi, deftly reminded him that the party was his idea in the first place. She also reminded him of the many times he told her that variety was the spice of life and that men were wired to sample different flavours; otherwise, their tastebuds got tired quickly. Obinna confirmed saying that to her, although it was said in a different context and about a different subject matter. Not wanting to prolong the argument any further, he extolled her culinary skills and quietly left the kitchen to rest for a little bit.

Obinna was tired from all the cleaning, arranging, and rearranging of furniture he did in the family room and in the rest of the house. He also had to stay up late, assisting Nkechi with chopping vegetables and preparing the ingredients while she cooked. Even their three young children were conscripted and paid thirty dollars each to join in the preparation. They were made to slice and dice, set out cups and plates, take out the garbage and wash pots, pans, and utensils so their mother didn't have too much to do after cooking.

Even more enthralling than the food at a Nigerian event was the music, so Obinna spent some time organizing a playlist that was sure to keep his guests on their feet throughout the evening. A lot of people didn't know this about him, but he once deejayed at a nightclub in Enugu, so he had the music angle covered. Knowing their invitees weren't all in the same age bracket, his selection included the likes of Fela Kuti, Chris Okotie, and Felix Liberty from the 80s and 90s, as well as songs by newer artists like Davido, Buju, Ladipoe, Burna Boy, and CKay. The old-school stuff was mostly to evoke nostalgia, while the contemporary music was to sustain the party vibe.

Obinna and Nkechi didn't say anything about a dress code, but as guests arrived, it seemed there was a memo he and his family didn't get. Everyone who walked through the door, kids and adults alike, had on at least one item of clothing that was green or white or a combination of both colours. Noticing how well the green-white-green of his country's flag blended with the neutral colours in his dining and living room pleased him no end, and Obinna couldn't remember another time he felt prouder being Nigerian.

As expected, within minutes, the conversations in the room became quite loud and boisterous, and it had nothing to do with alcohol. People were shouting and speaking over each other as if the more animated they got, the better their argument became. Despite the noise and heated debates, it was a good day to reminisce about things they missed the most about their home country.

While the women were busy in the kitchen, Obinna and his friends talked about the good and not-so-good things that local and international media constantly reported about Nigeria. They traded stories and shared personal recollections of their country when they left, as well as their expectations from its leaders and citizens now that they are part of the diaspora community.

In one corner of the room, some of Obinna's friends were projecting into the future and wondering what would happen to the Nigerian economy when the oil wells dried up and the federation account became depleted. In another corner, a different set of friends were in deep conversation about the boxer Anthony Joshua and the music artist, Wizkid because someone had suggested that they were both doing more as ambassadors of Nigeria than all the politicians in leadership positions put together. Still, all the talks about Nigeria and Nigerians didn't stop the men from discussing football and getting into the Cristiano Ronaldo versus Lionel Messi Greatest-Of-All-Time debate.

At intervals, Obinna would leave the men and their heated arguments to check on the women. Apart from wanting to know how they were doing, his mission to the kitchen was also to ask for something to eat or drink for someone just arriving or someone needing a second portion. All in all, Obinna was glad their friends were happy and everything was going on satisfactorily.

When he went into the kitchen to get pepper soup, he noticed Oroma standing alone by the refrigerator. Sensing she might be feeling a certain kind of way, being the only unmarried woman in the room, he walked up to her to ask how she was faring. He wasn't happy seeing her all by herself and told her as much.

"I'm doing okay, Obinna. Don't worry about me," Oroma said to him when he expressed his concerns. "My friend, I'm a big girl. It's the kids running all over the place and messing up your beautiful house you should worry about."

"You're a big girl, eh? Okay, that's good to know. Anyway, thank you so much for coming, Oroma. I really appreciate that you are here."

"Well, thanks for inviting me. I can't think of another place I'd rather be on October 1st than here with my fellow Nigerians, eating, drinking, and dancing."

"Except that you, my friend, aren't doing any of the things you just mentioned."

Obinna stopped talking like he had an epiphany. His eyes glistened with a mischievousness that wasn't there when he first walked up to her.

"Look, Oroma, there's someone here I'd like you to meet."

Oroma froze when he said that. She wondered who it could be. She hadn't been into the Nigerian scene since Chike left her, and she was happy with her antisocial life.

"I-- I-- I hope I'm not in trouble?"

"Just follow me, Oroma. Don't be scared. You're not in trouble. And I'm sure you know that I'm not a troublemaker."

Oroma dropped her half-empty glass on the dining table and followed him to the living room, where the men were still engrossed in their shouting match about politics in Nigeria. They stopped by a group of five men discussing potential presidential candidates in the next general elections only a few months away.

The man who had the floor spoke with so much passion and conviction he could have been an analyst on a live radio or television show. Obinna waited patiently for the man to make his point before pulling him away from his cohort.

"Owoicho, meet Oroma. Oroma, this is my very good friend, Owoicho."

45.

Winter came with a ferocity Owoicho wasn't prepared for. His dread of the cold weather kept him indoors for more than a week. Whenever he was up in the main building and looked out the window, he marvelled at how people, including newcomers like himself, could be going out, walking their dogs, or waiting at the bus station at -30°/40°C temperature. In spite of his recent conversation with Governor Ochepo and the prospect of returning to Nigeria, he knew he should be out there networking, making cold calls, and doing anything within his power to find a job. But he couldn't. Winter sucked for him. It made him sad and depressed, and if he had never questioned his decision to relocate to Canada, the windchill made him do it every time he checked the weather forecast on his phone.

The combined effect of the blistering cold and the brownish-white soggy mess on the streets and sidewalks looked nothing like the portrayal of snow in all of the Christmas movies he had watched on Hallmark Channel and Netflix while in Nigeria, and it left him completely immobilized. His mood worsened when he lost his parking spot in the garage because the Browns ordered some household items from Amazon. When the things arrived, they did not have the time to unpack them and put them where they should be, so the couple converted Owoicho's parking space into temporary storage and asked him to park his car in front of the house. Now he had to spend precious minutes scraping snow from his car every time he went to drop off or pick up Ochanya from school.

It also didn't help that in the nearly three months since he had been in Saskatoon, none of the organizations he applied to, either through referrals by acquaintances or in direct response to online job postings, as much as acknowledged his email to them.

This, more than anything else, left him devastated and completely demoralized. It was hard for him to stay motivated and continue contemplating a future in Canada when nothing seemed to be working for him. Bimpe and Damiete noticed his mood and tried to bring him out of the brink of depression he was sliding into. Their best endeavours, however, did very little to improve his spirits.

When Obinna called to invite him to dinner at the Red Lobster, Owoicho accepted the invitation. He wasn't quite ready to end his hiatus, but he also knew that one more day of self-isolation might push him over the edge.

They met at the restaurant's parking lot and walked into the beautifully lit property together.

"Bro, how you dey na?" Obinna asked, hanging his jacket on the backrest of the chair. Owoicho did the same thing.

"Chairman, I dey oh."

"How you see the cold na? Have you experienced winter before?"

"Never. I never see this kind cold weather before, I swear. People described it to me when we came in from Nigeria in the summer, but my friend, this is ten times worse than any description or the assumption I made about it. In fact, it is indescribable. People in Nigeria have to experience it to believe it. The other day, when the windchill was like -51, I was forced to ask myself if it wasn't an evil spirit from my village that had embodied the cold to frustrate me out of this country. Honestly, this cold is human. It knows what it is doing."

"Did you get winter tires?" Obinna said, laughing at Owoicho's description of the cold.

"No, I'm still using my all-season tires. And I don't have any plans of changing them either. Maybe I will change them next winter, but for now, they're all I've got, and if I perish with them, I perish."

"Well, I only started using winter tires this season. The first year, I simply couldn't afford them, and last season, I wasn't on the road very much so I figured my car would be fine without them."

"We go dey all right, bro," Owoicho chuckled. "You guys that are married shouldn't even be complaining about this weather at all. In Canada, two is definitely better than one. Aside from the obvious benefits of two incomes and all of the tax benefits married people enjoy, you and your wife at least have each other to cherish and to hold on cold nights. What will single men like us do?"

"You nor be single man na, you be widower."

"All join body."

"Wetin me I sabi be say pillow and blanket dey everywhere for this town and e no too cost to buy," Obinna laughed again. "And don't for a second think that all married couples are having it easy in this winter o. You remember my friend, Jide? He's the other Nigerian guy who worked with us in the cold room when you were there. Well, I just heard that he and his wife are having serious problems in their marriage. When the pastor in their church called them for counselling, do you know what his wife told the pastor?"

"What did she tell him?"

"She told him Jide had only slept with her twice this year. And she ma, dey young and fine scatter."

"But why?"

"When dem want to find time do the thing? The man dey work three jobs, and she ma come dey do shift work follow. As she dey enter house, the guy dey go work. When him dey come back, she dey go her own. In fact, if Jide true-true sleep with her two times since January, the guy try, I tell you."

"Men, this country no easy."

"I tell you."

Obinna waited for the server to take their orders before continuing. "You know, sometimes it feels like we are in a conveyor belt. We come in as skilled workers but get tossed into the world of unskilled labourers. We stay there and do the job for several years because we don't have Canadian education or work experience. After we improve ourselves through hard work and government student loans, which we have to pay back with interest, and move on to skilled or semi-skilled positions, another set of skilled workers come in to take our place as unskilled workers, and the circle continues."

"You're absolutely right, my brother."

"Enough of gloomy talk," Obinna was prepared to move on to another topic. "When we spoke this morning, you sounded like you had something you wanted to talk to me about?"

"Actually, I do," Owoicho suddenly had a serious look on his face. "I have just been offered a very good job. But the job is in Nigeria. I've been so confused since I got the offer because I don't know if I should take it or let it go. It's all so confusing to me right now."

"Can I ask what the job is and if it pays well?"

"For sure. I'll be heading the Benue Media Agency. Good salary, big cars, big house, local and international travels, all the works. The problem is that I don't know whether or not I should take it. You know how rough I've had it since I got here, so it's really tempting to pack up and go back to the life of luxury that awaits me."

"What's stopping you?"

"Ochanya and my Canadian citizenship."

"There you go. That's your answer right there for you."

"But concerning Ochanya, she has already moved in with my late wife's friend, Bree, and her family. The girl was exhibiting some kind of teenage girl wahala, so Bree asked her to move into one of the spare rooms in the main house so they could monitor her more closely. About the Canadian citizenship thing, I don't know. It really doesn't mean that much to me, and in any case, I have a five-year window to accomplish it, as you know."

"If you decide to go back sha, I pray you'll be safe. Things aren't any better since we left. Every time you connect to Nigerian television stations, it's always one bad news or the other. Honestly, that country na cruise. E don reach make e get hin own YouTube channel abi na Netflix series sef. We all monitor developments back in Nigeria."

"You know what I've realized since coming here, though? A city is like a person. It has its good sides and bad sides. The first time my car was broken into, it didn't happen in Abuja; it happened here. My first encounter with homeless people in large numbers didn't happen in Makurdi; it happened here. I don't remember the last time I saw drug addicts on the streets of Lagos; I saw them two weeks ago in Saskatoon. And in all the years I did school runs in Nigeria, I never saw my kids' schoolmates smoking or vaping anywhere near their school premises, but I see Ochanya's schoolmates doing it all the time. In the final analysis, no city or country is perfect."

"If you were to leave Saskatoon, what would you miss the most?" Obinna wanted to know.

"Let me see, I like the look of the townhouses. I'll miss that. I absolutely enjoyed the one-time Ochanya and I took a walk along River Landing all the way to Broadway and back. I remember we took selfies on Traffic Bridge and she almost got knocked down by a skater when she stopped to tie the lace of her sneakers at Spadina. That evening we had an amazing father-and-daughter moment, eating ice cream and discussing her future as we watched the gorgeous sunset above Traffic Bridge. I'll really miss that. I'll also miss all the drive-throughs–carwash, fast food places–even ATMs have them. I'll miss Tim Horton's coffee and their sugary Timbits. I'll miss all the cranberry juices in my fridge, for sure. I'll miss the voices of Rob and Shauna as they banter on the radio and share funny stories about their lives, work, and families. Let me see, what else will I miss? Yes! I'll definitely miss those child benefit payments that come in monthly for Ochanya."

"See as you like money, after you go dey call me Igbo man."

Both men laughed. They waited for the server to put their food on the table, then laughed again.

"Come o, Owoicho, but seriously when you said you wanted us to talk, I thought it was about Oroma."

"Wetin you wan hear? You this Obinna, you too like gist. E be like say you don forget say you be married man, abi."

"I no forget anything, Owoicho. If anyone is forgetting anything, it is you who has forgotten that I introduced both of you."

"I be widower. I don't have time for women."

"Ah, so that thing my father told me about widowers that year is true."

"What did he tell you?"

"Him tell me say when man wife die, him prick no go stand again," Obinna replied with a straight face.

This time, they laughed so hard and for so long that they didn't notice the other patrons in the restaurant staring at them in a funny way.

46.

"Alegwu, I'm in trouble."

"What is it? Are they deporting you?"

"Why does your mind always go to bad things?"

"Fifteen, you said you are in trouble. Where did you think my mind would go? What did you expect me to think?"

"Okay, maybe it's my fault. I shouldn't have put it that way. I'm not being deported. I got a job offer only a fool would refuse."

"I've learnt my lessons, so I won't ask how that has put you in trouble. Instead of doing that, I'll just say congratulations."

"I don't know if you should be saying that just yet. I haven't accepted the job. That's why I'm calling you."

"Why haven't you accepted the job? Haven't you been job hunting for like two, three, four months now?"

"Three months, but it feels like three years, I tell you. Anyway, the job isn't in Canada. It's in Nigeria."

"Guy, what are you telling me na? Have you stopped following the news here, abi you and your colleagues in your former TV station don't talk anymore?"

"They removed me from the office WhatsApp group shortly after I got here, but that's beside the point. I know everything that's been going on in Nigeria. I read about the killings and kidnappings, the ban on Twitter, and how the government is now toying with the idea of restricting free speech. Alegwu, I know everything happening there because I make it a duty to be up-to-date with news about Nigeria. Besides, I'm a journalist; that's what I'm trained to do. But then, let's be truthful, people still live there. You and your family are still in Lagos, and I don't see you guys relocating to another country any time soon."

"I know what you're doing. You've already made up your mind to come back, and you only made this call so I can tell you that you've made the right decision. Owoicho, as much as I'd love to be that friend, I can't do that just yet because I don't have all the facts."

"Ochepo has given me a juicy appointment as General Manager of the media agency in our state. That is the full story. Now my guy, is that an offer any sane person should turn down?"

"The answer is in the word 'sane.' No sane person can refuse such an offer, and Owoicho Adakole, you are not insane."

"What about Ochanya?"

"Don't they have boarding schools down there? Then again, didn't you tell me that she now lives with your friends in another part of your building? Look, Fifteen, you've always been the ajebutter type. Maybe that Canada and all the hustling and bustling you tell me about no good for you. Ochanya can remain there with Breeze --"

"Bree."

"Yes, Bree. Ochanya can stay with her while you come back."

"I feel like a failure, Alegwu. People come here from all over the world and they stay. They adjust. They don't just pack up and run away. Why can't I do the same thing? Why can't I be like them?"

"Because you're not them. Owoicho, No one would laugh at you because you came back to head a government agency you are qualified to run. How many people can turn down an offer like that? You are not a failure, Owoicho. Don't even think about it that way."

"But I am. Alegwu, I got fired from yet another job today."

"Oh no, not again. What happened this time?"

"When Ochepo and I spoke, he gave me one month to tidy up any business that needs tidying up here. I didn't immediately say yes or no to his offer, and he didn't press me for an answer either. His conclusion was that I get in touch with his ADC whenever I am ready to resume work in Makurdi. I'm still uncertain what my decision would be, so I kept looking for a job, and I found one as a Front Counter Attendant in a liquor store downtown.

"This afternoon, my fourth day on the job, by the way, I was taking trash bags to the dumpster because the cleaning guy called in sick, when this old pickup truck pulled up beside me. The driver was an elderly man, and his wife was beside him. They were probably in their late seventies or early eighties. I felt sorry for them. I felt bad that old people like them could not get someone to drive them around. The next thing I knew, the man was out of his truck, asking me to help him carry some wooden pallets beside the building into his truck.

"I didn't think twice about giving him and his wife a helping hand. It wasn't until they drove off that it hit me that I should have gone in to ask the manager if he knew about any old man picking up pallets he claimed he had paid for. Anyway, I denied knowing anything about the missing pallets when the manager asked me about them hours later. As a rookie employee, I didn't know that part of the building was under surveillance. The manager went back to watch the CCTV footage and saw me clearly assisting the pallet thieves to transfer the stolen items from the ground into the back of their vehicle. The old couple conned me."

"Oh my God!"

"I was fired for lying. He didn't say it outrightly, but the manager kind of insinuated that firing me was him being lenient because the store would have had me arrested for conniving with a third party to steal from them."

"Wow! You see why this offer from Governor Ochepo is a no-brainer. My friend, take the offer. My only regret be say Mercy don chop my money."

"What are you talking about? Which money your wife chop?"

"Mercy and I made a bet. I told her that in less than three years, you will marry a white woman. My madam said it is impossible. She said you will return to Nigeria to find a wife when you are ready to remarry. Now that you are coming back to work in Makurdi, it looks like she has won the bet. Abi what can I say? My one hundred thousand naira don go."

"Alegwu, right now, women and marriage are the farthest things on my mind. I need to pay my bills."

"But body no be wood na--"

"I know where this is going. Alegwu. Goodnight."

Owoicho ended the call. He was tempted to tell Alegwu about Oroma, but he knew his friend would keep him on the phone for another hour if he started that conversation.

Next on his list of people to call were Ene's parents. He suspected they'd be happy to hear that he was considering coming back home.

47.

"How was your day?" Owoicho asked, handing Oroma the box of Ferrero Rocher chocolate and bottle of wine he brought her.

"Not too bad. I've been cooking and doing some cleaning. That's it," Oroma smiled. "Wow, thanks for the gift. I really wasn't expecting anything." Her face lit up as she examined the content of the colourful goody bag containing the items he bought for her. "Thank you so much. Please make yourself comfortable."

"Thanks, Oroma."

"And how have you been?"

"Awesome. Apart from the cold, I don't think I have anything else to complain about," Owoicho said, taking off his black puffer jacket and handing it over to her because she already had her hands outstretched to collect it from him.

"How's your sister, Rama--?" he asked as he made his way to the loveseat she pointed him to.

"Ratamma."

"Yes, Ratamma. How is she doing? You told me the last time that she was still in the hospital. Has she been discharged now?"

"No, she hasn't been discharged yet," Oroma responded. It was a Sunday afternoon and he was visiting with her at her apartment on the Westside. It was his first time in her house. At first, Oroma was nervous about having him over, but when she remembered that only a handful of people had bothered checking up on her since Chike ended their relationship, she was happy to start a friendship with someone far removed from all the drama in her past. Someone who felt comfortable enough to want to spend time with her both in private and in public.

When she received Owoicho's text message asking if he could see her again, her immediate reaction was to say no so they could slow things down. She didn't want him to have ideas. Even more importantly, she didn't want to have ideas. The probability of another betrayal and abandonment filled her heart with fear and she wanted walls. She wanted to take her time and not rush into anything she would regret. But then, Owoicho gave her a glimpse of how terrible his week had been and his stories broke her. He wasn't needy or insistent. She gave in on her own. Despite her initial hesitancy, Oroma was happy that it wasn't going to be another boring evening for her.

"Why hasn't she been discharged yet? Were there some new complications?"

"To the best of my knowledge, no. The doctors decided to keep her with them for a little longer to closely monitor her and the baby. My mother can't stop praising God that she didn't have a miscarriage. Jesus, I still can't believe the child in her womb survived the beating Ratamma received that day. It would have been so painful if she had lost a baby she didn't even know she was carrying. Honestly, those women who attacked her should be jailed. All of them."

"Thank God the enemy is not rejoicing over your family."

"As always, God has put them to shame."

"Yes, He has. By the way, your house is really beautiful. I love the simple yet tasteful furnishing. How many rooms did you say it is again?"

"Two rooms," Oroma replied. She thought she knew why Owoicho abruptly changed the subject and it made her feel bad. Evidently, her mention of death and a child in a sentence was triggering for him.

"Wow! Looking at the block from the outside, you will never know that each apartment inside has two rooms. I really love the layout."

"I like it too. Maybe I can give you a tour of the house after we eat," Oroma offered. "It was a lucky find, I tell you. But you know what I would really, really like? Someday, when I'm qualified for a mortgage, I want to have my own house in a nicer neighbourhood. A three-bedroom duplex with lots of space, a garage, a garden for flowers and vegetables, and a picket fence, including two Bolognese dogs."

"Two dogs?"

"Yes. One black and the other white. I would name the black one White and the white one Black."

"This is the craziest thing I've heard all week." Owoicho couldn't stop himself from laughing. "This one you are already planning to buy dogs, not just one, but two; you have turned full Canadian be that."

"I dey tell you. One hundred percent Canadian. In fact, when I'm ready to write my will, I will put it there in black and white: 'Bury my body in Saskatoon'."

Owoicho cracked up some more.

"Be there laughing. Meanwhile, please excuse me for a bit. I think I hear the kettle whistling. Let me go and make the eba." Oroma left for the kitchen to attend to her cooking.

It was the second time they would see each other after the party. This time, she opted to cook instead of meeting him at a restaurant. She knew he hadn't found a job yet, and so the last thing she wanted was for him to pay for an expensive dinner he probably wouldn't enjoy as much as he would her hot eba and ogbono soup. She was also concerned about the strain that eating out on two dates in a row might have on his budget and personal finances when it was certain he had rent and other important bills to worry about. Their first outing was interesting. Oroma thought it went really well.

She suggested they meet at Eron Coffee House on 8th and McKercher. Owoicho was happy with her choice since he was still exploring the city and discovering new places to dine out. It was a Friday evening, but being their first time hanging out as friends, Oroma thought they'd be done with dinner in an hour and she could go back home to her nightly cup of hot chocolate and the Ukamaka Olisakwe's novel she was reading. However, things didn't go quite the way she had expected. What was intended as a quick, one-hour conversation about each other turned into a three-hour exposé of what it means to be an immigrant in Canada and how to manage or maximize expectations. They conversed like old friends.

As a result of his background in media and communications, Oroma was not surprised that Owoicho was lively and had fascinating opinions about almost everything. From global events to Funke Akindele's antics in Jenifa's Diary, Owoicho had rib-cracking yet insightful anecdotes to share. Oroma liked that he didn't pretend not to have heard her story and everything she had been through in Saskatoon. He let her know right away that Obinna had told him everything. She was quite touched when he said he wasn't about the past but the future.

Oroma liked that he didn't have airs. She was surprised at how down-to-earth he was, even though many people, including herself, had watched him on television for years. She also liked that he was dealing with the drastic change in circumstances with so much positivity and that he could laugh at himself.

When he told her about his late wife and children, she noticed the tears forming in his eyes, but he held himself together. Considering her own recent experience with pain, she thought she had seen it all, but his was different. His was death. Not just the death of one person, but four family members in one day. She knew about the incident that took them, but she didn't learn of it when it happened because she had gone off social media after her breakup with Chike. Then she also got tired of following up on her sister's shenanigans, so she deactivated all her accounts. But Obinna told her all about it. He even forwarded a video of the incident to her. Watching it made her heart bleed for Owoicho and his remaining daughter, whom he couldn't stop talking about.

When Obinna called her two days after the Independence Day party to inquire about her job and everything else, Obinna thought he was being circumspect, but Oroma saw right through his feeble attempt at hiding his true intention. It was obvious he felt guilty about something, and now playing matchmaker between her and his new friend was his way of assuaging his conscience and letting her know that he had her back no matter what.

※

Owoicho had a small list of people he wanted to consult before accepting the BMA job in Makurdi, and his brother was on it. He was going to call Onjefu in the morning about the offer and inform him of the possibility that he'd be returning to Nigeria soon, but his younger sibling beat him to it. Or so he thought.

Since their last conversation, when Onjefu more or less told him off for keeping his relocation to Canada a secret from him, they hadn't spoken to each other again. Owoicho had sent him a message on his mother's posthumous birthday a few weeks back. Not surprising, Onjefu's response to his effort at reaching out was one blue heart, two wine glasses, and three dazed smiley face emojis.

Why don't people talk to each other anymore? What's with the emojis? Is it now such a bad thing to express real emotions and hide them behind shallow symbols and images instead?

"Biggest bro, how you dey?" Owoicho was surprised at how chirpy his brother's voice sounded on the other end of the phone.

Hmmm. He seems happy. Tipsy? A little too much to drink, maybe.

"I'm good, Onjefu. You?"

"Not too shabby, not too shabby. You already know the motto Fela gave us in this country when he was alive – 'suffering and smiling.' Anyway, we are grateful to God for health and life. And those of us who can afford three regular meals daily, plus a little luxury on top when we feel like it, cannot complain when people who are not as privileged are angry. God will not be happy with us."

Is He happy with you now that you are defrauding people of their hard-earned money and robbing them of the fruit of their labour?

"Onjefu, you called. What should I slaughter in celebration of this surprise phone call I am receiving from you this night – chicken, cow, or goat?" Owoicho waited to hear his brother's reaction to his goading. Onjefu didn't do random calls. Knowing him, Owoicho suspected there was more.

For sure, the crafty guy must have heard something about my moving back to Nigeria and only wants to harass me for not telling him.

"Bro, why are you talking like this? So, I can't call my Canadian brother again or what? Remember, me and you haven't really spoken since you and Ochanya left some months back. To be honest, most times, I worry about you because I don't know how you are settling into your new life there. I don't know anything. Like, are you even working now? Are you in school? How are you able to pay your bills? You know what I mean, right? I mean, I know people, friends, and very tight ones, for that matter, who have travelled abroad, and they tell me that the first few years of trying to settle down can be tough. That's why I sometimes think about you and wonder if all is well. How are you finding Saskatoon, Owoicho?"

His brother's questions caught him off guard. For a minute, Owoicho didn't know how to tackle them.

The truth. Tell him the truth. Tell him how much you've tried to fit in and it hasn't worked out for you. Tell him how courageous you've been, braving the harsh winter to go out hunting for jobs. Tell him you're still unemployed.

"Thanks for asking, Onjefu. I am fine. Ochanya and I are doing just great."

"But I haven't seen you post any photos on Facebook since you left. I thought pictures of you busy at work would have blessed our timelines by now. You know, we'd like to see pictures of you doing stuff in your place of work. You did that a lot at the TV station when you were still here."

He knows something. This isn't random. For sure, Onjefu knows something. He is going somewhere with all this talk about pictures.

"When I start posting pictures, you will be the one begging me to stop, trust me. And you, how have you been?" Owoicho knew he had to change the subject because he wasn't comfortable with the prying his brother was doing.

"I've been well."

"Anything new happening you'd want me to know about?" Owoicho continued. Any new arrest? Is Interpol or the FBI after you now?

"Owoicho, I won't even lie to you. I need your help."

Again, the way Onjefu went straight to the point so Owoicho knew the call wasn't about a friendly chit-chat took him by surprise.

What does he want from me now?

"You're not in trouble with the law again, I hope?"

I said it, another police case. It has to be another police case.

"Someone has asked me to marry her."

"Wow! That's great news. Congrats."

Okay. I wasn't expecting that. I wasn't expecting that at all.

"Don't congratulate me just yet, Owoicho. She's sixty-two years old, and her family owns one of the biggest ranches in Nantucket. Owoicho, she's very, very rich. Very, very, very rich. She's been sending me dollars from America and buying me things since we started dating seven months ago. This one is a big catch, bro."

I knew it!

"What about her husband and children?"

"Her husband died many years ago, and she's never remarried. She has a grown-up daughter she doesn't speak to anymore. I don't know what the problem is between the two of them–crack cocaine or something– I don't know. She doesn't like talking about her. She calls her a junkie. But this my woman, she's really into animals. She has cats and dogs. And lots of horses."

Rich, lonely white woman.

"How did you meet her?"

Let me guess. Online.

"We met online. A dating site. She's madly in love with me and wants to visit Nigeria soon. She wants to meet my family and spend time with me before the wedding next month."

"How come you don't sound as excited as I expected? Hasn't this always been your dream?"

"It has, Owoicho. But there's a problem. She thinks you are me-- I am you. We are each other-- I don't even know which one is the correct English, but I'm sure you understand what I am trying to say."

"Ha! What are you trying to say? Onjefu, how could you involve me in your catfishing business? How?"

"It's not the way you are seeing it. This one is genuine and you won't get into any trouble. This woman, she really likes me-- she likes us-- she likes-- What am I saying? Look, bro, she has money. Plenty of it. Honestly, I didn't know things would get serious like this and that she would want to visit Nigeria and even want marriage. That was why I used your name and photo."

"Jesus of Nazareth. So, I can just be in my house eating or sleeping and minding my business, and law enforcement people will come and arrest me for something I know nothing about? Onjefu, why didn't you use your picture? Why did you have to involve me in this nonsense lie?"

"My legs, Owoicho. I'm in a wheelchair, remember. If I had used my real picture, do you think things would have progressed the way they did with her? Do you think she would have fallen in love with me? Who wants to leave America and come all the way to Nigeria because of a cripple? Ko le work. That was why I was asking about you and how life is treating you in Canada."

"Do you have someone spying on me here?"

"Owoicho, if you find things difficult there, why don't you just come back and marry this woman. I swear, Owoicho, if you marry her for me, you will never have to work again in your life. I swear."

"Because you are my brother, I will quietly hang up this phone and not tell anyone we had this conversation. And please, for your own good, take down my picture from anywhere you've been catfishing with it. I don't want anything to do with your 419 schemes. I have enough I'm dealing with here, don't come and add to my problems. And please, for the love of God, I will say this one last time – leave me out of your yahoo-yahoo schemes."

"Owoicho, I know you are angry, and I don't blame you. I also know that you will end this call now without hearing how wealthy this woman is and how marrying her would change your life forever. You can end the call now if you want, but before you do, please promise me you'll think about what I told you."

Hours after Owoicho ended the call with his brother, he kept asking himself one question over and over again. It was the only thing he could think about.

If I go back to Nigeria to head a government agency, I'll be awarding and supervising contracts. I'll make money. Plenty of it. But it will be money meant to develop the state and not to enrich me. That is stealing. And if, by the wildest stretch of my imagination, Onjefu convinces me to marry this old woman and I move to America with her, I'll be living off an old woman who genuinely has feelings for me. I'll also make money. Plenty of it. The only thing is that I'd be pretending to be the version of me my brother created.

That is stealing.

God! What do I do?

Owoicho fell asleep wondering how many more women were out there sending money to Onjefu because they thought he was him.

48.

THE WINNER OF THE RECONCILIATION, INCLUSION AND diversity arts competition was to be notified by a personal email from the Premier of Saskatchewan. The other two finalists will receive a similar email; only theirs won't say they won. It will simply thank them for participating in the competition while encouraging them to continue creating beautiful art for the community and using their bourgeoning creativity for the advancement of the province, Canada, and the rest of humanity.

Seeing as the usually composed Ochanya was growing increasingly tense and uncharacteristically restless twenty-four hours to the big announcement, her father frenetically contemplated ways to distract her. He wanted something that would take her mind away from the competition and assure her of his love and support, irrespective of the outcome and the content of the letter from the Premier.

Thankfully, it was Sunday, and since he knew she hadn't eaten anything, Owoicho thought taking her out to lunch might be fun. Convincing her to drop the book she was reading, Buchi Emecheta's, The Bride Price, wasn't easy, but he succeeded in the end. Owoicho didn't want her to know they were going to Fuddruckers, her favourite place in the city for burgers and fries, so he lied that he wanted to get gas for his car and would like her to come along. He said something about wanting to explain traffic lights and road signs to her before the formal start of her school driving lessons, which caught her attention.

When they were done at the gas station, an excited Owoicho revealed his real intention to her, and Ochanya gave him a high-five.

"Thanks, dad. I appreciate your wanting to do something nice for me today. And thank you for teaching me about traffic lights and speed limits. I promise never to violate traffic rules so I don't get a ticket you'd have to pay for."

"Oh, you really think I will pay? My dear, you are on your own. And why would I even do that when you're earning so much money babysitting Jason?"

"But, dad, I already told you what I'm saving the money for. I want to buy my own car when I turn seventeen."

They drove in silence for a minute or two, and then Owoicho spoke again.

"Did you and Bree discuss anything about me yesterday?" Owoicho asked.

"No, we didn't discuss you, dad. Did you do something we should be discussing?"

"I'm moving back to Nigeria." He didn't know how else to break the news of his imminent return home to her, so he just blurted it out. He prayed she wouldn't ask him to stop the car so she could run away.

"We're going back to Nigeria?" Her father was right, but for the seatbelt, she would have jumped out of the car for sure. "But why, dad? We only just got here, and I like Saskatoon."

"I'm going back to Nigeria. Alone. You won't be coming with me. I know this looks like me leaving you in Makurdi all over again, but trust me, this time, it's nothing like that. Then, it was your grandparents' idea. I went along with it, not caring how you felt, and I take ownership of that mistake. I was confused about a lot of things. We all were. Your mum, Inalegwu, Okopi, and Ejuma had just been killed, and it was going to be the two of us alone in the house. I didn't think I was prepared to be a single father. I was terrified that I would suck at it. That was why I caved in and left you in Makurdi."

"And now, who are you leaving me with?"

"I'm not leaving you," Owoicho stressed. "I spoke to Bree, and she will help me take care of you. Thank God you already live in their part of the house. It is true what they say that God moves in mysterious ways. When she first made that suggestion to me, I wasn't happy that you were leaving the basement, but now I know why. God was preparing all of us for a time like this. I'm happy you both get along really well. Ochanya, you know I won't be doing this if it wasn't absolutely necessary, right? I promise I'll call you every day. I'll visit as often as I can."

"But you haven't even told me why you're going back."

"I got a very good job, something that would change our lives for good, and I don't want to throw away the opportunity. You know it has been rough for me since we got here. It's been tough with bills, and it's been tough for me personally because I'm not used to staying at home doing nothing. Ochanya, it'd be nice to know how you feel about what I just said because it is important to me that you are fine with the idea of me going back. My mind won't be at peace if you don't feel safe or happy here by yourself."

"I like that you explained things to me this time, dad. And I will be fine."

"Thank you, Ochanya. Everyone tells me how smart you are, and I'm really proud of you."

"Thank you, dad."

"And when I'm gone, I don't want you worrying about stories you might hear or read concerning happenings in Nigeria. I will be fine by the grace of God. You just keep working hard, stay out of trouble, and always remember your roots and whose daughter you are."

"I will never forget that, dad."

"You and I don't really have these types of conversations, but seeing your entry to the competition, and the synopsis you and Cheyenne wrote up, I know you are passionate about equality, discrimination, and things like that. And I'm happy you care about the world and the people who live in it. I encourage you to keep it up. Never blur the truth with a lie, and if you are ever confused about life or anything at all, please call me so we can talk about it."

"I will, dad."

"Whether or not Bones gets selected tomorrow, I like how you explained it to me–people treat people badly because of ethnicity and racism and when the dynamism of power favours them. That really left an impression on me, Ochanya. You really don't know what people are like until they have power and are in control or think they are in control. There's so much going on in the world right now. Sadly, communication is now in the hands of the uninformed, so be careful what you consume on social media, and always speak the truth."

"I will, dad. Miss Riley tells us the same thing all the time. She says we should be hopeful for humanity."

"I like that. Let's all stay hopeful for humanity."

"Dad, when I get married, I'd like to be on Family Feud. It would be me, you, my husband and maybe Bree and Uncle Damiete. We'd make a formidable team."

"Where is this Family Feud thing coming from?" Owoicho was surprised at the abrupt change in subject, which made him laugh hard. He didn't wait for her to respond because he already knew what her answer would be. Ochanya was hungry, and it was her way of telling him they had stayed too long in the parking lot of Fuddruckers.

"Dad, I love you. I really, really do, but can we go in now? Those onion rings won't come out here to meet us."

"I love you too, Ochanya."

🍁

Ochanya knew her father had a sweet tooth, so she made him an upside-down pineapple cake for his birthday. But she didn't do it all by herself. She enlisted the help of Bimpe, who also helped with the fried rice and chicken, as well as the vegetable soup and goat meat stew. Damiete bought the drinks while the pizzas and donairs came from this Afghanistan place that had just opened on Circle Drive and Faithful Avenue. They had all that food and drinks because it wasn't just a birthday celebration for Owoicho. It was a celebration of many things all at once.

It was a celebration of how much closer Ochanya and her father had become in the last weeks. When Bimpe told him about Oche and his antics, Ochanya had thought he would be mad at her and withdraw all her privileges, including access to her phone, but he didn't. Rather than ground her and have her locked up in her room as punishment, her father asked her down to the basement for a heart-to-heart conversation about boys and how much of a distraction some of them can be to even the most focused and responsible girls.

Her father apologized for not trying hard enough to know and understand her, for focusing on his own grief, and for neglecting to acknowledge hers and how she was dealing with the traumatic loss of her mother and siblings. She forgave him; she didn't have a choice. He was the only family she had.

On her part, Ochanya promised to be more open and intentional in sharing things about her life he should know about and be involved in. And when it came to boys, she promised not to hide anything from him again. Based on that promise, she confessed to having feelings for Cheyenne EagleFeather. He liked her, and she liked him too, but they decided not to date because it might ruin their friendship and future arts collaboration. Her father agreed that she had made a good decision and encouraged her to keep her grades up so she could get a good scholarship to a good college.

The party was a celebration of her father's new job. It was his farewell party, and the few friends he made in the short period he lived in Saskatoon were invited to rejoice with him. Ochanya knew she would miss him, but she also knew that his leaving for Makurdi was for the best. The speech she prepared for later that evening was replete with glowing tributes to him. She was going to use the speech to let him know that she appreciated the sacrifice he made by bringing her to Canada and that she was proud of him.

The party was also a celebration of Ochanya and Cheyenne. They didn't win the prize, but coming second in a province-wide competition was no mean feat, and everyone acknowledged their effort. Miss Riley was particularly proud of Ochanya. In her message to the school, she reminded everyone that Ochanya didn't let the fact that she was new to the country stop her from showcasing her strength and talent.

Ochanya was also proud of herself and how she was settling in. Now that her father was leaving her in Saskatoon, she was more determined not to fall his hand, as Oche told her when he constantly pestered her for her nudes.

49.

Two days after Governor Ochepo's ADC sent him his ticket, Owoicho went shopping for gifts and souvenirs for people back home in Nigeria. Alegwu wanted a leather bag for his laptop; his father-in-law asked for books on leadership, while his mother-in-law sent him the names of people living in her house and some members of her church she wanted him to shop for. Her request ranged from socks and ties to shirts and dresses. It was hard deciding what to get for the people on his personal list because he just wasn't good at shopping. Besides, he had a small budget to work with. Alegwu had lent him another one million naira, but after he converted it to Canadian dollars and gave half of it to Bree for Ochanya's upkeep, what was left could barely pay for the things he wanted for himself and the others.

To stretch the money in his account, Owoicho went from shop to shop in search of stores that had items on sale or that were offering significant discounts on multiple purchases. It was the only way he could get the quality and quantity he wanted at prices he could afford. His quest for bargain prices kept him in the mall longer than he anticipated. Hurrying to his car because he had promised Ochanya that they'd go see a movie together later in the evening, he typed in his home address and searched for the fastest route to Silverwood.

The first indicator of trouble he noticed was seeing so many bags on the deck. Who would put out bags in the backyard with two inches of snow from the previous night that hadn't even been shovelled off the landing? Owoicho wondered as he struggled to make it up the stairs without slipping and falling flat on melting ice. Even more worrisome than the bags on the deck was seeing Ochanya by the door. It was as if she was waiting to welcome him back home. She never did that. Considering how cold it was outside, she wasn't even supposed to be out there.

"Ochanya, what are you doing here?" Owoicho followed her into the living room. He didn't even take his boots and jacket off.

"Dad, something happened while you were away."

"What happened?" Owoicho's heart was racing. He couldn't imagine what it was, but he prayed everyone was all right.

"The cops just left the house. Bree and Uncle Damiete were in a fight. They calmed down when the policeman was here, but the moment he left, they started quarrelling again."

His first instinct after listening to his daughter was to mind his business. Sometimes couples quarrel and get into arguments. It was a fact of life. Going up to see them might appear meddlesome, and Owoicho wasn't a nosey person. He loved minding his business and staying in his lane. But seeing the bags out in the snow, he knew he couldn't pretend like he didn't know what was going on. And if, like Ochanya said, they were still arguing even after the police left, then perhaps intervening might be a better strategy than pretending he didn't know what was happening.

"You stay here. Let me quickly go see what is happening. I'll be back soon, then we can go see our movie," Owoicho said to Ochanya, who was already looking through some of the bags her father brought in.

Owoicho knocked on the door to the main building, and Bimpe let him in.

"Talk to your friend o. You better talk to your friend," Bimpe said without acknowledging Owoicho's greeting.

"Bimpe, if anyone needs to be spoken to, it is you. You are the one who has been acting crazy since yesterday," Damiete screamed from the couch, where he sat shaking and sweating.

"Be running your mouth, Damiete. You will leave my house today."

"Guys, guys, what's going on? Please calm down, Damiete. Bree, what's happening? I have never seen the two of you like this since we've been here."

"Is it not your friend? If he doesn't have shame, tell him to tell you what he did. Shameless man."

"Damiete, what is the problem?" Owoicho was puzzled by how different they seemed all of a sudden. The couple he was looking at was nothing like the image of marital perfection they had given off since he and Ochanya had been their house guests and tenants.

"I didn't do this woman anything o. I was sleeping in the room jeje and the next thing I heard a man's voice calling my name. I went down to the living room, and I saw a policeman. He told me my wife had called 911 to complain about a domestic violence situation. Meanwhile, I was sleeping in the room. In fact, if your daughter, Ochanya, hadn't come to my rescue, I'm sure the cop wouldn't have believed I wasn't lying. This wicked woman had the boldness to call the cops on me when I didn't do anything wrong to her. Can you imagine that?"

"I don't get," Owoicho looked at husband and wife, perplexed. "Why would she call the police when you two weren't fighting?"

"It all started yesterday. In fact, it started last year when I went to Port Harcourt for my mother's burial. I met this lady, and one thing led to another. When I returned to Saskatoon, this girl told me she was pregnant and that it was mine. The last time I spoke to her, she said she was going to get an abortion because she wasn't ready to be a single mother, and that was it."

"Liar. Damiete, you're a big liar."

"And you are a pathological liar," Damiete retorted. "Why will you even say I am lying? Were you there when I was discussing the pregnancy with her?"

"Owoicho, this man is a liar, and he will leave my house today."

"Your house indeed," Damiete scoffed. "Let me see you kick me out."

"Damiete, leave my house. Useless man. I will finish you in this Canada. I will jail you and make sure you languish there.

How dare you go and get another woman pregnant when you are staying under my roof?"

"Let's even say that you are right and I got someone pregnant, is that why you will call the cops on me? In this era of the Black Lives Matter movement, when it feels like Black men are endangered species in this part of the world, you go and call the cops on me over trumped-up allegations. Tell me the section of the law in Canada or Nigeria where it is a crime to impregnate another woman? Tell me."

"Be talking o, instead of you to go and pack your things quietly, you are running your mouth. I will show you and that dirty thing you call your baby mama. Owoicho, you won't believe this foolish man has been sending my hard-earned money to that dirty bitch. He has been sending my per-hour labour and all the sleepless nights working night shifts and doing extra hours to some illiterate ashawo in Nigeria. Ha, I have suffered."

"My hard-earned money, my hard-earned money,'" Damiete mimicked his wife. "You keep saying that as if I don't have a job and earn my own money."

"You have a job, but is this house yours? Did you pay for any single thing in this house with this so-called money you earn? You must leave my house today. And when you leave, Damiete, I swear on my mother's grave, you will never see Jason ever again. Bet me."

"Is that a threat? Bimpe, are you threatening me?"

"It is not a threat. This one I called police is just Season One of the series. Watch out for Season Two. You will leave my house today whether you like it or not because I am done with your womanizing."

"Your house, your house. If you don't stop saying that, I will tell him. I will tell Owoicho everything."

"I dare you. Damiete, I dare you to tell him, and we will see who he will believe."

"Tell me what?" Owoicho was surprised that he might be linked to their fight in ways he didn't care to discover.

"Are you daring me?"

"Yes, I dare you. Damiete, I dare you."

"Okay. Owoicho, this house we live in, we bought it with your money."

"My money? Damiete, what are you talking about?"

"This house, the car, the furniture, and so many other things I can point to, came from the money your wife gave Bimpe to keep for her."

"I don't get," Owoicho was really and truly confused now, and he sat down to take it all in. "Please, Damiete, Bimpe, can you guys tell me what is going on?"

"Owoicho, it's not what you think. It isn't even the way Damiete is saying it."

"Then what is it, Bimpe. What is it?" Owoicho was confounded. He didn't know what to think anymore. All he wanted was for them to tell him what was going on and spare him the mystery.

"Look, my friend, don't let this evil woman deceive you. I will tell you everything. I don't know how she did it, but this wicked woman convinced your wife to transfer money from Nigeria to her bank account here."

"Damiete, Damiete, I won't allow you to twist this story so you can come out smelling like roses. You know how it all started, and you were very happy spending the money and even getting some runs girl in Nigeria pregnant when you know how much I wanted to have another child after Jason."

At this point, Bimpe collapsed to the floor, crying. "Damiete, I told you I wanted another child, but you told me to wait until Jason got a bit older because of his special needs and learning difficulties. Then you went and got another woman pregnant. You went and got another person pregnant, knowing very well that I'm menopausal and can no longer conceive. Damiete, you are wicked. Damiete, God will punish you."

"The money; can we talk about the money?" Owoicho interjected. He had heard enough of their family drama. His only interest at this point was in finding out about Ene's money. "I need to know about this money."

"Like I was saying, it was all Bimpe's idea. She and her incestuous uncle in America."

"Please don't bring my uncle into your stupid lies. It wasn't Uncle Okin's idea that we spend the money; it was yours. And by the way, he and I do not have an incestuous relationship."

"Didn't you tell me that Remi, your unhappy elder sister, told your mother that he was always inappropriate with you and her when you guys were growing up, and that was why he ran away to America?"

"Liar. Damiete, you are a liar."

"You are the one who's lying."

"Please! God! The money, tell me what happened to the money?"

"I didn't know Ene was going to die. No one saw that coming, so how can anybody accuse me of stealing her money? When I advised her to start changing her money from naira to dollars and sending it to me to keep for her, I did it from a good place. I didn't want her to suffer the same loss we suffered when we arrived and needed to buy dollars only to discover how badly the naira had depreciated. And honestly, I thought she would discuss the idea with you, but she preferred not to. She said she wanted it to be a surprise, and I couldn't question her wish. When you called that day to tell me what had happened to her and the children, I wanted to tell you about the money. I really wanted to."

"I told her to tell you immediately because you might be looking for money for burial and things like that. But does Bimpe listen to me? No. Instead, she called her incestuous uncle, who dictates everything that happens in our home, by the way. They speak Yoruba for a couple of hours, and the next thing I know, she's transferring money to him to invest in cryptocurrency for both of them."

"That's not true. You were the one who brought up the cryptocurrency investment and not my uncle, agbaya! Why are you lying like this?"

"Owoicho, I wish there was a way I could prove this to you, but that was exactly what happened. It was all Bimpe and her uncle's idea."

"I bet the mortgage and the cars were also me and my uncle's idea, right?"

"It was your idea, Bimpe; it was all your freaking idea. I kept telling you to call Owoicho and tell him about the money, but you went on spending from it. When you weren't buying things for yourself, you were sending money to America."

"Liar!"

"You accuse me of getting a girl pregnant. When you gave that old fool Okin and your adulterous sister Remi money to buy land and start building a house for you in Abeokuta, did you tell me?"

"Liar!"

"Abi I should also tell Owoicho how you deliberately left him and Ochanya at the airport because you weren't happy that they were coming to Saskatoon, and you feared that somehow they would learn the truth and realize how two-faced you are? Well, guess what, Madam 'I-am-now-a-Canadian-and-this-is-my-house'? He knows the truth now. He knows you are a fake and manipulative money-grabbing liar."

Owoicho looked from husband to wife and back to husband again. If they were confessing to what really happened, irrespective of who was telling the truth, then he could not risk spending another night in their house with his daughter. He didn't even want to be in their presence anymore.

Some questions kept ringing in his ears, though. Knowing that the down payment for their house came from money that was rightfully his, why did they trick him into paying rent for the same property? Why did Bimpe insist that he should give her three hundred dollars monthly for Ochanya's upkeep when they could have just welcomed her into their home like a daughter? Owoicho was mad at the deception and dishonesty, but he wasn't ready to let them know just how mad he was. He would save that for later when he had processed everything.

"Why did you do it? How could you sleep at night and look my daughter and me in the eye, knowing that you stole from a dead woman? Not just any woman, Bimpe; you stole from your friend."

"Owoicho, it isn't the way you are making it sound."

"Please, Bimpe and Damiete, right now. I'm not interested in your stories. I just want to know – how much is this money we are talking about?"

"Thirty-two million naira," Damiete blurted out.

"Liar. It was only ten million naira," Bimpe screamed.

"Are you willing to print out your bank statement for Owoicho to see?"

"Are you now a judge? For your information, Damiete, Canadian law protects me from disclosing details of my financial dealings to anyone unless I am ordered by a court to do so. So, ask another question."

"There's only one question for you to answer, Bimpe. Will you let Owoicho see how much his wife paid into your account?"

"Useless man. Liar. If you continue with these lies, I will call the cops on you again. You think this is Nigeria? We are in Canada, and I will deal with you. I will make sure you sleep on the streets this night."

Listening to Bimpe and Damiete go back and forth about the money they hid from him, as well as their messy matrimonial situation, convinced Owoicho again that he'd be making the biggest mistake of his life if he left Ochanya in their care.

The couple were still screaming and shouting at each other when he left their living room. Back in the basement, Owoicho didn't reply to his daughter's question about the situation in the other part of the house. Muttering a barely audible response, he went straight to his room, checked the top dresser drawer for his stack of business cards, and scattered them on the bed.

Thankfully, he hadn't gotten around to discarding the ones that weren't useful to him. When he found what he was looking for, he carried his laptop to the dining table, turned it on and typed in the email address before moving on to the body of the mail he was writing to Isabella Ramos. The bombshell revelation from the Browns that evening had changed everything. And now, it was imperative that he set up an appointment to meet with her immediately.

But even before the meeting with Isabella was the very pressing problem of where he and his daughter would spend the night. In his confusion, only one name came to his mind.

Owoicho brought out his phone and called Oroma.

50.

"My apologies. I had to take that call. It was my daughter, Anna. She said one of the boys just threw up and she didn't know what to do."

"I'm so sorry to hear that."

"Oh, no worries, it's not your fault," Isabella said, putting her phone down so she could focus on Owoicho again. "He'll be fine; he likes to act up sometimes. You know how kids can get when they need attention. Apparently, he swallowed something that shouldn't even have been in his mouth in the first place."

"Yeah, kids can be like that. I hope it isn't that serious, though, and he wouldn't need to see a doctor?" Owoicho asked.

"Anna was worried, but I was able to calm her down. I believe she can take care of him until I get home. From what she described to me, I don't think it's something that requires him to see a doctor."

"That's good. I'm happy it's not an emergency, and your boy will be fine."

"For sure, he'll be all right."

"Thank God. So, how many boys do you have?"

"I have two – Kane and Hunter."

"I had two boys myself, Inalegwu and Okopi. They were killed by bandits a few months before we relocated here."

"I remember your daughter telling me that the last time at the airport. I'm so, so sorry, Oworchu. Please accept my condolences." Owoicho had heard worse pronunciation of his name since being in Canada, so he didn't bother correcting her.

"Thank you so much. It's been tough without them, but I believe they're in a better place. So, how old are your boys?"

"They are seven and ten, and mischievous as hell," Isabella answered with a smile.

Owoicho was meeting her for the first time since that afternoon she gave him and his daughter a ride from the airport. After reading his email, she had asked him to come in for an in-person meeting.

"I remember when my kids were that age, they were all over the place too. My wife and I had to be on our toes so they didn't get into trouble and damage everything in the house. They say boys will be boys, right?"

"You're absolutely right. Boys will be boys."

"So, what grade are your boys? They are in elementary school, right?"

"Elementary school? No, they're not in elementary school."

"They are not?" A surprised Owoicho asked Isabella. "Are they being home-schooled?"

"As much as I'd like my dogs to be educated, I'm yet to see a school for dogs in Saskatoon. And no, they aren't being home-schooled either," an obviously amused Isabella replied.

"Wait. You mean Kane and Hunter are not human beings but dogs?" An embarrassed Owoicho wanted to bury his head in shame. "I'm so ashamed of myself right now. When you said boys, I automatically assumed you were referring to your male biological offspring."

"There's nothing to be ashamed of, Oworchu. Trust me, you wouldn't be the first person jumping to that conclusion," Isabella said, still smiling so Owoicho didn't feel bad about his blunder.

"My apologies. Honestly, I feel terrible."

"Oh, it's nothing, really. Now, can we please go back to what we were discussing before my daughter's call came in?"

"Yes, please."

"So, I was saying that my uncle, Derek Alonso, you may not have heard of him because you are new to Canada, but he's quite famous from his days as a reporter and much later as a news anchor for one of the biggest television stations in the country. Derek is now in charge of programming for another big but newer network in Toronto."

"That's great."

"Yes, it is. We are all really happy for him. Anyway, Derek is visiting the city for work, and just yesterday, he invited me over to have lunch with him. You don't know how happy I am that you are contacting me now, Oworchu, because, at lunch, he told me that his station is looking to employ reporters with your kind of experience and background to fill up spots in their newsroom. I looked at your resume just before you came in, and I think you'd be a great hire for what they are looking for. With your permission, I will forward your resume to Derek."

Owoicho couldn't believe his luck. "Please, go ahead. You don't need my permission to do that. Should I send you a cover letter as well?"

"Don't worry about that for now. I'm sure there'd be a portal on their website when they announce the opening. You will be told what to do at that time. For now, I just want him to look at your resume and tell me if you'd be eligible to apply and if perhaps you have what they're looking for."

"Thank you so much, Isabella."

"No need to thank me. I see you've had a rough time since you got here, and if I can help in any way, I'll gladly do it. Yesterday, I met with two newcomers. One of them literally got his fingers burnt on his first day at work in a local juice-making and canning plant. The second one lost the use of his left eye working in a restaurant. It was an accident with a simple wine opener. I'm telling you this so you know that I understand how challenging things can be for newcomers and pretty much anyone looking for work in this country. But I know that there's a silver lining too. There have been bad cases, but it isn't all gloom and doom. I have seen, time and time again, because of the work we do here, that for every challenging start, there are many more successful endings."

"I should have come here earlier. I shouldn't have waited this long."

"Don't feel bad about that. Thing happen for a reason."

"Thank you so much. I really appreciate this."

"Thank you."

"I should be on my way. Let me not keep you from attending to other people."

"You bet. I'll definitely let you know how things go with Derek."

"Thank you again. And my regards to your husband."

Isabella's reaction when he said those words was like someone hit unexpectedly by a bat. She was immobilized for a few seconds, and when she could move again, her eyes went from Owoicho and the binder in front of her to the framed photograph of her husband on the filing cabinet behind her brown chair.

"My husband died two months ago. An accident in his workplace."

"My condolences." It was the second time he would make an inapposite remark in less than an hour, and he apologized profusely for it. His experience with widowerhood had taught him that the pain of losing a loving spouse never really goes away. He had a million things to share with her about his own experience, but since he was only just learning that she had become a widow, and he really didn't know her that well, he decided to bridle his tongue. Perhaps, there will be other opportunities, and then they can talk about grief and loneliness and maybe even learn to feel something for someone else again.

Owoicho left Isabella's office and drove to meet with a lady he had contacted on Kijiji. Her basement was up for rent. If he liked it and she liked him, perhaps he and Ochanya would move in with her immediately. He didn't want anything to do with Bimpe and her husband ever again, and he couldn't squat with Oroma forever either.

As a result of the blizzard from two nights before, there was slight traffic leaving University Bridge and heading towards College Drive, but that didn't bother Owoicho one bit. After the good meeting with Isabella, he refused to focus on obstacles. His gaze was on possibilities.

51.

Oyale Lucky Ondujum woke up feeling lucky. His meeting with Governor Lazarus Ochepo the day before went really well. His request for one hundred million naira to pay for the soundproofing of the newsroom in the newly constructed eleven-story building of the Benue Media Agency complex was approved without questions. He didn't have to defend the project or even the budget. The governor was in such a good mood that he even sent for the state's Accountant-General to ensure that the company that got the contract immediately received the money. He told Oyale that the president was visiting Makurdi at the end of the month and that he wanted to include the complex as one of the projects to be commissioned during his two-day working visit to the state.

The governor's enthusiasm for the project and his magnanimity in leaving his request untouched meant that he could pay for the roofing of the eight buildings in the mini-estate he was building in Agbadu. Like all the other contractors involved in the construction, from foundation laying to furnishing, this company also agreed to the thirty percent markup he instructed them to build into their proposal before submitting their bid to the State Tender Board.

Oyale Lucky Ondujum could hardly believe that in less than two years of being appointed to serve in Ochepo's government, he had bought two new cars for himself, married a second wife, bought a second house in GRA, sent his eldest son, Kingdom to Coventry University and his last son Oche to the University of Saskatchewan. For the first time in his life, Oyale had good money in his bank accounts. And soon, thanks to his wiliness, he too will own properties in Abuja and Lagos.

Even though he didn't know him in person, Oyale was thankful to Owoicho Adakole for declining the position of

General Manager of the flourishing Benue Media Agency. If Owoicho had accepted the position and returned home, none of the good things he and his family were enjoying would have been thinkable. God had indeed been faithful to him, and one day, he hoped to visit his pastor with a fat thanksgiving envelope.

🍁

Coincidentally, at that same moment Oyale was thanking God for his good fortune, within the walls of a classy recording studio located in downtown Ottawa, an excited Owoicho was preparing for the taping of his syndicated weekly talk show programme, This Week in Diversity. He was seconds away from interviewing his biggest guest yet since the show launched.

"Five, four, three, two--"

Through his in-ear monitor, he heard his producer's voice countdown to the big moment.

"Ladies and gentlemen," Owoicho paused for effect and applause from his live studio audience. When he spoke again, he couldn't contain his excitement. "Let's welcome our guest tonight, the second female Prime Minister of Canada, Madam Farheen Chaudry!"

Meanwhile, back in Saskatoon, a heavily pregnant Oroma and her stepdaughter, Ochanya, waited for him to call and tell them how it went. They were proud of him and how far he had come, and they couldn't wait to tell him so.

Author's Note

THE PHOTOGRAPHS USED FOR THIS BOOK'S COVER ARE FROM MY FRIEND BOB HOLTSMAN. I met Bob soon after I arrived in Canada. He had come to cover an event I was volunteering at, got talking and became friends. Some weeks later, we met for coffee at the Tim Hortons in University Heights, and I recall Bob asking me to follow him to his car afterwards. He brought out a winter jacket and said something to the effect that winter was coming and that he didn't know how prepared I was for the freezing temperatures, the city would experience in the coming months. He offered me the jacket.

I was surprised by his kindness. Being new to Canada, that gesture meant a lot to me. Without a steady job or source of income at the time, I was grateful for the coat, the conversations and other acts of generosity that followed the gift. The jacket protected me from the cold that first winter when I couldn't find work. Bob's wise counsel and friendship helped me get through challenging moments in the coming years. I am happy and feel honored that Bob permitted me to have his photographs of Saskatoon on the cover of Leave My Bones in Saskatoon. Thank you, Bob.

Front cover photo shows the Broadway Bridge spanning the South Saskatchewan River. The castle in the background is the Delta Bessborough Hotel by Marriott, a Saskatoon landmark since 1935. To the left is the Renaissance Condominium Tower.

Back cover photo shows the Pioneer Cairn at the top of the Broadway Bridge, built in 1952.

Acknowledgements

SOMETIMES WE MEET PEOPLE WHO DO NOT EXACTLY SAY IT, but by their actions, we know that they have our back and support us. Ibiso Graham-Douglas is like that. So, here I am, saying to Ibiso and everyone on her team at Paperworth Books Limited that I am grateful for working with me on this story. It means a lot to me. It is hard work, but you make it so much fun.

No pun intended, but I call them my backbone. Without their advice, support, and encouragement, you probably would not be holding this book—Emmanuel Frank-Opigo, Ayi Torubeli, James Ogah, Bukola Akinyemi, Awom Kenneth. Johnson Ochulayi, Kemelayefa Otue, Taiwo Oladele and David Nwaokocha, thank you for everything.

To Biboye Afenfia and Weniebi Afenfia, you always have my love and appreciation.

Lastly, I reserve my most sincere gratitude to you, who have loved my writing, particularly this book.

QUEEN ELIZABETH ISLANDS
NUNAVUT
YUKON
NORTHWEST TERRITORIES
SASKATCHEWAN
ALBERTA
BRITISH COLUMBIA
MANITOBA
Saskatoon
ONTARIO
QUEBEC
NEWFOUNDLAND AND LABRADOR
PRINCE EDWARD ISLAND
NOVA SCOTIA
NEW BRUNSWEEK
CANADA

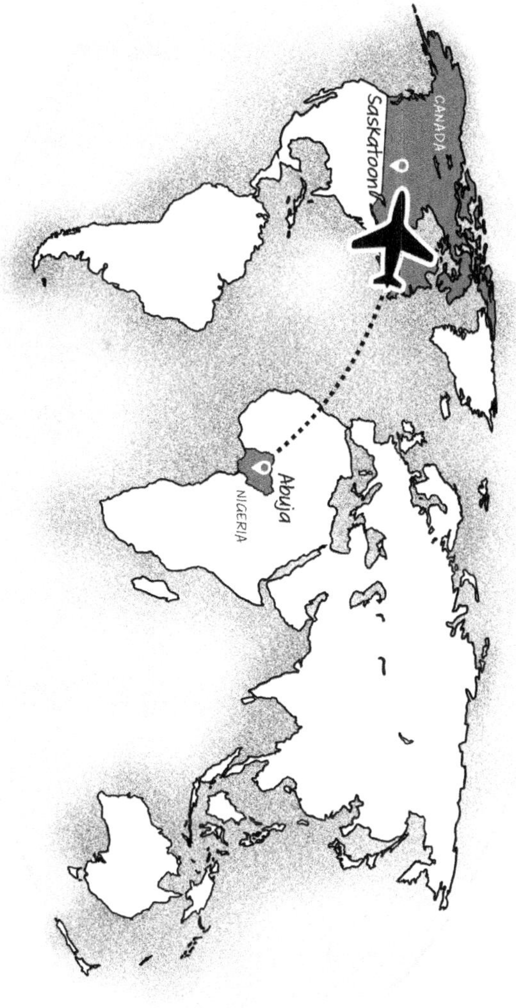
CANADA
Saskatoon
Abuja
NIGERIA

Other Fiction Titles by Paperworth Books

Rain Can Never Know by Michael Afenfia

Trading Places and Other Plays by Paul Ugbede

Dear Alaere by Eriye Onagoruwa

Piece & Pieces by Paul Ugbede

Authentic Mama by Olunosen Louisa Ibhaze

Tomorrow Died Yesterday by Chimeka Garricks

Other Books by Michael Afenfia

When the Moon Caught Fire

A Street Called Lonely

Don't Die on Wednesday

The Mechanics of Yenagoa

Rain Can Never Know

MICHAEL AFENFIA

Michael Afenfia was born in Port Harcourt, Nigeria but now resides in Saskatoon, Canada. Two of his novels, *Don't Die on Wednesday (2010)* and *Rain Can Never Know (2021)* made the shortlist for the Association of Nigerian Authors Prize for literature. A born storyteller, Michael expresses himself through his novels, short stories, and performances. Since arriving in Canada, Michael has learnt to cook. It hasn't happened yet, but he hopes to one day find the confidence to share his recipes with the world.

Printed in Great Britain
by Amazon